2   6/16

THE
RESTORATION
of
OTTO
LAIRD

The Restoration of OTTO LAIRD

NIGEL PACKER

St. Martin's Press ⚞ New York

This is a work of fiction. All of the characters, organizations, and events portrayed in this novel are either products of the author's imagination or are used fictitiously.

www.stmartins.com

The Library of Congress Cataloging-in-Publication Data

Packer, Nigel.
   The restoration of Otto Laird : a novel / Nigel Packer.
     p. cm.
   ISBN 978-1-250-07154-5 (hardcover)
   ISBN 978-1-4668-8268-3 (e-book)
   1. Retirees—Fiction. 2. Architects—Fiction. 3. Life change events—Fiction.
I. Title.
   PR6116.A335R48 2015
   823'.92—dc23

                                                      2015025063

Our books may be purchased in bulk for promotional, educational, or business use. Please contact your local bookseller or the Macmillan Corporate and Premium Sales Department at (800) 221-7945, extension 5442, or by e-mail at MacmillanSpecialMarkets@macmillan.com.

First published in Great Britain by Sphere, an imprint of Little, Brown Book Group, an Hachette UK company

First U.S. Edition: November 2015

10 9 8 7 6 5 4 3 2 1

For my parents, Judith and John.

Acknowledgements

Many thanks to all those who have made this book possible, including my agent, Hannah Ferguson, for finding the manuscript a good home, and my editor, Lucy Malagoni, for her patient work and invaluable advice during the process of revision. Thanks also to desk editor Thalia Proctor, copyeditor Celia Levett, proofreader Peter McAdie, cover designer Hannah Wood and everyone else at Sphere involved in its production and promotion.

Special thanks to my parents, brother Neil and nephew Arvo for their support and humour, and to all the friends and colleagues who have offered words of encouragement over the years.

The RESTORATION of OTTO LAIRD

One

It was not uncommon, these days, for Anika Laird to return from one of her morning trips to town to find her husband standing naked in the kitchen window. The first time it happened she was mildly surprised; by now it had become the stuff of routine. She would catch a peripheral glimpse of Otto as she cycled up the pathway, but the oblique angle of her approach, and a remnant of brick wall standing just beyond the window, prevented a more detailed study as she pedalled round the side of the villa to the front door. Once she was inside, the image that greeted her as she propped up her bicycle and paused in the kitchen doorway was always the same. Otto stood with his back to her, his pale buttocks luminous in the gloom, and stared through the window with a still intensity. Sometimes, during rain, she would discover him pressing his fingertips lightly to the pane, one arm stretched before him in an attitude of silent reverence.

Anika watched in fascination from the cinnamon-scented

doorway. Otto's ageing body was transformed by the quivering half-light into something elegant and weightless: an elderly sea lion, moving through the depths. He never seemed to hear her enter the house, or wheel her creaking bicycle through the hallway, and so she would watch him quietly for minutes at a time, breaking the silence with a soft call of his name. Invariably Otto came to with a start, the rimless spectacles (his sole attire) bouncing on the bridge of his nose.

'Anika,' he would say, turning without embarrassment, 'such terrible weather we are having – you must be soaked right through. Let me fix some luncheon for you while you change.'

Then he would gather up his discarded silk kimono from the stone floor, pull it about his unusually tall frame and tie the strings firmly round his scarred belly, closing each episode with a decisive gesture that seemed to rule out any need for explanation.

Rubbing a towel through her hair before the bathroom mirror, Anika pondered this odd, recurring scene with her husband. It troubled her to find Otto staring into space like that, not least because the kitchen window had no view. It was the only room in the house without one. Positioned immediately beyond it, the crumbling section of wall – part of an old cottage that once stood upon the plot – effectively blocked any sight of the surrounding hills, save for a hint of open landscape through a gap where some bricks had eroded. Despite Anika's protests, Otto had insisted on leaving the wall in place when overseeing construction of the villa some eighteen years earlier. This was done partly from a sentimental attachment to vernacular architecture, partly from a sensuous

2

attraction to the rough mauve bricks, with their regular inter-vals of vivid moss strata.

All the same, Otto's choice of this particular window for his episodes of silent communion struck Anika as perverse. They had chosen this location specifically for its spectacu-lar natural setting. Otto had designed their home with the greatest of care in order to maximise its potential. For anyone lucky enough to enter the Lairds' hillside villa, the interior of the building never failed to draw gasps. It offered a dizzying profusion of light, glass and distant vistas; a three-dimensional frame through which to admire the pristine beauty of the Franco-Swiss borderlands. The blue hills of the Jura could be seen to the north; southward, the giant peaks of the Savoy Alps. Broken and discoloured as a dentist's dream during summer, they were restored each year to a glinting perfection by the first winter snows. Underscoring this rampant geology was the wide expanse of Lake Geneva: implausibly blue when bathed in sunlight, impregnably grey when not. This, all of this, was available to the Lairds for moments of quiet contemplation; the same timeless land-scapes that had once inspired Voltaire, the Shelleys and Byron. Yet Otto – thinker, visionary, the avant-garde's answer to Sir Christopher Wren – Otto seemed much happier with his piece of crumbling wall.

'The inscrutability of genius,' Anika told her reflection in the bathroom mirror.

In truth, she was not convinced by the term, but others had used it when describing her husband, so who was she to argue?

Wandering about naked, too. He must be losing his marbles. Thank God we don't have neighbours for him to scare.

She thought of a Dutch phrase, and spoke it aloud.

'*Een gek.* A crazy man. Whatever was I thinking?'

But she smiled to herself as she spoke.

Combing out the damp strands of vanilla hair, as long and striking now, when she was in her early sixties, as it had been when she first met Otto more than twenty years before, Anika glided from the bathroom to the south-facing lounge, pausing for a moment before its great wall of glass. An autumn breeze rippled the surface of the lake, while Mont Blanc in the distance lay truncated by the dark clouds troubling its heights, a legacy of the morning's storm.

I could always knock it down, she told herself, thinking once more of the length of wall. One day when he's off at a conference somewhere.

She would blame it on the *bise*, the brutal northerly wind that sometimes froze the lake-edge solid during winter, and could turn even the mildest spring days suddenly raw and hostile.

Otto entered the room, looking perplexed. He was carrying a tray laden with two mugs and a silver coffee pot. Setting down the tray on a low glass table, he retrieved a rolled-up magazine from the silk folds beneath his armpit, tossing it down with venom.

'Unbelievable,' he said, pausing to find a better word, before settling on the one he had already. 'Quite unbelievable.'

Recognising the masthead of *The Architectural Eye* – Otto's last remaining link, via monthly subscription, to a profession he had once helped to shape – Anika searched out her glasses in the pocket of her bathrobe and slid them onto her nose. The contours of the masthead sharpened before her as she picked up the magazine.

'What's upset you?' she asked.

'Page five, bastards,' said Otto, whose habit of compressing two separate thoughts into a single phrase was familiar enough to Anika for her not to take offence. The expletive, she realised, wasn't directed at her. She found the page and absorbed the headline.

MARLOWE HOUSE TO GO.

'One of yours,' she said.

'They want to demolish it, buggers,' said Otto.

There was a pause. Anika was browsing through a mental scrapbook of Otto's landmark buildings, but she couldn't place Marlowe House with any certainty. She took a chance.

'London.'

He nodded.

'The concrete tower block south of the river. The one that looks a little off balance?'

'That's the one,' he replied, somewhat testily.

Built in the early 1960s, Marlowe House had been one of Unit 5's defining achievements. Anika remembered Otto once telling her it had won a major architectural prize.

'And what's their reasoning?'

'People don't like living there, apparently. The local news-papers have been campaigning for years. Finally they have their wish. The plan is to knock it down and replace it with private apartments. Stupid arseholes, the lot of them.'

Otto bent angrily to pour out the coffee. He struggled to tailor his movements to the task in hand, spoiling the delicate operation with a spill and a low muttering.

Anika was reading the article.

'But I thought it was listed,' she said, looking up at him above the frame of her glasses.

'They listed its twin, Taylor House, the building out west. But not Marlowe House. It was always the more problematic of the two. The wrong part of London. Social problems and poor maintenance. No fashionable young people to buy up the apartments and trumpet their architectural value. Still consists almost entirely of local-authority tenants, as far as I'm aware. Damned shame we never tried for a listing, though. It's much the better building.'

He became lost in memory then, an increasingly common occurrence during recent years. Unlike most of his work, scattered around the world and rarely visited by Otto after completion, Marlowe House was a building he had observed for many years at first hand. This came about by chance, rather than design, as its distinctive profile could clearly be seen from the stands at the Oval cricket ground, a place where Otto, a keen follower of the game, had spent many a spare summer day during his three-and-a-half decades in England. Consequently, during quieter moments in matches, or in the blissful afternoon reverie that usually followed a teatime scotch, he would find his attention wandering from the field of play, over the gasworks and across the skyline, before coming to rest upon Marlowe House, its lines in the lowering sunlight as crisp and elegant as a well-timed shot to the boundary.

During the early 1960s, Otto had watched with paternal pride as the construction reached its full height of twenty-seven storeys, thereafter looking on with quiet satisfaction as it matured and settled into the urban fabric of south-east London. It had been joined over time by buildings of a similar scale, stretching out in all directions, transforming genteel suburbs into inner-city badlands, and pushing the dark smudge of the Surrey Hills ever further into the distance. Yet despite the burgeoning development around it, the heroic mass of Marlowe House had refused to be overshadowed. Even when finally outgrown by a 1970s upstart several storeys higher (the architect responsible was a long-time rival of Otto's), it had somehow retained its dominant position on the skyline. For Otto, therefore, it remained throughout the 1970s, and into the 1980s, an object of aesthetic contemplation; one to rival the finest sweep shot or a giant blow for six.

He felt a frisson of excitement even now at the thought of Marlowe House, followed by a different sort of frisson at the thought of its destruction. Familiarity with this structure – with its myriad grey moods, the play of sun and cloudlight on its richly textured surface – must, at some point, have blossomed into love. But it was only now, many years later and when it was on the point of extinction, that he had come to fully appreciate it.

Anika noticed his expression darken.

'Is there nothing you can do?' she asked.

Otto thought.

'We can fight the proposals.'

'And how do you do that?'

'I can't quite remember. I'm a little out of touch with these things. We have to write some letters, I expect.'

Otto rarely read *The Architectural Eye* in any detail these days. He would devour with relish any interviews with his peers, commenting out loud on their idiocy or philistinism, but he rarely bothered with the more technical articles. It had been more than twenty years since he moved to Switzerland, and the intricacies of the British planning system seemed as alien to him now as when he had first arrived in England, back in the early 1950s.

'Well, surely there's someone you could ask for help. How about Daniel?'

Otto winced at the sound of this name. Relations with Daniel were a little awkward at present, and the idea of contacting him to ask any kind of favour was disagreeable. Furthermore, Otto had taught him everything he knew about the architectural profession, or so he had come to convince himself in later years. What would it say about his own diminished status, not to mention his waning powers of recall, if he were reduced to calling up his own son in order to seek advice?

All this passed through Otto's mind as he stood scanning the lake's far shore, the steaming cup of coffee poised beneath his nose. Finally, his eyes found what they sought – the distant lights of Evian-les-Bains, rippling in the murky lee of the Alpine foothills. He had felt a strange affinity with this town since being advised to drink more mineral water following the onset of his prostate problems. At least three litres a day, the doctors had told him, and Anika had imposed the regime with unwavering rigour. For much of the past decade, therefore, barely a waking hour seemed to pass without Otto either ingesting, or attempting to expel, the town's famous waters, often to the accompanying strains of deep discomfort. Given such associations, Otto's feelings for Evian were ambivalent at best, yet there was no doubting the intimacy of his connection with the place. It resonated within him at the molecular level.

How is the body composed again? Are we sixty per cent or seventy per cent water? I once knew of such things.

He turned from the window and blew on his coffee.

'I shan't trouble Daniel – he'll be busy with the project in Mumbai. I'll call Angelo instead.'

Angelo Morretti, once a junior partner with Otto's firm, had since gone on to achieve considerable success with his own London-based partnership. Personable and discreet, he had managed to remain a friend and confidant of both Otto and Daniel, despite their difficult relationship. He could be trusted not to speak out of turn to either.

Otto reached for the phone, while Anika drifted off to the bedroom in search of a hairdryer. Perched on the edge of the four-poster, she ran the warm nozzle over her locks, and could just make out Otto's distinctive baritone, rumbling away beneath the airy blast.

He's very upset, she thought. But I'm not really sure what he can do. They seem to be knocking down everything from Otto's era these days. Anything large and made of concrete is fair game.

It had become a regular topic of conversation between them. Each month, Otto would leaf through *The Architectural Eye* and tell Anika which of his peers' buildings had been condemned to the wrecking ball. It was clear from the tightness in his voice that his feelings on the matter were complex. On the one hand, he couldn't resist indulging in a certain *schadenfreude* when reading of the misfortunes of former rivals or friends. Yet he knew that it was only a matter of time before he, too, fell victim to these changes in architectural fashion. He had been shocked, therefore, but hardly surprised by that morning's headline.

Anika switched off the dryer as Otto appeared in the doorway.

'Well?' she asked.

'There's still hope. Angelo's going to make a few calls about it, including one to his lawyer. The fightback will soon be under way . . . the counter-offensive has started.'

Otto's face flushed and his eyes glittered. He drummed *The Architectural Eye* into his palm.

'We've a lot of work to do. Angelo agrees with me that we shouldn't take this lying down. He says I owe it to posterity, and to myself, to fight this through to the end. He's quite right – we must act, and act fast. I won't let those pen pushers obliterate *my* oeuvre!'

Otto's breathing sounded harshly across the threshold as he awaited Anika's response. It was some time since she had seen him in this kind of state, but she knew the right tone with which to calm him.

'I admire your spirit, Otto,' she said, sympathetic but cool as she sat poised on the edge of the bed. 'And of course you must do everything possible to save your building. But please remember both your age *and* your current state of health. You're seventy-nine years old – it's only a few months since your last operation. There's a balance to be struck here. You need to look after yourself. And when all is said and done, I'd much rather keep *you* for posterity than one of your buildings, however important it might be.'

The flame in Otto's eyes lowered a notch.

'Of course,' he said, 'you have a point, which is exactly why Angelo is going to get his people to do the lion's share of the work. He said I can't be expected to take on too much, given recent circumstances.'

His fingers brushed lightly across his abdomen as he spoke.

'Well, that's good,' replied Anika. 'I'm glad you're both being sensible about it.'

Bending her head forward, she flicked back her hair in a fluid motion that Otto paused to admire.

'So what happens next?' she asked.

'We won't know much for a couple of weeks. Angelo told me to sit tight and wait for his call.'

He looked around, as if for something specific.

'In the meantime, I'll need to keep myself busy. It won't be easy. Patience never was my greatest virtue, as you know.'

'I'm sure I can find plenty for you to do. Didn't you promise to cook us lunch for a start?'

'So I did.'

'An omelette would be perfect. There are eggs in the pantry, freshly laid. I collected them this morning.'

'Right – an omelette it is.'

Anika switched on the dryer once more and dipped her head forward to complete the routine, disappearing behind the vanilla wave. When she emerged again, a minute or two later, Otto was still standing in the doorway.

'Eggs,' said Anika, as she flicked off the dryer.

'Eggs, yes,' said Otto, turning away as the jet of air revived.

Half an hour later, he still hadn't returned.

Leave him alone with his wall a little longer, thought Anika, who by this time had settled onto the sofa with the latest edition of *Paris Match*. He'll make his way back, when he's ready.

For Anika, who had a literary turn of mind, the fragment of wall beyond the kitchen window had come to represent a metaphor for something lost and irretrievable in Otto's life.

11

Cynthia, his first wife, was the obvious candidate, which explained why Anika felt a slight pang of resentment every time she cycled up the pathway and past the pile of bricks, nurturing fantasies of demolition.

You can't be jealous of a wall, she thought, smiling to herself, setting aside her magazine and bending an elegant knee to paint a toenail. That would make you even crazier than he is.

There were other reasons for Anika's frustration. She was aware that the wall must have certain aesthetic qualities that she, with her untrained eye, couldn't appreciate. Cynthia, of course, would have seen them immediately. A gifted architect in her own right, Cynthia had shared Otto's eccentric passion for buildings in need of a lick of paint. Even as students, the two of them had gone on tours of the English countryside, seeking out ruined farmsteads in order to photograph them. But then hadn't Cynthia been, in the final analysis, Otto's 'intellectual soulmate', a painfully memorable phrase Anika had once read in *The Architectural Eye*?

Cynthia would have been cranky about that fucking wall, too, she thought – instantly regretting her spite.

How could she still harbour such feelings? They were unbecoming, undignified. The poor girl had not been around for many years. And besides, Anika knew that her own place in Otto's life was permanently secured. The passing of time, and Otto's increasing fragility, meant that to all intents and purposes he was now entirely dependent upon her, as much errant child as doting husband. His philandering days had long passed into history, giving way to a strange docility and the creeping vagueness of old age. It was Anika, in fact, who played the gadabout in this relationship. It was she who had the affairs, usually with men somewhat younger than herself. She found them to be less bothersome than men her own age, who invariably spoiled everything by asking her to do the one impossible thing and leave her elderly husband. And if Otto suspected anything (he occasionally hinted as much, during pillow talk), then he didn't appear to object (he was careful to hint at this, too).

Despite the relatively contented state of their marriage, Otto's behaviour in recent months had unsettled Anika. She sensed that she was finally losing her husband – not to someone else, but to his memories. It was not so much that he was *losing* his memory, the usual assumption made about those experiencing the profound effects of old age, but the very opposite. Otto's memory was *growing*, consuming him, making the present seem fuzzy and obscure, an ever-shrinking space in which he increasingly struggled to function. During conversations with Anika, he would sometimes lose his thread of logic and sputter into silence, something painful to see in a man of once formidable intellect. Or else he would set out to undertake some practical task, only to become lost in reverie, forgetting to wash up, or feed the chickens, even on occasion to dress himself. Until Anika discovered him – absently stroking the folds of a shirt, or studying the grains of feed as they slid through his fingers – and gently reminded him of what he had set out to do.

It was clear to her that Otto was suffering from some form of mental deterioration, the kind people of a certain age dread as much as the physical. Alzheimer's ... Dementia ... The words, as she recalled them, touched Anika like a sore spot. She ought to go online and check out the symptoms more thoroughly, maybe arrange for Otto to see a specialist in

13

Geneva. But she preferred not to face up to this eventuality just yet. She knew exactly how he would react. Unlike his libido, his temper had not yet faded entirely. For now, at least, he remained lucid and coordinated enough not to be a danger to himself.

Later, she thought, fastening her robe and preparing to go in search of her wayward husband. When things have deteriorated beyond doubt. When he's either too weak, or too confused, to cause a scene. Then I'll make the call.

Two

The egg in Otto's hand was palest blue; its cool weight pregnant on his palm. He was kneeling in the shade of the pantry, clad in his kimono and stroking the shell with a trembling thumb. The texture was extraordinary, granular yet smooth. Its surface formed an endless curve, held in perfect tension.

How does nature do this? Such engineering . . .

Raising the egg to eye level and rotating it slowly, he studied its proportion and balance; savoured its equilibrium.

Brunelleschi couldn't have achieved this. Not even Phidias and the Greeks.

A line came to him from somewhere:

Geometry and poetry, indivisible.

He must write that one down. Or had he done so already? From one of his books, perhaps? Fearing that he might drop the egg, Otto lowered it back carefully into the wooden crate and covered it over with his handkerchief. An omelette seemed impossible now, to break the delicate shells would be sacrilege. He would fix them both a sandwich instead.

Otto's knees on the stone floor throbbed with pain, and it took him a few seconds to climb to his feet, clutching a low wooden shelf for support. The dust on the hem of his gown required attention, but the thought of stretching down again deterred him, and he hobbled over to the fridge to fetch some cheese.

These moments of epiphany came regularly to him now; an overwhelming sense of the world's great beauty. He wasn't turning religious in his old age, surely? His younger self would have laughed at such flakiness.

No, he thought. It's nothing spiritual – just a heightened appreciation of matter.

Viewed from this perspective, Otto's moments of revelation formed the final stage in his intellectual odyssey; the culmination of a lifelong quest. His passion for raw materials, the physical stuff of which buildings were made, was legendary. The need to respect the integrity of those materials was always a guiding principle in his work. Whatever materials he built with – wood or brick, concrete or steel – Otto sought with the utmost sensitivity to draw out their aesthetic potential. He explored through trial and error their colouring and grain, the way the light struck them at different times of day, revealing new qualities and hidden imperfections. He wanted others to appreciate those qualities as much as he did, and considered any attempt to disguise the beauty of raw materials as the very gravest of architectural sins. He said as much in his first manifesto, typed out quickly on an old Olivetti while sitting in his Lambeth bedsit. In the long years since 1952, he had never really shifted position.

'If a building is made of concrete, then *show* that it's made of concrete,' he once told an audience while lecturing at Yale.

'Don't go hiding it behind cladding or paint – explore the possibilities of its concreteness.'

Otto was a great fan of concrete. He considered it to be among the most beautiful of all materials, and he waged a constant battle against those who believed otherwise. This campaign was fought on two fronts: out on the streets, in the form of his buildings, and in the world's lecture halls, where he regularly gave provocative talks comparing Auguste Perret's Le Havre to Haussmann's Paris. Otto's passion for concrete hadn't waned with the years, but the tide of public opinion against which he swam had finally exhausted him. Nowadays, he sought refuge in designing in the vernacular of the Jura, a labour of love he could pursue in perfect peace, without ever needing to defend his actions. A few years ago he had undertaken a detailed study of transhumance in the region, visiting the remains of abandoned huts and taking copious notes in his sketchbook. Recently, he had designed a contemporary eco-house, constructed on the forested slopes near his home from pine and local stone. It was an exquisite piece of work, but hardly original – the kind of building even his harshest critics would struggle to find offensive. These days, Otto aimed to please as much as to provoke with his work, taking on small private commissions as they caught his fancy. He no longer cared for the ideological fray.

As he cut deep into the loaf and contemplated the challenge awaiting him in London, his earlier resolve began to waver. People in Britain had never really understood his work, so why should they do so now? He was especially concerned about Angelo's suggestion that he might want to consider giving some telephone interviews to the press. It wasn't much to ask, given that Angelo would take care of the campaign to

17

save the building. Yet despite having promised that he would give it some thought, he had his misgivings.

Otto missed many things about his adopted homeland, but its press, in general, was not one of them. Throughout his career, he had encountered problems with journalists, the result of his natural aloofness and a refusal to curb his ferocious intellect in their presence. They found Otto to be short-tempered, arrogant and slightly baffling. He saw them as irredeemably shallow. Some of them left the interview room with a sense that he had deliberately humiliated them. But in truth he rarely noticed as they struggled to keep pace with his acrobatic mind. This gained him a reputation for being difficult and obscure. For some people, at least, the opportunity to poke fun at him was too much to resist. Back in the early 1970s, for instance, when Otto had taken part in a series of highbrow televised debates on the state of late twentieth-century culture, a well-known satirist had parodied him in a series of sketches, mimicking to a T his tangential flights of logic.

More than forty years later, Otto remained wary of the British media. The feeling would doubtless be mutual. From what friends had told him, the country's innate mistrust of intellectuals had grown even stronger since his departure. To a new generation of writers and broadcasters – cynical, irreverent and respectful of no one – the bookish and serious Otto would seem like a man out of time; a hopeless historical anomaly, like his buildings. In short, they would eat him alive.

He contemplated the prospect as he laid out slices of Emmental, searching the shelves for the black pepper.

Do I still have the stomach for the fight? he thought, smiling at his unfortunate choice of words.

Much of Otto's stomach, like his prostate some years earlier, had been removed during a series of operations. The last of these had taken place just three months before.

Show a little gumption, he thought to himself, firmly turning the pepper grinder in his hands. If you can cope with evisceration, you can certainly handle a few newspaper hacks.

He finished constructing Anika's sandwich and started on his own. He had developed a fondness for the local Bleu de Gex, admiring the stray blue threads of its marbling as much as its taste. He split the block of cheese with a knife, popping a thick slice into his mouth as he laid out the rest. Its flavour stopped him in his tracks, an emotional response – way beyond thought – sparking in his cortex.

If sight and touch had gained a near-hallucinatory quality for Otto, then taste, too, had an added intensity these days. All his senses, in fact, seemed to be firing on overload. It dated back to his recent batch of operations, as though the trauma of the experience had enhanced his awareness of the body's capacity for registering sensation. Of all kinds. Alongside – and countering – his daily pain and discomfort, the continual pitfalls of old age, he also felt a deeper and more profound awareness: of the body's ability to feel pleasure, fleeting and intense; of its extreme sensitivity, if properly nurtured, to its surrounding environment. With this deepening awareness, he had become alert to each passing sensation, to every nuance of his own physical experience. And the days without pain, when they came now and then, were a source of boundless joy. It was like retreating through time. Everything again felt fresh to him. On days such as those, he was awake to sensuous experience as almost never before.

19

He remembered the first time it had happened. It had been some weeks earlier, shortly after the discomfort that followed his last operation had started to ease. Sitting at his writing desk one summer afternoon, he had suddenly savoured as never before the slight breeze through his study window, the sweet scent of pine from the adjacent forest, the dense canopy of birdsong. Laying down his pen, he had wandered into the forest in a state of unthinking rapture; bending to stroke the wild flowers carpeting its banks; pausing to enjoy a shaft of light as it fell between the trees, briefly illuminating a patch of blue gentians. He pursued a white butterfly, agile as a fly half, and drank in the mossy air, the hints of wild garlic and woodsmoke, the omnipresent symphony of the birds. Like a modern-day Wordsworth, Otto was drunk on nature; drunk on existence, his own above all. That surge of elation had resurfaced often in the weeks that followed. It seemed as though, faced with the failings of his anatomy, he had embarked on the one act of defiance now left him: to turn whatever remained of his life into a conscious celebration of the physical world.

There was a cruelty about the timing of all this, he realised – his senses reaching a peak of refinement just as his physical powers were deserting him. Even as he found the wisdom to fully savour bodily experience, some of its greatest pleasures were closing off to him. Take sex, for example. Surely that would have felt incredible to him now. If the shape of an egg or a slice of cheese could bring him such transcendence, just imagine what coitus might do. But it wasn't to be. Several episodes of surgery had put paid to that possibility. Instead, Otto experienced sexual excitement vicariously, through Anika, whose generous sensuality had gradually become a substitute for his own. In the afternoons when she had no appointments, she would stretch her long body on the bed beside him and suggest that he undress her. She would guide his movements with little gasps and exhalations, his hands caressing her breasts and belly with a curious, detached intensity; his fingers following her own inside as she drew him towards her great cry of release. It was a beautiful experience, but cerebral rather than physical, despite the pliant wonders of Anika's flesh beneath his hands, and the way she bit his bottom lip as she came.

Otto was grateful to her for this facsimile of lovemaking. He knew it was done for his benefit alone, as she could experience the real thing whenever she wanted with any of her small squad of lovers. Yet try as he might, he could never completely lose himself to its rhythms. An orgasm felt through the fingertips was no substitute for the real thing; and passion recalled, but no longer experienced, was like a memory of music unheard.

'Any sign of lunch?' asked Anika, appearing in the kitchen just as Otto finished making the sandwiches.

'I'm not sure about those eggs,' he replied. 'I think they might be off.'

'I'll throw them out,' she said, making for the pantry.

He blocked her path with the proffered sandwich.

'I'll do it later. I've made us these.'

Three

The following day, as the weather had improved, they decided to eat lunch together on the rooftop terrace. Anika had prepared two mushroom omelettes, served as Otto liked them with a sprig of parsley and a salad of green leaves. With the clouds of the previous day deserting the wide sky, the autumn sun had regained its strength and now emitted a heat that was almost Mediterranean in its intensity. Even this late in the year it could surprise unwary hikers, but Anika understood its moods and sat wearing a wide-brimmed hat for protection. Otto chose to sit in the shade.

The strong afternoon light gave the surrounding hills an insubstantial quality, their liquid shimmer contrasting with the raw physicality of the Alpine giants across the valley. With the change in light and visibility (a celestial telescope, finding its range), Mont Blanc and its companions appeared much closer than the day before, their white peaks outlined with shocking clarity against a topaz sky. The lake below, a deeper blue, lay sunken in its own haze.

Anika and Otto sat quietly, their eyes half closed in the languid warmth, and listened to the spirited scraping of the year's last cicadas. Sometimes, the Lairds enjoyed a leisurely glass of wine with their lunch. A fragrant white from the Valais was their current favourite. But they both had things to do that afternoon, and Otto couldn't spare the hour or two needed to sleep it off. He sipped a glass of sparkling water instead.

'What time's your tennis lesson?' he asked.

Anika had recently joined a new club in town and was currently working on her topspin. She was keeping herself busy following her retirement from a desk job at the United Nations.

'Three-thirty,' she replied. 'You won't be needing the car?'

She raised her sunglasses as she spoke.

'Not today. It will take me a couple of hours at least to get through all that paperwork. I'll go later in the week.'

Otto's current passion was eco-housing. Once a week he drove to Lausanne to conduct some research at the institute of technology. But a large pile of correspondence awaited him in his study, and he decided he could delay it no longer. Shortly afterwards, drawing up a chair at his mahogany desk, he ran a hand forlornly through the thick wad of letters and listened to the Bentley pulling away over the gravel. He paused to remove something from his pocket – the egg, now wrapped in his handkerchief – and slipped it into a drawer. At least one had been saved from the wrecking ball.

He wearily lifted a letter from the pile and looked at the postmark on the buff envelope. Paris: the 10th arrondissement. It was from Pierre, his old friend at the Sorbonne. Otto had always been a voluminous writer, exchanging regular letters with influential friends from academia and the arts. Often he used this correspondence as a sounding board for his never-ending flow of ideas. In recent years, however, he found that he had less and less to say. Now he was starting to regret his former wordiness. The letters were becoming a chore, but he didn't know how to halt them. He couldn't just admit that he had given up on thinking. To his academic friends, it would be like admitting that he had given up on breathing.

'Should have kept your mouth shut all these years,' he muttered to himself, taking a paper knife and slicing open Pierre's letter.

As ever, it was composed in perfect English. The handwriting was microscopically small and claustrophobically spaced. Thirteen pages of the stuff. Otto sighed, flicked briefly through its contents and noted the references to the usual suspects: Foucault and his panopticon, Lefebvre and space production. It was like some game of academic tennis, this ferocious hitting back and forth of different names and systems of thought. Pierre and Otto were in the depths of a discussion about the architecture of control, its uses by various political regimes as a way of securing and maintaining power. It was an important topic, but one with little bearing upon Otto's current field of research. It was a misunderstanding between them, really; a sign that, with the passing years, Pierre and he were steadily drifting apart. The themes of their discussions were broadly the same as they had been many decades before. But Otto, at least, had moved on.

Pierre still thought of Otto as a pioneer of the 'Brutalist' style of building. He remembered him as the energetic and committed young socialist who saw in architecture – the art of arranging space – the means to contribute to both social and personal liberation. Architecture in those days was a political act, no less. Otto and many others at the time believed that by creating large housing estates it would be possible to ensure that everyone lived in a clean, safe and comfortable environment. The well-kept public spaces would encourage interaction and neighbourliness; the uniform size of the apartments would abolish notions of hierarchy. People from all backgrounds, he had argued, would eventually want to inhabit these estates. They would become a microcosm and a foretaste of the society to come: peaceful, progressive, egalitarian, and free from all physical and social division.

That was more than fifty years ago and things had, of course, worked out differently. Otto himself had also changed. Unlike some of his fellow travellers, he hadn't abandoned his ideals completely in the rush to embrace Neoliberalism, a trend that began as a trickle in the late 1970s and became a great flood after 1989. But he *had* let those ideals quietly slip. He had laid them carelessly aside, one day, and conveniently forgotten where he had left them. Now all he wanted was to build unobtrusive houses in the Jura hills and tend to his broken body, grabbing moments of happiness where he could. And if most days he barely had the energy to walk down the hill in order to fetch a baguette from the local store, then battling the worst excesses of capitalism was clearly no longer on the agenda.

Pierre, on the other hand, remained up for the fight. His energy could be terrifying – even now, when he was well into his seventies, it showed no signs of dissipating. He regularly worked eighteen-hour days, while writing a new book, and three times a week ran the circumference of the Bois de Boulogne, usually clocking up a time of less than three hours. Politically, Pierre remained deeply immured in the spirit of 1968 – he had played no small part in the events that unfolded in Paris that May. He knew about the long-term waning of Otto's political commitment, but there were passages in their correspondence when he remained convinced that the small red flame in his old friend's heart had not yet died out entirely.

Otto would not have agreed.

He doesn't realise how far it's gone, he thought, noting with a slight sense of shame Pierre's tireless activism, and then remembering his own recent afternoon spent communing with an egg.

It's not his fault – I've kept it all from him. The Bentley, the golf clubs, the beneficial tax arrangements, the underpaid cleaner from the developing world who visits twice a week and tends to our expensive mess. I'm hopelessly bourgeois now, I'm afraid. *I'm* the class enemy – perhaps I always was.

But then he knew how hard it was to really change people. He had seen it in others and experienced it in himself. All those noble intentions, abandoned to self-interest. Cynicism, winning out each time.

It's such a struggle, trying to keep up the struggle. I don't know how Pierre manages to do it.

Otto had learned his lessons the hard way. Throughout his career, he had encountered the brute forces of capital on a regular basis, and he knew the machinations of which it was capable. He had come up against its iron laws many times, when fighting to maintain the integrity of his projects, and usually he had lost. Apartments in his own Taylor House, for example, developed as a serious experiment in social housing, now sold for large sums of money to wealthy young people with a taste for 'retro' and 'urban grit'. The building had even featured on some TV property show: Angelo had sent him the link. The imbecile of a presenter called it 'funky', whatever that meant.

No, Otto thought. Everything has become a commodity nowadays; and maybe every person, too. All of us have become commodities to each other. The profit motive has entered every sphere of life, and its hegemony is complete.

He was among those who had seen this coming – he had fought against its spread for decades. Finally, sometime in the mid-1980s, he had thrown in the towel, sickened by the grasping cynicism of the emerging generation. Cynthia's loss had been the final straw, sapping the last of his once steely resolve. And so he had fled to France, where he hid himself away in the mountains, buried in perfect seclusion until he encountered Anika one day in a hillside café overlooking Lake Annecy. She had approached him as he sat nursing a coffee at a terrace table and asked if she could borrow his binoculars. And then, much to his surprise, life had begun again.

But how could Otto explain all this to Pierre? How could he explain the long and tortuous journey that had brought him to his hillside villa in the Jura?

Pierre's a sociologist at the Sorbonne, Otto thought. The man lives in a time capsule.

Lectures, seminars, late-night discussions at literary cafés – Otto had seen it all first-hand during his visits there in the

1970s. And from the tone of Pierre's letters it was clear that nothing much had changed. Otto knew the slow, eternal rhythms of academia. He also knew that, for all their brilliance and fine intentions, the people who inhabited that world were as far removed from everyday reality as the average rock star. Otto loved Pierre like a brother. They had been through a great deal together in the old days. But he no longer wanted to read his long and rather boring letters about Foucault. Or reply to them, for that matter. Otto's powers of recall were not what they had been, for one thing, and he struggled to keep up with all the changes in terminology, especially now that his voracious appetite for books had waned. There were moments when he didn't have a clue what Pierre was writing about. Well, now was the time to draw a line. He must put a stop to it, once and for all, and either re-establish their friendship on a sounder footing, or abandon it altogether.

He picked up his pen.

Dear Pierre,

Thank you very much indeed for your latest letter. I should say at the outset that I agreed with everything you said – something of a first, I know. Your argument was beautifully crafted and I have little else to add. In our games of intellectual head-tennis, you take game, set and match every time. You're a clever old bugger, aren't you?

Sorry if my opening remarks appear flippant – I realise you were probably expecting a more considered response. But I'll have to ask you to show some compassion and forgive an old friend his crassness. I'm rather frail these days, you see, and losing my mental sharpness. Many of your more subtle arguments are simply lost on me. These are my *shortcomings, of course — not yours. I'm sure that your discourses remain as lucid as ever. But my mental energies are somewhat depleted nowadays, and those that have been left to me are largely dispersed in concerns more pressing than a long meditation upon architecture as a tool of political control. I have to deal with this pain in my gut, for a start, and I also find myself teetering on the brink of mysticism — an odd thing for a man of science, I realise, but I'm trying to work it through.*

In short, I'm no longer the coherent and articulate figure of old, bursting with a passionate commitment to social transformation and global justice — the person you befriended in the late 1950s, in other words. My ambitions these days are more modest ones. I want my stomach to hurt less, I want Anika to be happy and I want to design a building that's as perfect as an egg. That's about it. Oh yes, and I want to try to save Marlowe House from destruction. That's the run-down tower block in south London, by the way, not the mystifyingly fashionable one out west. They announced a few days ago that they plan to demolish it.

I know you'll welcome my attempt to fight this decision, but I feel duty bound to confess that the reason I'm trying to save Marlowe House is not because of the high ideals it once represented. I could pretend that's the reason — it would certainly make me appear nobler in my intentions. But any such claim would be less than honest. No, I want to save Marlowe House for other reasons. For itself, and for myself. *Because I think it's a good building and I'm still rather proud of it, despite the decades of neglect, its terrible reputation for crime . . . and three generations of yobs, pissing in its stairwells. Yes, despite all these negatives, I still think that Marlowe House is a building worth saving. It probably has something to do with Cynthia as well. I haven't really thought about that one, but I expect it's the case. She played a large part in its design, after all, and I think she would probably have wanted me to do something. Finally, I'm doing it just to keep myself occupied, to wake myself up a bit, and maybe ward off some of this encroaching senility. I know there's something not quite right with my mind, these days, although it's so hard to tell what exactly, when one is living on the inside of these things.*

I danced with a butterfly recently, you know. Can you imagine? An elderly man, prancing round the forest like a wood nymph. I nearly gave myself heart failure. And I've started taking my clothes off at inappropriate times. Poor Anika got a terrible fright the first time it happened. So I think it's pretty obvious that something is amiss. I find myself in an odd situation, mentally. Is it like this for everyone at a certain age, do you think? So little serious work has been done on the psychology of ageing. I find that there are moments of great clarity, even wisdom of a kind. But there are also moments of terrible confusion – perhaps that's the price for those of wisdom. And I keep thinking about the past. It swamps me, sometimes; more vividly than I've ever known before.

So, you see, it's important that I keep myself busy, although not – I regret to inform you – by reading any more Foucault. I hope that doesn't upset you. Do you think we could write about other things instead? How is your body bearing up these days, for instance? Do you still get laid, now and then? Do you regret your failed marriage to the

violinist? Are you as frightened of ageing as I am? My guess
is that you must be, judging by your behaviour. Racing round
the Bois de Boulogne like a man possessed. You ought to be
careful at your age, you know. They'll find you dead under
the trees, one of these days, and think you were up to no
good.

Anyway, I hope you don't mind the rather candid tone of
this letter. I realise it's somewhat out of keeping with our
usual discussions, but please don't take any offence, because
absolutely none is intended. I'm attempting to save our
friendship, not destroy it. It's been so many years since we
spoke honestly to each other. I think now is the time to scrape
off this crust of formality that has developed between us, and
get back to basics while there is still time. We used to have so
much fun together, do you remember?

I hope to hear from you soon, old dear, and sorry once
more for my rambling thoughts. Look after yourself and good
luck with the launch of the new book. Friday week, isn't it?
With deepest affection,
Otto

He read the letter back to himself, correcting one or two
grammatical errors as he did so. Should he send it? If he was
going to, then he must do so quickly, before he had a chance
to change his mind. Pierre was an unpredictable fellow, and
there was no telling how he might react to Otto's irreverent
tone. It was decades since they had spoken like this, before the
accolades and awards began to weigh them down with their
own self-importance. Pierre might laugh delightedly, with
that deep, infectious bellow of his. Or he might catch the first
flight over and punch Otto's lights out.

Sod it – just send it to him, thought Otto. I can walk to the postbox this minute. I'm feeling well enough today. Then I'll come back and write some more, now that I'm in the right frame of mind.

He was already planning how to tackle the next letter on the pile. It was from his old friend Laszlo – an architect turned avant-garde composer. But just as he was searching out his jacket in the hallway, the telephone rang in his study.

Four

'Otto, it's Angelo.'

'That was quick.'

'Quicker than expected – which is a good sign, hopefully. I've several developments to report, if you have a few minutes.'

'Of course.'

Otto sat down.

'Firstly, I've been in touch with my lawyer and she's already preparing the paperwork. We have a strong case – there are precedents – and your name will be a factor, too. Secondly, a number of influential people have indicated that they are willing to help out with the campaign. The Twentieth Century Society are definitely interested. English Heritage have said they will take a look. And I've also spoken to several of your friends and former colleagues in the profession. Norman, Richard, Rowena – even Jorge has said he'll write something on your behalf.'

'My goodness, has he really?'

Jorge was the rival who had designed Marlowe House's loftier neighbour.

'You'd be surprised at the levels of support we're receiving. As I told you yesterday, the situation is nowhere near as hopeless as you appear to think. Things have begun to change in the past few years. People are revising their views about postwar architecture. Did you get a chance to look at that link I sent you last month?'

'You mean to that ridiculous property programme? Yes, I did take a look.'

Angelo seemed a little thrown by Otto's tone and hesitated before continuing.

'I know that sort of thing isn't really to your taste, but it can be a useful way to generate support in a situation like this.'

'I suppose it can,' Otto replied, with little enthusiasm.

'Helps spread the message to a broader public, educates them about the value of twentieth-century architecture, you know the sort of thing.'

'I'd hardly call programmes of that sort educational,' said Otto. 'Vacuous morons, leaping about with paintbrushes, working out how many thousands they can add to the value of their investment. Those apartments weren't built for *their* benefit,' he added. 'They were meant to improve the lives of the socially excluded.'

'And that's exactly what Marlowe House *has* done,' broke in Angelo. 'Well, that's what we'll be trying to argue. If Taylor House, which is now largely privately owned, has received a listing, then surely Marlowe House – earlier, architecturally more significant *and* still serving the purpose for which it was designed – well, surely that deserves a listing, too.'

'It's a nice argument,' said Otto, 'but there are some voices missing in all this.'

'And whose are those?'

'The residents. What do they think? From what I read in *The Architectural Eye*, they were pretty much unanimous in their condemnation. People hate living in Marlowe House, apparently. That's why they want to knock the thing down.'

The disappointment in Otto's voice was clear.

'And ultimately, whatever the architectural merits of the building, whatever its place as a piece of post-war social history, if the people who actually live there regard it as a failure, then perhaps one should admit that it probably *is* a failure.'

Angelo sought to pluck Otto free of his descending gloom. He had strong ideas of his own on the subject.

'You can't blame yourself for the current condition of Marlowe House,' he said. '*You're* not responsible for the direction British society has taken over the past thirty years. The lack of public investment, the crumbling social fabric, drugs, crime, everyone for themselves, the rampant materialism, turning our built heritage into a used-car lot.'

Angelo was getting into his stride now. It was obvious he had spent time as Otto's apprentice.

'If Marlowe House has become emblematic of the modern urban nightmare, then that's the result of multiple social and economic factors – *not* the fact that it's made of bloody concrete, whatever the authorities might say. Look at Taylor House, it's becoming a popular place to live. Marlowe House is very similar, physically. The only difference is that it's in a more deprived part of town. If it had been properly maintained by the authorities, and if society hadn't long ago pulled the plug on the poor sods who live there, we wouldn't have a fraction of the problems that exist there today. Don't let the politicians try to push the blame for this onto you, Otto. It's *their* failure – not yours.'

Angelo paused to draw breath, while Otto considered his answer.

'You have a point,' he conceded. 'And I'm almost convinced . . . but I'd still like to know what the residents think.'

Angelo paused. Should he say it now? Why not?

'There's another reason I've called you back this soon.'

'Go on,' said Otto, sensing the reticence in Angelo's voice.

'I got a call this morning' – *say it*, he told himself – 'from a television director.'

The involuntary sound in Otto's throat might have come from *The Exorcist*.

Angelo pressed on.

'They're launching a new cultural show on television next month. It sounds as if it could be reasonably highbrow.'

Angelo was frantically pushing all the right buttons he could think of, before Otto made that terrible sound again.

'Chloe, the show's director, thought that the planned demolition of Marlowe House would make an interesting feature for the programme. She lives in Taylor House, as a matter of fact.'

'Of course she does,' said Otto, darkly.

'That's how the problem with its twin across London came to her attention. Chloe's lifestyle coach, who lives on the floor above, showed her the story.'

From the snort on the end of the line, Angelo guessed that maybe he shouldn't have added this last piece of information.

'She was especially interested when I mentioned the appeal,

and when I told her that you were taking a personal involve-
ment in the campaign. I must admit to you here, she was
surprised to discover you were still alive.'

'That's understandable,' said Otto. 'I'm surprised to discover
it myself most mornings.'

Good, thought Angelo, he's regained his sense of humour.
Now it's time for a touch of flattery.

'She's been doing some research about you. She said she
didn't realise you were such a well-known celebrity during
the 1960s.'

'I exchanged some ideas on contemporary culture with a
group of fellow intellectuals, and there happened to be television cameras positioned in the room, if that's what she
means,' replied Otto.

Angelo was losing him again. It was the word 'celebrity'
that had done it. He must tailor his vocabulary more to Otto's
world-view.

'She thought it a great shame that you never appear on television any more. She said from what she had seen you had an
engaging personality, a brilliant mind and were very "televi-
sual". Between you and me, I think that means she thought
you were *quite the dish* in your younger days.'

Over the years Angelo had gathered a rich treasure trove of
phrases from Otto, who sometimes sounded like a living
Pathé newsreel. He had recovered one of those phrases for
Otto's benefit now.

'*Do* get on with it,' said Otto, who knew what was coming
and had already prepared his answer.

'She asked some more about you – where you were living,
what you were up to these days. And then she asked if you
might be interested in appearing in person on the programme.'

At last, thought Otto, before launching into his reply.

'I don't feel entirely comfortable about appearing on television, as I explained to you yesterday. There are various reasons for this, not the least of which, I've now come to realise, is plain old vanity. I don't particularly want people of an older generation sitting in front of their television screens and saying: "Good God – look what happened to him."'

At the other end of the line, Angelo smiled.

'But I've thought it through, since we spoke, and I realise that the media are a necessary evil. If we're going to campaign to save Marlowe House, then we ought to do it properly – not half-heartedly. A slight humiliation in front of a couple of million people would be a small price to pay, if we eventually won. So I'm willing to at least discuss the possibility of doing an interview.'

'I'm glad to hear it.'

'Where would she like to do it, if I happened to agree? Here or back in England?'

Now for the difficult part, thought Angelo.

'Well, a straight "interview" as such is not really what she had in mind. You know what television is like these days. They've lost the taste for talking heads. Producers are always looking for a new angle, something to make their programmes more palatable to the contemporary public.'

A small shiver ran up Otto's spine. What was coming?

'She said that rather than you simply *talking* about Marlowe House, it might be interesting for you to do something more' – he braced himself to say the next word – '*interactive*.'

This was too much for Otto.

'If she wants me to dress up in costumes and play bloody parlour games she can forget it!'

'No, nothing like that,' Angelo reassured him. 'It's quite an inventive idea, really.'

'Which is?'

'While she was looking through various clips on YouTube, Chloe found an old documentary you appeared in during the mid-1960s. Do you remember it?'

Oh God – not that, thought Otto, but he replied: 'It's slipped my mind just now. You'll have to remind me.'

'When you spent a month living in Marlowe House?'

'I seem to remember *something* . . . '

As if he could ever forget.

'I must admit, I'd never heard about it myself. At just the time when debate was raging about whether or not people wanted to inhabit these "streets in the sky", they managed to persuade one of Britain's leading young architects to live for a while in a recently built tower block he and his partners had designed. And then they filmed the result. It was a great idea, and you were pretty game to take part.'

I didn't feel I had a great deal of choice, thought Otto, although he managed to summon a low grunt of assent for an answer.

'Well, Chloe wondered if you might be interested in doing it all again.'

The moment of truth had arrived. Otto paused to consider his response.

'What about my health?'

'I told her about that. She was very understanding. They wouldn't expect you to spend a month there now. Not given your age and, well, the crime problem, frankly. Neither Marlowe House nor you are in quite the same shape you were in the mid-1960s. But she wondered if you might be able to do five days. Just walking around, reminiscing . . . meeting one or two of the residents. It could make for quite a nice piece. And security won't be an issue. They'll hire some people to look after you. What do you think?'

Otto would have been hard pressed to express his exact thoughts at that moment. They were a curious mixture. His innate dislike of appearing on television told against the project, as did his rather unpleasant memories of making the original documentary. It was nothing to do with the residents – they had been fine with him. But he had been unhappy with the final edit of the film, which he felt had been deliberately tailored to make him appear a snob and a hypocrite.

Counteracting these doubts, however, was his curiosity. He hadn't even *seen* Marlowe House for over a quarter of a century, since the last of those summer days at the Oval. More than forty-five years had passed since he had actually stepped inside the place. On balance, therefore, and much to his own surprise, he found himself inclined to say yes.

'It's not a bad idea,' he said, 'although much will depend on how it is all put together.'

Angelo gave a small grin of satisfaction as Otto continued, 'I agree to it in principle, although I'll want to know a little more beforehand about how we approach this and how it will be presented to the public.'

'Of course. I'll ask Chloe some questions and get back to you.'

'I'm not saying I wish to exercise editorial control, but at the same time I don't want to be the victim of a stitch-up like before.'

So he does remember. 'I fully understand.'

'I want the integrity of the residents protected, too. I don't want any exploitative nonsense that sets out to demonise the people who live there. I know there are problems with crime but I don't want them exaggerated. And I'm really not sure I want to walk around accompanied by a bunch of heavies!'

'It's something we can discuss. We'll need to talk through the practicalities at a later stage.'

They seemed to be progressing rapidly, although there was still one formidable barrier to overcome. Angelo braved the subject.

'What about Anika? Will she mind you doing this?'

'I'm not sure how she'll feel about it, to be perfectly honest. She can be very protective towards me, as you know. Too protective, sometimes. And it's only got more pronounced since the surgery. If anything, she's become convinced that I'm a lot more doddery than I actually am. She'll hardly let me do anything around the house these days. It can be very frustrating.'

'I'm sure it can, Otto.'

They both sensed the slight embarrassment that had descended. Otto never usually discussed his marriage during conversations with Angelo, perhaps as a consequence of the age difference between the two men. Somehow they had strayed inadvertently onto the topic now.

'I'll do my best,' Otto concluded brusquely. 'I'll talk to Anika when she gets back from the tennis club this evening. Will you be in the office again tomorrow? I'll call you then.'

As Otto had suspected, Anika was unhappy about the idea. She pointed her racquet towards him like a long, accusing finger. Did he *want* to kill himself? Was he out of his mind? He had recently undergone three episodes of major surgery,

41

there were days when he was too frail to even leave the house, and now he wanted to do *what*?

She paused for a moment, breathing heavily, and then rallied again to an even faster tempo.

Just think of the stress he would be under, away from his routine, in unfamiliar and hostile surroundings – this wasn't the 1950s, London wasn't Switzerland – did he know the dangers? Well, she could tell him a thing or two. *She* still read the English newspapers, even if he chose to avoid them. There were guns in London, nowadays – did he know that? *There were guns.* People used them . . . all the time. And where exactly was Angelo in all this? He *wanted* him to do it? She had thought that Angelo cared about Otto, who used to be his mentor, after all.

Anika's emotional response – and the pointing racquet of doom – seemed a little over the top to Otto. But her concern for his well-being was genuine enough. He was sorry to have upset her. The storm passed after several minutes, and she apologised. Yet it was clear from the way she fidgeted on the couch that her anxiety hadn't left her.

'It's only a television documentary,' Otto told her. 'I'm not joining Special Forces.'

It raised a reluctant smile, and things were a little better after that. He offered her the same reassurances that Angelo had offered him.

'Two nights in a hotel, followed by four in Marlowe House. What could possibly go wrong? I'll be well looked after.'

But he felt absurd even having to say this.

How did it come to this? he thought, sadly. A few short years ago we were travelling the world together. We were staying in a tent in the Australian Outback when I first noticed that my stomach wasn't quite right. Five years on and she doesn't trust me to survive a week in London.

'Why do you want to do this, Otto?'

'I told you. Because it will help the campaign to save the building. It wouldn't be fair of me to expect poor Angelo to do all the work. He's being generous enough as it is.'

She inspected his expression closely. He was reluctant to look her in the eye.

'No,' she said. 'There's more to it than that. More than just a sense of fair play or professional pride. There's another reason, a deeper reason, something you're reluctant to explain.'

Dammit, he thought. She's found me out again. It was quite uncanny, this forensic ability to dissect his motives. Beneath her unflinching gaze, he sometimes felt like a disorientated traveller, cowering in the glare of a desert sun.

'All right,' he said to her. 'I'll tell you what it is. I need to find a purpose again. I need to feel that I still have something to offer. I'm sick and tired of twiddling my thumbs all day, waiting for a special delivery from the Grim Reaper.'

Anika thought this over.

'You feel you have no purpose?'

'I don't. Not any more.'

'Is this a recent feeling? You've said nothing before.'

'I'd never really noticed it before. It's not something I've been consciously withholding.'

'So why now? Why do you suddenly feel this way? We have a lovely life here in Switzerland, the two of us . . . don't we?'

'Of course we do. I'm an extremely lucky man. I really couldn't ask for anything more. It's the surgery, I suppose. These aches and pains have brought it home to me. I'm getting old,

43

Anika, time is passing. I don't know how many years I may have left.'

She looked alarmed, momentarily, and he sought to intercept her fears as they surfaced.

'Please don't misunderstand me. There'll be *many* more years, I hope. The journey of my life hasn't yet reached its terminus, even if the buffet car has closed. I just need to feel that I'm doing more than marking time.'

Anika nodded, as though in confirmation of some private and long-standing doubt.

'You're unhappy,' she said. 'I knew as much, if I'm honest with myself. I just didn't want to admit it all this time.'

Otto realised just how his explanation must have sounded and immediately felt terrible for having spoken. Taking hold of her hands – slightly callused, from practising her topspin – he sought through touch to reassure her. Suddenly, *he* was no longer the child. It happened like that, sometimes.

'Of course I'm happy,' he told her, gently. 'Very happy indeed. I didn't mean it to sound as significant as it did. I just want to do something different for a while, embark on a new adventure. And besides, it's hardly a trip to outer space I'm undertaking. It will all be over and done with in no time.'

And his words appeared to work.

'Well, I hope you know what you're doing,' she said, her signal that she was about to concede defeat.

So do I, thought Otto, stroking her hands apologetically.

But he replied to her with a cheerful: 'I'll be fine.'

Five

Otto's fingers were stained with blackberry juice as he crouched before the hedgerows lining the garden. He had already filled one plastic bag with berries, and was about to start on a second, when he raised his head to contemplate the ripening season. Autumn's tones were dominant now in the depths of the forested slopes: soft reds, wilting browns and bright explosions of yellow, immersing summer's green.

'There's no dissonance in nature,' he remembered Cynthia once telling him, searching the hedgerows for blackberries in another place and time. 'There's no bad taste, or excess – not a single colour jars. Left alone, its elements always harmonise.'

When Anika appeared at the french window and saw her husband at the bottom of the garden, her heart gave a little jump. Otto was kneeling before the hedgerow, his head bowed forwards and his body completely still. She made her way quickly across the lawn, calling out his name, and was relieved when he turned and looked towards her. By the time she reached him, he was struggling to his feet with the help of his cane. A fistful of crushed blackberries had slid to the ground beside him.

'Otto,' she said. 'What on earth are you doing? Didn't you hear me calling from the house?'

'I'd forgotten about the blackberries.'

'There isn't time for the blackberries. You're going to miss your flight!'

'But it may be too late by the time I come back. Some of them have rotted already.'

'*I'll* do them while you're away in London. I'll put them on my to-do list.'

Otto wanted to tell her that this wasn't the point; that it wasn't about the blackberries themselves. The important thing was that *he* should gather them, as he had done every year since building the villa. He couldn't believe he had forgotten to do it, something of such significance. How on earth could the matter have slipped his mind?

'Please, Otto. Don't just stand there staring at the hedgerow. You *have* to get a move on. You have to go and make your documentary. Go and get changed at once. I'm really not sure we'll have time to get to the airport.'

Otto hobbled up the garden path beside Anika, who fished in the pocket of her cardigan and removed his letter to Pierre.

'I found this in your study. Would you like me to post it on for you?'

Otto reached out with unusual swiftness and took it from her hand.

'I'll deal with it later.'

He slipped the letter into his pocket. He must remember to put it into the bin before he left.

'Oh, and do try to keep your study in a more hygienic

condition,' Anika added, sliding back the french window and shepherding him inside. 'It's starting to smell quite horribly of rotten eggs.'

By the time they arrived at the airport in Geneva, the atmosphere between them had grown tense. Due to a number of conferences taking place across the city, there were no spaces left in which Anika could park.

'It's okay,' Otto told her. 'You don't have to see me all the way onto the aircraft. I can find my own way there. Why don't you just drop me off outside the Departures building? It's getting late.'

And whose fault is that? thought Anika.

But she held her tongue.

She agreed to Otto's suggestion, but sought at the final moment to establish a compromise. Pulling up in front of Departures, she helped Otto out with his case and then attempted to wheel it on his behalf into the building. It was the last of these stages that got to him.

'I'm fine,' he said, as they began to wrestle for control of the gently rocking case. 'I'm *fine*, I tell you. Get back to the Bentley, or the bastards will tow it away!'

Still Anika persisted, refusing to let go of the case. Her strength was more than a match for his, these days. Gaining a grip on its extendable handle, she fended off his feeble efforts to prise her fingers free, and looked around for someone in a uniform to ask for assistance.

'Don't be silly, Otto,' she said to him. 'If you won't allow me to take it for you, at least let me find someone else who can help you. There must be a member of staff around here somewhere.'

Otto's temper finally snapped.

'I can pull a fucking luggage case, for heaven's sake! Why do you have to treat me like an invalid all the time?'

He sensed the jolt that his angry words had given Anika. He had overreacted, he knew, but he was worried about missing his flight. His irritation had been worsened by the amused glances of one or two passers-by.

'As you wish,' Anika answered calmly, choosing to retreat.

Letting go of the handle, she stepped forward to kiss him, formal and frosty, upon both cheeks. Then she turned and walked back to the Bentley, not even glancing back as she settled behind the wheel and shut the door. Otto sighed as he raised the handle of his case, turning and wheeling it slowly – and with more effort than he had anticipated – in the direction of the glass doors of the Departures building. They were just opening for him when a kerfuffle behind caught his attention. He turned and saw Anika running towards him, waving a holdall in her hand. It had been left on the back seat of the Bentley. She had glimpsed it in the rear-view mirror as she was pulling out.

'Otto . . . ' she was calling to him.

It was unusual for Anika to forget any detail like that. Normally she organised their lives with military precision. It was a sign that she was not quite herself today. Otto waited on the pavement for her to reach him. She handed over the holdall, containing a thick ream of notepaper he had been unable to fit into his suitcase, together with a photograph of the two of them standing arm-in-arm before the Matterhorn. Anika had put it there herself.

Suddenly, she threw her arms around him in a tight and unforeseen embrace. He felt a painful compression on his midriff, weakened by the surgery, closely followed by a mysterious gurgling sound.

'My stomach!' he cried hurriedly (and yet awkwardly, almost an apology), causing Anika to jump back with a sudden gasp of remembrance. The handsome bone structure in her face appeared to disintegrate.

'I can't even hug you properly any more,' she said, her voice now cracking completely.

It was the tipping point Anika had been working hard to avoid. She had tried throughout that day to remain composed, determined to maintain her usual decorum. But now her breath began to catch because of the tears she was suppressing, and suddenly it all went badly wrong for her. She surprised even herself with the loud and wrenching sob, a sound that was not quite her own. The emotion was released along with a great strand of mucus, which she hastily wiped from a cheek in mortification. She quickly regained her composure; it was almost instantaneous, but too late to stop the message that had been sent. For a moment Otto stood looking at her, shocked and embarrassed on her behalf. She had always been such a graceful person, an archetype of elegance and bodily control. Even in the deepest throes of their lovemaking she had always exhibited an underlying restraint. He couldn't quite believe what he had just seen, and in a public place as well. But then he was stirred, at a deeper level, by this sudden sign of vulnerability, written across and then cleared from Anika's face. It was a similar feeling of compassion, he realised, that had caused her to hug him so tightly just now, and it took him an effort to avoid reciprocating the gesture. Instead he gently stroked the offending cheek.

Otto's intestines and Anika's snot: two unlikely catalysts for the rediscovery of love. Yet each felt oddly moved now by these signs of the other's humanity; by the body's secrets, cruelly exposed. They stood gazing at each other in empathy – not quite sure how to express the depths of what they felt. Then a quick peck on the cheek and she was on her way back to the car.

'Phone me when you get there,' she called from across the bonnet.

Otto gave a little wave of acknowledgement.

Six

It was a shock when he first saw her. The same pale-blue eyes, lightly hooded, sharply intelligent; the same small crease beside the mouth as she smiled; and then a flash of teeth, behind the full lips, followed by a downward tilt of the head and an upward glance of the eyes, suggesting a well-hidden shyness. The hair was different, though – what did he expect? It was almost sixty years later. Shorter, messier, no soft wave falling across the forehead. It was uncanny, though. It was uncanny.

I think this is going to be rather difficult, thought Otto, rising to his feet for the introductions.

They were about to dine in a restaurant on the South Bank, where Angelo had suggested they meet.

Otto had felt surprisingly nervous on the plane across from Geneva; not from any fear of flying, but a fear of what he was flying *to*. It was twenty-five years since he had left England. He had no idea how he had managed to avoid it for so long. Or had he been avoiding it? Was it just the way things had worked out? He didn't know the answer to that.

Throughout the short flight he experienced a strange inner turbulence. He had a queasy sensation that he was re-establishing a connection with the past; flying backwards into his own memories. He would no longer be experiencing them from a distance, but in the city where they had once been real.

At least you'll have some time to acclimatise, he told himself. You can relax in the hotel for a couple of nights. You're not moving into Marlowe House immediately.

As he pondered the days to come, Otto shifted about uncomfortably in his seat. The air pressure in the cabin unsettled him. He began to worry that he might encounter problems with his stomach, and tried relaxing to some anodyne music station, the most soothing thing he could find on the in-flight entertainment menu. But every few minutes he would take off his headphones and listen for tell-tale gurgling sounds. Everything was fine, it was just his paranoia, but he could tell from the glances of the air steward patrolling the aisles that he hadn't covered his agitation as well as he had hoped.

Arriving at Heathrow, he felt a little better. The familiar rhythms of transition – escalators, ambient music, the steady churning of the baggage carousel – began to soothe him. By the time Angelo had met him at the gate and ushered him into the passenger seat of his car, Otto was feeling quite chatty. The mood stayed with him throughout that day: hotel, café, sightseeing along the Embankment. Even as they sat in the restaurant, awaiting their evening appointment, Otto found himself enjoying a light-headed nostalgia. It washed softly through him like the Thames below their window.

And then *she* walked into the room.

Feeling sick as he climbed to his feet, Otto reached out a hand. He heard, as through a haze, Angelo's voice addressing him.

'Otto – this is Chloe, your director.'

She took his hand. The touch was different ... Thank God for that. It meant he could speak, at least.

'Delighted to meet you, Chloe.'

'Hello, Otto.'

The voice, too, was different. Lighter, less serious. The giddiness was dispersing now.

'These are the other members of my film crew – Simon and Paul.'

In his shock, Otto had not even noticed there were others. Now he saw their faces. Young, kind, compassionate; the eyes meeting his, the hands outstretched.

'Hello, Otto.'

'Nice to meet you.'

Their faces now turned away from him – the hands reaching out to Angelo.

As they retook their places and prepared for the opening volley of conversation, Otto felt her eyes upon him. But he could cope with no more than a glimmer of contact, the merest of smiles, and then he had to look away. He reached for his glass of water, welcomed its coolness in his throat ... seized the chance to briefly shut his eyes.

Their switch into the preliminaries was effortless. Angelo was good at these rituals, and the others seemed practised, too. Otto felt grateful for their conversational polish. He could take a back seat in all this. Just the occasional interjection. Yes, the flight was fine – about twenty-five years now – yes, it certainly had changed – he had caught only a glimpse of the Shard earlier, but he hoped to see it properly tomorrow. He soon established his role. If they were a small orchestra, then he was the timpani player, sitting tight on the sidelines and making his presence felt with an occasional well-timed flourish. His age was a help (he didn't often think that, nowadays) and they were perhaps a little overawed by his natural gravitas.

Otto felt so diminished, sometimes, that he didn't realise what an impressive physical presence he remained. Very tall, lightly tanned, thin and with a full head of longish white hair, swept back rakishly from striking brown eyes. When dressed for the occasion – today he wore a blue blazer and a silk cravat, the white hair tumbling down over his collar – he could still attract admiring female glances, much to his astonishment.

So he could take it easy, then, play the wise owl, not make too much of an effort to impress. Moreover, it was clear from the shape of the conversation, and the way that Chloe and her colleagues often finished their sentences with a quick glance over to seek his approval, that, if anything, *they* were here to impress *him*. He felt relieved about that. It took the pressure off. And it bought him some time to regain his mental balance.

Otto had arrived at the restaurant with plenty of questions. There were many things he wanted to know about their plans for the television feature, which was scheduled to begin filming the day after tomorrow. But then he had caught sight of her as she walked into the restaurant and his brain had been completely overturned. The lurching sensation had struck him like seasickness, as if the restaurant were suddenly a small ship and the Thames a raging ocean.

A waiter took their order, and with no more impending interruptions on the horizon the conversation deepened. It looked as if it would be a while until they got down to the nitty-gritty of talking about the documentary, becoming side-tracked into a general discussion about the merits of post-war architecture. Angelo could never resist the topic. Freed from any need to follow the thread too closely, Otto repeated his initial thought once more to himself, in order to confirm it.

She looks exactly like a young Cynthia.

Followed by a question.

What does that signify?

On the plane, he had been struck by that odd sense of foreboding that he was somehow flying back into his past. Now, within a few hours of landing, he had met someone whom a less rational man might suspect to be the reincarnation of his late wife.

When did Cynthia leave us again? he thought. And how old do you think this young woman is?

He caught himself making some mental calculations and stopped.

Idiot. But the resemblance is remarkable, isn't it?

He glanced over at Angelo, who was explaining some of the central precepts of Modernism, and tried to work out whether he had spotted it, too. But from his effusive manner and gently waving hands, it appeared that Angelo had noticed nothing.

But then he had hardly known Cynthia, having been in his mid-twenties when she died. He had very recently joined the practice at the time. Besides, he only ever saw Cyn in middle age – when she was already sick and somewhat changed. He had never known her when she was like this.

As Chloe leaned forward to speak to Angelo and the others, Otto took the opportunity to study her face more closely. He still didn't think he could handle any eye contact, and would have to glance away again if she suddenly aimed those pale-blue eyes towards him. As he had already noted, the similarities lay not just in her features – and my goodness, they are close enough, he thought – but in the gestures, the expressions. That was the most striking part. There was her mode of eye contact as she spoke, moving methodically from one face to the next, gauging and including. Her laugh, too; not so much the sound, but the little throw back of the head – delighting in the moment. And then she did something that truly floored him. As she listened to Angelo, she took off the small bracelet she wore on her left wrist (unthinkingly, as she was still intent on the conversation), and spun it between the fingers of her right hand. Three times in one direction, then three times in the other. Quickly, dextrously – no one else at the table even noticed – and then slipped it back onto her wrist.

Otto sat back in his chair.

I thought I'd never see that again.

The first time he had done so – the first time they had spoken – was in a student café in Bloomsbury in the mid-1950s. But they had already spotted each other some weeks before, at the Architectural Association on Bedford Square, a prestigious college with a reputation for cutting-edge design where the two of them were working towards their professional qualifications. Otto had already been studying there several years. She was newly arrived from the United States. Strange, now, to think that he had ever lived in this city without her.

56

Cynthia was impressed at first sight by the rake-thin young man with the luminous skin and soulful eyes, whose presentation on Le Corbusier confirmed for her the reputation she had already heard about from others. She and her friends would track around the library the progression of this enigmatic figure, who apparently preferred to live among the poorer communities of Lambeth, rather than take his rightful place among the fashionable young bohemians of Bloomsbury. Otto's evasiveness, together with his obvious intelligence, only added to his allure, and within a few weeks of Cynthia's arrival at the college, he was already firmly established on her radar. For the time being, however, she kept her distance, knowing she was not short of allure herself.

It was common knowledge that Cynthia had taken her first degree at New York's Columbia University. It was also known that she had lived for a while in fashionable Greenwich Village. Rumour had it that she once drank coffee just two tables away from James Dean. The first thing that drew Otto's attention, however, was her headwear. Most days she wore a stylish black beret, tilted down slightly to the left, which she could use very effectively to either shelter from view, or offer up for contemplation, the blue eyes beneath the auburn wave. With the smoke from a cigarette curling constantly around her face, she had all the credentials of an authentic beatnik. Not only was she the kind of person who could appreciate Abstract Expressionism, she looked like someone who might understand the complexities of modern jazz.

Walking alone into the café that particular day, Otto spotted her at a table by the window. She was reading a dog-eared copy of *Orlando*, pausing now and then to stir her coffee with a silver spoon. Settling down at an adjacent table, and calculating the best strategy for interrupting her reading, he was spared further anguish by her glance, smile of recognition and offer of a place at her table. He was impressed at once by her confidence and maturity, if a little taken aback by her cut-glass English accent.

'You're not from New York, then?'

'No, I'm Home Counties born and bred. My spell at Columbia was the first time I'd ever been to the States. My father has business contacts in America, you see, which is how I came to study there.'

'New York must have been exciting.'

'Yes, I enjoyed it, greatly. But I decided to come back home to complete my studies. And you're Austrian, I hear?'

'Technically, yes, although I haven't actually lived there since I was young. German remains my first language, however, and the accent I have kept, or so I am told. Are you living near to the college?'

'Not too far away. I have a place on Marchmont Street – just up the road from here.'

'And you are renting there?'

She looked a little awkward.

'No, it's a family heirloom. My parents have owned it for years. It's convenient for my studies and great for the West End. I've heard a rumour that you live somewhere in the far south, is that right?'

'It's not so far, but it is south of the river. I have a room in Lambeth.'

'And what drew you down there?'

'At first, there was a mixing-up with the accommodation. This was a few years ago, when I first came to study here. The forms I filled out for the college were lost, and so I had to find somewhere quickly. And then, once I was there, I grew to like it. The atmosphere is different. They are maybe more like human beings down there.'

They both laughed.

'You will have to excuse me. My English is still not always so good. I express myself a little oddly on occasion.'

'It's okay. I understand what you mean. And I think there is probably more truth to your words than you intended. Bloomsbury can feel a little artificial sometimes, although it's a shame that you're so cut off from everyone. You're missing out on a lot – there's quite a vibrant community up here. You should think about leaving the human beings and coming up to live with the Bloomsbury Set. We don't want you sitting down there all alone, brooding away in your attic like some mad genius. You're clearly well ahead on your reading – well ahead of some of the lecturers, from what I've heard. Come north and broaden your scope.'

'My scope?'

'Your outlook – your potential.'

'You think I have potential?'

Cynthia gave him a look, then, holding his eyes with confidence as she drew on her cigarette, the smoke wreathing sensuously around her face.

'I think you have lots of potential, Otto.'

She paused and stubbed out her cigarette into the ashtray. Her restless hands detached the silver bracelet and spun it between her fingers . . .

Otto's throat began to tighten at the memory. He was becoming emotional. Tears were squeezing their way out of the corners of his eyes.

Steady, you old fool. Calm yourself. Start blubbing now and the game is up. They'll lock you away for ever.

With a considerable effort, he forced his attention away from the bracelet – how many times he had seen that, in so many places, but don't give in to it, not here – and back to the conversation taking place around him. He was relieved when the food arrived shortly afterwards, and they moved on to the business in hand.

Otto voiced some of the concerns he had previously mentioned to Angelo, but this time only in the most cursory of ways. All pride and suspicion seemed to have drained from him as if the evening's events had sapped his will. He had seen enough to convince him that these young people had sufficient integrity to do their job properly. He should leave them alone to get on with it. Besides, in a sense he felt that he had no choice but to go along with whatever came his way. The bizarre coincidence that he had just come to terms with over dinner seemed to have effectively ruled out any alternative. There was no backing away now, even if he wanted to.

Fate was one of those words Otto detested – a hangover from the superstitious past. When it came to explaining baffling occurrences, he preferred to think in terms of autonomous bodies, circulating through space-time, and sometimes forming chance events that to the irrational mind might seem to have been preordained. To him, it was a simple question of physics. Nevertheless, he was forced to admit that this particular chance event had affected him strangely. He felt that something was under way over which he had little control.

'Do you have an itinerary for the filming?' he asked Chloe, for the sake of finding something to discuss.

'Yes,' she said, 'it's pretty straightforward. We'll start with three full days, but after that things should be easier for you. Just the afternoon, on the fourth day, and the morning on the fifth. That will give you a little recovery time.'

Good God, thought Otto. They think I might keel over halfway through.

But the news that he would be given some time to himself was welcome.

'And would it be presumptuous of me to ask what sort of questions you might throw at me? I don't wish to be awkward, but I was hoping for some time to prepare my answers. I'm not as good at speaking off the cuff as I once was.'

'I won't ask anything especially challenging. But if it's all the same to you, I'd rather not give too much away in advance. Better to keep things fresh, I think, for the cameras.'

'Of course. I understand.'

'In general terms, we'll be looking at a number of issues. The condition of the building, the possibilities for a listing, the debate about the merits of post-war architecture. But we don't want anything too heavy or technical. We want the film to be more personal in tone.'

'I see,' said Otto.

The tone of his voice caused Angelo to look up quickly.

'We want to explore your emotional journey – your feelings on seeing the building again. That will be the core theme of the documentary. I imagine it will be quite a nostalgic experience for you, and we'd like to capture that as best we can.'

Angelo wondered what Otto might say. His expression looked oddly frozen. Was he about to ruin everything at the last?

Otto's face relaxed.

'I'm afraid I'm not terribly good at expressing emotion; rather difficult to prise from my shell. But you're welcome to give it a try, of course, if you feel it might be of interest to your viewers.'

He smiled pleasantly at Chloe, and she returned the gesture.

'Thank you for the opportunity,' she said.

Angelo breathed a silent sigh of relief.

Seven

'So you're happy then?' Angelo asked Otto, once they were ensconced in the taxi and crossing over Blackfriars Bridge once more. He was surprised at how straightforward it had all seemed.

'Yes, they seem very nice. I can't say I'm exactly relishing the prospect, but I'm sure they'll make it as painless as possible.'

'Good ... good ...'

Angelo glanced over at Otto, but he was looking out of the window, his body turned slightly away. Now wasn't the time for a post-mortem on the evening's proceedings.

A few minutes earlier, as they climbed into the back of the taxi, Angelo – buoyed by the evening's success – had asked Otto if he would like to take a detour via Marlowe House.

'We needn't get out, or even stop,' he had told him. 'Just take a peek before the filming begins.'

But he had misjudged the mood.

'It's late,' Otto said, 'and I'm feeling tired. I'd rather just get back to my hotel, if you don't mind. I'll see it again, soon enough.'

Angelo sensed that something was wrong, but Otto's seniority and the peculiar dynamics of their relationship – close in some ways, distant in others – meant that he couldn't possibly ask him outright. So he spent much of the cab journey trying to work it out for himself.

At first, he wondered whether Otto was unhappy about being in a taxi with him at all. Angelo had secretly promised Anika that he would see Otto safely back to his hotel. Perhaps Otto had guessed that some arrangement had been made. He certainly seemed a little put out when Angelo insisted on sharing a cab with him. Otto was fully aware that Angelo's house in Dulwich was in the opposite direction to his Marylebone hotel.

Or perhaps Otto still harboured secret doubts about the television programme.

Have I pushed him into this? thought Angelo. Just a little?

The problem with Otto was that he was such a powerful personality, so innately strong-willed, that it was easy to forget, sometimes, that he was now elderly. Anika was right in many ways. She didn't see Otto as Angelo did, as a gifted architect and a man of near-superhuman qualities. Because she was not part of the profession herself, and hadn't known Otto until his best days were behind him, she saw him for what he currently was: her weak and vulnerable husband, who had very nearly died on the operating table a few months before. Angelo had always thought of Anika as a bit of an obstacle; as someone who didn't quite appreciate or understand the man she had married. Yet he had been unfair to her.

I'm the one with the skewed perspective, he thought. She sees Otto as he is, not as he was. She sees the person and not the reputation. I really must make more effort to see it from her side.

Then Angelo thought of Daniel. Was it *he* who was bothering Otto? In all their discussions of recent weeks, Otto had never once mentioned Daniel; even here, in the city where his son was born, and where he still lived with his own young family.

Angelo glanced over at Otto, who remained staring out of the window. The rapidly passing street lights played across an inscrutable face, fluttering between light and darkness in a roll of moving stills.

They were entering the heart of the Square Mile. There was some interesting architecture in this part of town. Otto looked out for examples now to distract himself from other thoughts. St Paul's, the Old Bailey, the meat market at Smithfield. He glimpsed a fragment of Roman wall as they swung around a corner of the Barbican. Otto was consciously emptying London of all emotional content, regarding it in purely professional terms, with the detached eye of the connoisseur.

As they reached the busy West End, his attention broadened from individual structures to the scene as a whole. From the back of the cab it seemed to be a city of shape-shifters. Buildings, traffic, streets and people became hybrid, animate beings in perpetual flux. At night, he thought, new evolutionary orders seemed possible; all types of matter appeared equally alive. The brightly lit advertisements were clearly in rudest health, the species best adapted to this strange primordial world. The figures moving beneath them were at a lower stage of development: submerged beneath the neon's glare; drifting through the murky depths in states of flickering consciousness.

Otto suddenly spoke, his gaze not stirring from the window.

'Where's Marchmont Street from here? I'm afraid I'm a little lost.'

Otto had moved into Cynthia's apartment there the day after they were married at a local registry office. The summer of 1956. He had almost no possessions. The books that filled his rented room were all loans from the college library. On the day of the move he condensed his life to the size of two small suitcases, which Cynthia helped him carry across from Russell Square tube station.

'Marchmont Street? It's some way behind us. We passed it a while ago.'

Angelo was about to ask if they should turn around, but he sensed that this was not what Otto wanted. Instead he sought to draw him out of himself.

'What was the apartment like?' he asked.

'Small, functional, prone to draughts and cold. It was located above a small grocery shop. I would pop downstairs in my dressing gown and slippers whenever we needed milk or bread.'

Even now he could hear the heavy jangling of the bell; smell the fresh spices as he pushed open the door.

Angelo waited to see if Otto would expand any further, but he was gazing once more out of the window. A reflective silence returned to the cab. This time, Angelo allowed it to settle.

*

In his hotel bedroom, Otto lifted his suitcase onto a chair. He was feeling tired and not especially looking forward to the lengthy routine of preparing for bed. With a yawn, he removed the various items that were needed for his nightly ablutions. After taking off his clothing, he gathered up the materials and headed for the bathroom.

Back at home, the lighting was dim and discreet, allowing him to wash in a welcome soft focus. It was bright enough for him to see what he was doing, yet hazy enough to allow him to avoid the graphic detail. When he switched on the bathroom light now, however, and saw himself naked in its full-length mirror, Otto gasped in shock. The bathroom itself was luxuriously appointed: large sunken tub, marble tiles and a bidet. But its lighting was the stuff of nightmares. By creating a strong chiaroscuro effect, bathing parts of the room in a lurid brightness while hiding others in shadow, it threw his body into pitilessly stark relief. Not only did it emphasise every nook, cranny, scar, wrinkle, sag, vein, liver-spot and blemish on his grey and collapsing body, it elevated them all to some kind of hyper-reality.

'Well,' said Otto, transfixed and repulsed by his own reflection, 'there's nothing beautiful about *this* raw material.'

He was amazed at his own skin, which appeared to have acquired the shade and texture of beaten concrete. For one surreal moment, he saw himself metamorphose into one of his own buildings; one in urgent need of heavy maintenance.

When did this happen? he asked himself. I know my body is on the downward slide – it has been for the past forty years or so. But I didn't realise things had sunk quite this low.

Were the lights at home in the villa really that flattering? Or had the ones in the hotel bathroom been installed by a sadist?

There was no sign now of the dashing silver gentleman in the blue blazer and cravat. What a cruel illusion *that* had turned out to be.

Fighting back squeamishness, Otto began to study the scars from his operations, then the other marks and blemishes recording a long, long lifetime of accidents, injuries and illnesses. He had taken quite a battering. The knots and weals remained etched upon his flesh, as deep and vivid as a Dürer woodcut. Each one represented a different memory – a different crisis or trauma in his life. Otto ran his fingers across these marks in fascination, recalling each incident, when he could, and wondering how on earth he had managed to get this far at all. He marvelled at the resilience of the human body, of the human beings who suffered these blows and still kept bouncing back. All was laid before him here, nothing now was hidden. In the unforgiving light of the hotel bathroom, Otto had become a living map of almost a century of pain.

Twenty minutes later, he re-emerged from the bathroom. It was too late to call Anika – he would do it in the morning. He put on his pyjamas – yes, hide it all away now, please – and climbed into one side of the large double bed. Stretching behind him, he rearranged the pillows to his satisfaction, then set and checked the alarm clock that would wake him far too soon.

Perhaps they should list *me*, he thought, reaching out to the bedside light to welcome darkness.

Eight

Otto telephoned Angelo the next morning, to tell him he wasn't feeling too good. In truth he felt fine; surprisingly so, given what he had witnessed in the bathroom mirror the previous evening. He felt oddly rejuvenated – mentally, at least – and decided to cancel their sightseeing in order to pursue an alternative itinerary.

'Do you need a doctor?' asked Angelo, sounding concerned.

'I need a conservator,' Otto replied. 'But there's nothing especially wrong with me this morning, if that's what you mean. I'm feeling a little tired, that is all, and would like a quiet day reading in the hotel.'

After telephoning Anika, he repeated the previous night's procedure, but found that by opening the curtains and propping open the bathroom door he could avoid switching on any lights. While showering, he drew up a shortlist of possible locations, but it was a delicate matter that required him to second-guess his own psychological state.

Having faced up to, and faced down, his physical scars the

night before – a difficult experience, but a strangely cathartic one – Otto resolved that it was time to approach the mental ones. He was back where it had all happened, for the next few days at least. So it was time to stop avoiding it; time to stop pretending that London was a city, for him, like any other. Some interesting buildings, a neatly packaged history, a passing glimpse of Abbey, Tower and Gherkin. Then perhaps a pint of bitter in a welcoming pub. Who was he trying to fool? The capital he knew couldn't be condensed to a postcard. The physical past mapped onto Otto's body had its echo and its counterpoint: a psychological past, mapped onto the fabric of London itself. As with his flesh the night before, it was time for him to explore that past as unflinchingly as possible.

Otto carried a detailed map of his personal geography, buried and ignored within his psyche. He knew the location of every mental blemish, each emotional welt and scar – places he had avoided thinking about, in some cases for decades. Joyous memories, too, but sometimes made painful by subsequent events. Now it was time to unearth this map of memories and go in search of them once more. He must be careful, though, he realised. He couldn't go just anywhere. Not yet. His giddiness in the restaurant the previous evening should act as a warning. There were some locations that remained off-limits, at least until he had properly broken himself in. The Royal Free Hospital in Hampstead, for instance – he would certainly not be going anywhere near there. Here be dragons, Otto thought. Kenwood House, up on the Heath, that would also have to wait for another day, perhaps indefinitely. Even their old house in Hampstead would be too much for him now. No, he would have to try something more straightforward. Somewhere quotidian; less emotive. A source of unequivocally happy memories, or at least relatively neutral ones.

Drawing back the curtain, Otto peered at the traffic rumbling along Marylebone Road. The autumn day was grey, but no rain appeared to threaten. Perhaps he should start with a short walk. Nothing too ambitious – nothing involving the crush or confusion of public transport. Angelo had mentioned something about an Oyster Card to him. What on earth could that be? No, he should go easy on himself. Start with a short stroll somewhere near by, indulge in a little light nostalgia, and then back again to the safety of his hotel.

Otto consulted the virtual *A to Z* that to his great surprise, and with the precision of a cab driver, he still retained inside his head. The discovery pleased him, like a forgotten keepsake, uncovered in storage. An idea then came to him. If he was going to face the music, he might as well do so literally. He put on his overcoat and homburg, and sought out his wooden cane.

The area had changed, he noted, but not to the stage of disorientation. Marylebone High Street felt a little more chic, a little more monied, but as an area that had always exuded an air of comfort, it had not undergone the wholesale transformation he had heard about in some areas of the city. Passing the boutiques and gourmet food stores, he dusted the fallen leaves with his cane, looking out for dog-mess and uneven paving (he had quickly relearned *those* lessons the previous day). He took pleasure in the damp and heavy London air, its slight chill sharpening his thoughts. He absorbed the noise of pedestrians and traffic, enjoyed the familiar rattle of the passing black cabs.

71

At the corner of St Vincent Street, he stopped off for a coffee at an American chain. Intimidated by the menu's scale, its complex variations, he settled for a glass of fruit juice; pondered a detour; browsed a favourite bookshop that had survived. Wigmore Hall, on arrival, was comforting. No tightening of the thorax or quickening of the pulse. He had chosen wisely. Its iron and glass canopy remained unchanged, as did the promise of a free lunchtime concert, which had drawn them there so often when they worked in Portland Place. Otto made his way cautiously inside, as though intruding upon his own past.

The recital was excellent. A young Russian pianist played a late Schubert sonata. She sat hunched in anguish over the keys, the awkwardness of her posture running counter to the serene beauty of her playing. Each note seemed wrenched from her, but betrayed no sign of its cost. How different an experience it would be for those listening at home, he thought (the recitals were broadcast live on Radio 3).

A memory struck him; the first of that day.

Didn't we see Alfred Brendel here, playing this same piece? Around the time we were expecting Daniel?

She had sat curled against him, he remembered. He had felt the small stirrings of her belly against his side.

Outside the concert hall, Otto paused on the pavement and found his bearings. This way. His faded leather brogues led him instinctively onward, bodily memory outpacing his mind. So many times he had trodden these streets, in so many weathers and states of mind. When returning to the office with Cynthia following their lunchtime trips to Wigmore Hall, the bustling district through which they passed had seemed as insubstantial as air. Elevated as they were by the music to another plane, deep in conversation or a yet more intimate silence, their feet barely seemed to brush the pavement as they floated through the dissolving streets.

Otto now reached Portland Place and stood before the imposing Georgian terrace that had once sheltered, in its upper storeys, the offices of their long-disbanded architectural partnership. He climbed the steps to inspect the brass nameplates beside the door. A legal firm, financial advisors, someone fashionable in graphic design. Stepping back, he counted up to the fourth-floor window, its thick sill permitting just a glint of tall pane above. It was enough for him. He felt no wish to trouble the current occupants, no urge to enter the building and mount its winding stairs. Besides which, everything inside would doubtless be different. Only the dimensions of the rooms were likely to be the same. And Otto needed no assistance to recall the light-filled space of their former office. He could still see the brilliantined heads, bent in concentration over the worktables. He could sense the thick, creative silence — the slide and loop of set-square and compass; hear the scrape of pencil on paper, a reed-thin sound giving birth to new forms. The sensations Otto had experienced within its walls would stay with him all his life. They represented a time when he had been at his most productive; maybe at his happiest.

In another corner of Portland Place stood the headquarters of the Royal Institute of British Architects. In the mid-1960s, when moving their partnership across from Fitzrovia into offices on this square, Otto, Cynthia and their colleagues at Unit 5 had believed they were challenging the architectural establishment, as represented by this edifice. All these years later, however, Otto wondered if they had secretly been hankering to join it. He stood before the entrance, which was flanked by two nude statues in stone. Again he felt no impulse to go inside, not even to visit the bookshop near its entrance. There was a danger that he would be recognised, for one thing, and then he might find himself caught up in lots of interminable conversations.

More than sixty years earlier, in November 1951, it was exactly the opposite concern that had preoccupied the eighteen-year-old Otto. He was standing on this self-same spot, staring up at the giant building and shivering inside a rented tuxedo. A curious dampness seeped into the folds of his shirt, as his nervous sweat mingled with the oily secretions of the London night. His jet-black hair lay flattened across his scalp, parted and plastered down by the twin effects of Brylcreem and smog.

Then, as now, Otto stood hesitant before the RIBA, reluctant to step inside the lions' den. Deterred as usual by the cost of public transport, he had attempted to walk that evening from his distant bedsit to the drinks party being thrown for the recent intake of architectural students in the city. As a newcomer to this country, Otto had underestimated both the strangeness of its climate and his own physical reaction to the enfolding chill of autumn. He was feeling a little feverish, and had no great wish to join the party he could now see taking place at an upper-storey window.

The dense London smog, the first experienced by Otto, had descended on the city earlier that afternoon. In a few short hours it had oozed down, thick and heavy, onto the streets, worming its way through bridges and into alleyways, filling the interstices within and between buildings, the majority of which stood whole and complete. Others, mainly to the east of the city, had been damaged or shattered by falling bombs and by periods of long neglect. Having completed its silent act of effacement, the smog had hung immobile across the breadth of the capital, obliterating in the process all notions of space.

From his rented room on a Lambeth backstreet, where he had spent that day reading through a large pile of books, Otto remained unaware of the scale of the transformation outside. He realised that something had changed only when he rose from his desk to open the window. The stuffiness from the heater was making his head spin. As he lifted the grime-streaked pane, he searched in vain above the rooftops for a sign of Battersea Power Station, the one landmark, at present, that served to anchor him in this metropolis that was now his home. When he saw the shape of a giant chimney emerge faintly through the haze, the slight sense of panic that had risen in his breast began to wane. He decided to stick with his original plan and take his chances on foot. It was only a few miles to the West End, he reasoned, and he had been sent a map (rather a sketchy one, admittedly) along with the invitation to that evening's party.

A bowl of thin onion soup, heated on the single hob that occupied one corner of the room, took the edge off his hunger and prepared him for the long walk to come. He felt further emboldened by the warmth of the paraffin heater, its fumes clearly visible in the dimly lit room as he sat on the edge of the narrow bed drinking his soup.

Otto had not yet invested in one of the handsome tan over-coats he had seen worn by the commuters as they crossed over Lambeth Bridge each morning. The few pounds he kept in the dresser were always needed for a more pressing purpose: food, rent, the occasional trip to the cinema when his head was too full with reading. Yet he felt confident, on this particular evening, that the thick material of his rented suit, together with the natural swiftness of his stride, would protect him against any potential chill.

Otto took his turn in the communal shower that was stationed two floors below his room. The appearance of a growth of fungi in one corner of the cubicle had become a cause for concern in recent days. He returned to his room in order to brush his teeth and shave with difficulty in the low porcelain basin. Even for a person of average height, the modest mirror above it would have been hard to use. For Otto, it meant stooping down impossibly low, then peering into it to inspect his cheeks for signs of stray bristles.

His face still smarting from two quick splashes of eau de cologne, he unwrapped the black dinner suit he had rented for several shillings and dressed himself with care. But it was to no avail. At the sight of his pale ankles above the sock-line, and the long stretches of shirt that protruded from his jacket sleeves, he cursed again his freakish height and the limited range of choice at the local rental shop. For once, he welcomed the size and position of his bedsit's only mirror, which made a full-length inspection unthinkable.

Locking the door to his room, Otto carefully picked his way down the stairs, the carpet frayed and treacherous. Opposite the front door to the terraced house, the door of his landlady's apartment stood ajar. The sound of the Glenn Miller Orchestra blared from inside. After pausing for a moment, Otto decided to skip the usual ritual of wishing her a pleasant evening – one of the few opportunities he had found so far to practise his English. Instead he reached for the latch and stepped out into the smog.

Outside, all navigation proved impossible. Soon he was lost within this city in the clouds. He drifted blindly through the dreamlike streets, the shapes before him blurred or indistinguishable. His growing familiarity with this district had melted in a moment into confusion. The intersections between roads, even the order in which those roads appeared, had been rearranged at random by some malevolent hand. The glowing smudge of the constantly passing headlights disorientated him further.

Heading northwards towards the Thames, Otto sought out Albert Embankment, hailing passers-by to ask for directions. But on a night like this no one would stop, even for the briefest of exchanges. The commuters hurried past or ignored this exceptionally tall young man, who emerged from the fog to address them in an accent that evoked, for them, vague images of spies. Unaided by the figures brushing past him, Otto found his way across Lambeth Bridge and up towards Charing Cross Station. Cold, lost and now late for the party, he decided to board a passing bus, checking his pockets for the loose change he had brought as a precaution, and calculating that the remains of the onion soup must last him another day.

Standing inside the cramped and swaying carriage, he felt warmed by the bodies pressed around him. He tried to check his map, but gave up at the sound of a sharp tut, which came from a bowler-hatted man whose newspaper Otto's elbow had just nudged. Stepping off the footplate, somewhere along Oxford Street, he used a combination of map and intuition to guide him towards Portland Place. But arriving at last before his destination, and watching the shadows move across the lighted upstairs window, he longed once more for his paraffin heater and the comforting smell of stewed onions.

This desire to flee back to the safety of his digs was an instinct Otto had to fight on a daily basis. The scale of London itself did not intimidate him. He was used to labyrinthine cities, having been born and raised in Vienna, before fleeing with his family to the port of Antwerp. London's people, however, were a mystery he had yet to fathom. Here at the party, he realised, he must face their peculiarities undiluted.

For Otto, his three sisters and their frail and careworn mother, the British had been their wartime liberators, a fact that always moved him deeply. He remembered, even now, the tears that came to his mother's eyes whenever she spoke of the young soldier who had helped Otto bring her – almost blind – up from the darkness of the cellar and into the afternoon sunlight, one distant morning in September 1944. Otto, therefore, felt immensely proud when seven years later, at the age of eighteen, he was offered the chance to study in this country of ingenious and fair-minded people: the country of Sir Christopher Wren, Isambard Kingdom Brunel and David Niven. Yet shortly after he first set foot on English soil, the romantic stereotypes gleaned from those childhood trips to the cinema had faded, and a more complex picture of Britain and its people had emerged.

There was the coarse old woman in the launderette, for instance, who always made fun of Otto's accent, laughing at her own crude jokes and trying to draw the other customers into her cruel imitations. Usually they looked on, wholly uninterested, while a thin-lipped Otto sat listening to the churning of the suds in the monstrous machines. Then there was the pub on Streatham Hill, where a waxen young man, not much older than he was, started shouting drunken obscenities upon learning that Otto was Jewish, even drawing a knife with which to threaten him. The landlord of the pub forcibly ejected the culprit and apologised to Otto, yet he never felt the wish to go back there. This was by far the most troubling incident he had encountered since his arrival, yet others of a lesser magnitude occurred on a regular basis. Not hurtful events, exactly, but puzzling ones, which he often fretted about during the long nights alone in his digs.

While travelling on the Underground one morning, for example, a pretty young woman sitting opposite glanced repeatedly across at him. When eventually he dared smile at her, she firmly looked away, pausing only to glare at him as she rose to leave the train. There had been other inexplicable encounters of this kind. The smiling old gentleman in the local library would chat away warmly as he stamped Otto's books, but ignore him completely whenever they happened to pass each other on the street outside. Even at college, the behaviour of Otto's fellow students left him puzzled. They would nod and sometimes greet him with a smile outside the lecture hall, but showed no inclination to engage him in conversation, or invite him to the café where they routinely gathered.

In the weeks since Otto had come to Britain, the majority of people he had encountered had been polite but reserved. Not hostile towards him, but some way short of welcoming. Given his natural shyness and his problems with the English language, which he was rapidly mastering in its written form, but could not yet transfer into everyday conversation, he began to wonder whether he would ever break down the social barriers that existed here. The English were a strange and distant people, he decided, given to intricate and precise codes of behaviour, which to an outsider like him seemed impenetrable.

All these issues preyed on Otto's mind as he stood for the first time on the pavement outside the RIBA building. Damp, cold and faintly ridiculous in his undersized suit, he looked up at the severe stone sculptures, emerging intermittently from the smog, and wondered whether he had made a mistake in coming to this country. For all his sensitivities, however, he was a mentally tough young man. His life history so far had seen to that. He didn't give up easily on a challenge. Bracing himself, he mounted the steps to the assembled gathering, and there began his journey in from the English cold.

Looking at the entrance now, more than sixty years later, Otto saw himself emerge buoyant from the party.

It's even brought some colour to your cheeks, he observed from across the decades, with oddly paternal care.

The scenario the young Otto had most dreaded, standing alone and ignored in a corner while nursing a solitary glass of wine, had not materialised. Instead, the evening had turned into a personal triumph. A steady stream of guests had flowed towards him, thanking him for coming out on such a dreadful night and asking him lots of questions about his work. At no point did he have to seek out conversations for himself. On the contrary, he had to conduct two or three of them at once.

Otto began to notice, as the evening unfolded, that he was being treated somewhat differently to his peers. The other students approached him rather tentatively and respectfully, even those some years older than himself. A few of them asked if he would mind glancing over their work some day. Even the lecturers seemed eager to talk to him, waiting patiently in the wings for their moment to intervene. His suspicions that something was afoot were confirmed for him later on, when someone led across the room a venerable British architect, proudly introducing Otto as 'the young genius everyone is talking about'.

Until that moment, Otto had assumed himself to be a common-or-garden outsider; his considerable height and overseas origins setting him apart from his peers. Now he realised that there were other, more flattering reasons for their reluctance to invite him to the café. The other students were, it seemed, slightly in awe of him, especially when it became established that his work was of an order rarely seen in someone of his age. Otto had known before the party that he had a flair for architectural design. The award of a scholarship had been proof enough of that. But only now was he becoming aware of the scale of that talent, and the possible future it might open up for him; one far removed from tackling fungi in the communal shower.

Otto had never been an arrogant boy – confident, yes, but always measured in his self-belief – and the discovery of the expectations people had of him would later cause him considerable worry. Back in the darkness of his bedsit, for instance, with only the ticking of the paraffin heater for company, he would lie awake and question the extent of his abilities. This evening, however, with the discovery of these expanding horizons, he remained in a state of quiet elation. He hardly even noticed the slow lifting of the smog as he bounded down the steps outside and hurried to catch the bus back to Charing Cross.

Otto had returned to the scene of that debut triumph on countless occasions since. He could measure out the passage of his life in the changing reflection that greeted him in its smoked glass doors. One incident in particular struck him now. Some eight years on from the night of the shrunken tuxedo, he had been keynote speaker at a conference held on the RIBA premises. There he gave the first of what would come to be known as his Concrete Eulogies. It was not the speech itself that he recalled, however, but a small and seemingly insignificant incident that took place during the drinks party afterwards.

'The young fellow can certainly *talk* a good building, but can he actually *erect* one?' asked one smirking veteran of his colleagues, as they stood and sipped their glasses of wine. The timing of the question was unfortunate. Otto passed them at that very moment, in hot pursuit of a pile of canapés. He felt stung by the criticism, especially as it touched a raw nerve within him. Despite its growing reputation, Unit 5 had failed so far to secure any major commissions. They had produced plenty of tower blocks on paper; none, as yet, in the air. Far from allowing the overheard comment to crush him, however, he used it as a spur to strengthen his resolve. Working quietly from their small rented office in Fitzrovia, he and the others awaited the chance to finally put their theories into practice. The following year, with the launch of a high-profile competition to design Britain's Home of the Future, their moment to shine had finally arrived.

The thought of the resulting tower block – which was, after all, the reason for his presence in London – restored Otto to the present. He noticed a traffic warden approaching. From her expression, it was clear that his silent vigil had attracted concern.

'Are you lost, sir?' the young woman asked, just as the circle of memories surrounding Otto dispersed into the afternoon air. 'I noticed you've been standing there a while, and I was wondering if all was well.'

'I'm fine, thank you,' Otto replied. 'It's kind of you to ask. I lost my bearings for a moment or two, but it's all coming back to me now.'

And with a tilt of his homburg and a flourish of his cane, he set off in search of some food.

Nine

Dear Laszlo,

*I hope that this letter finds you well. Or, more realistically,
perhaps, given that we are of a similar age, that it finds you
not suffering too badly.*

*I am writing to you late at night from my hotel room in
Marylebone. The view from the window is unexceptional (the
nocturnal glow of offices; the traffic's constant passing) so I need
some conversation to distract me from my thoughts. To tell you
the truth, I'm feeling rather nervous, and finding it impossible
to sleep. What twists and turns the mind takes at this hour.*

*Tomorrow morning, I move into Marlowe House, a tower
block we designed many years ago, in order to take part in a
television feature about its proposed demolition. The aim, I
believe, is to capture my innermost feelings on observing the
blight that has occurred there. I would prefer the programme to
focus on the facts, and the arguments for retaining or
demolishing the building, but apparently that is not what is
required. It is not enough, apparently. Too dry, too obvious.*

Something to engage the viewers' emotions is needed, hence my tragi-nostalgic return to Marlowe House, where I must hobble around and haunt the ramparts like the ghost of Hamlet's father.

It is the way of the modern world, I suppose. Interests have changed, priorities altered. Emotion now trumps intellect every time. So be it. I cannot change that. What I can do, however, is withhold any emotions I do feel from the probing of the cameras.

The makers of the programme, I suspect, would not understand such a sentiment, kind and thoughtful though they undoubtedly are. There is a generational issue at play here. What they fail to understand is that for many people of my age, the public display of any private emotion is simply an abomination; to do so in front of millions, exponentially worse. The war, maybe, played a part in all that, establishing sensibilities in childhood that remain. For our generation, the sheer magnitude of the events that engulfed us, and the need to maintain great clarity of thought in order to survive the carnage all around us, meant that we had no time for emotional navel-gazing – we could not afford the luxury of self-indulgence. It might have cost us our lives.

If you are wondering why I am telling you all this, it's because there is no one else alive in whom I can confide such thoughts. Anika is off-limits. She doesn't really approve of my being here in London and has made it quite clear that she has no wish to discuss it further. Besides which, as someone who is 'post-war' in every respect, she is probably too young to comprehend my viewpoint. Of all my living friends, you are closest to me in age, and the one most likely to understand my perspective.

Since our little talk is going so well — no sign, yet, of any dissent on your part — I'd like to ask you a rather delicate question. It regards a matter that has puzzled me for years. You were an architect, when I first knew you, and a damned good one at that. Your work on any number of projects in the 1950s was simply outstanding. So given the success you had already enjoyed, your undeniable intelligence and talent, why on earth did you give it all up shortly afterwards in order to become a composer? It's an especially pertinent question, I feel, since your gifts in this field have always been — how shall I put this? — less apparent. I understand the similarities between these two great disciplines: the establishment of rhythm, of pattern, of balance and logical form; the sense of an unfolding (in architecture, of space — in music, of time). But despite all this, I don't understand why you abandoned completely the discipline that better suited your gifts and devoted yourself to one for which you have no obvious talent. Was the architectural endeavour too quiet for you? Did buildings not make enough noise? I sometimes suspect as much, judging by the infantile shrieks and clangs of some of your more challenging musical compositions. Or was it simply that you lost your mind, perhaps in a delayed reaction to the nightmare of war the previous decade? I have sometimes thought that, too, I must admit; for example, while watching you conduct your own five-hour opera, ten years ago during the festival in Darmstadt.

You looked extraordinary down there in the orchestra pit: the tics and the mutterings, the tossing of the head, the fluid expressions of fury and beatitude, lust and piety, playing in endless succession across your face. Then there were your huge, waving arms, your enormous shock of white hair, backlit and glowing like some mad explosion. Did you know the effect your hair had on the audience up in the gallery, distracting them constantly from the events on stage? Of course you did. Maybe you even arranged the lighting accordingly, to make yourself the radiant centre of attention. As a vain man myself, I cannot help but recognise the quality in others.

What you did not appear to recognise, however, was the effect your music had on the audience that evening. Did you really not notice? All the yawning and coughing? The checking of watches? The endless shifting about in our seats? Anika and I were clearly guilty on that last count. Three hours into the performance, she leaned across and told me that her buttocks felt like a boxer's face – and by that point we hadn't reached the interval. Even the orchestra and singers seemed a little confused, but then one can hardly blame them. There was the bizarre and stuttering overture, the meandering arias, the explosive, discordant choruses that went off like grenades, making us jump from our seats (at least they gave poor Anika's buttocks a momentary respite from their torture). Forty skilled musicians in search of a tune – that was how your opera felt to me. And I'm afraid they didn't find one, all evening long.

As for the plot, to this day I have no idea what I was watching. Wolves, bears, some people in togas – and then an astronaut appearing on stage? The relief at the end was palpable. You could see it in the fixed grins of the few members of the audience who remained.

But the only person who seemed oblivious to the sheer awfulness of it all was you, my dearest Laszlo. Beaming in delusional triumph, you bowed extravagantly and waved to

87

the gallery, despite the sparse and embarrassed ovation you received. And then you returned for a curtain call with the auditorium nearly empty.

I know my criticism of your music seems harsh, but please don't think of me as uncultured. I'm no musical reactionary, I assure you — not stuck entirely in the classicism of the eighteenth and nineteenth centuries. I enjoyed the musical experiments of the post-war avant-garde — of Stockhausen, Ligeti and Boulez. They were, after all, our cultural bedfellows. What they, and you, produced in sound, I suppose I produced in concrete. The intellectual currents in which we swam were much the same. I only wish that your own work hadn't left me quite so cold. When not cold, I must confess, then rather terrified.

Your music is unlistenable, incomprehensible. Yet still you persist with it after all this time. Part of me admires that persistence; another part believes you require treatment for it. You are eighty-four years old now, Laszlo — when are you going to give up? Apologies for not mentioning this to you sooner, but honesty on the epic scale is never easy. To put it bluntly, how does one tell an old friend that the past fifty years of his life have been an utter waste of time?

Yet, if it's of any comfort to you, and I sincerely hope that it shall be, I find myself in exactly the same position. Just look at my sad repertoire of dysfunctional buildings: leaking, creaking, longing to pull themselves down, standing evocations of alienation and violence — and those are just the ones I'd like to save. No, I'm hardly in a position to discuss legacies.

Am I too, then, guilty of a monumental waste of time? Is there really any difference between the two of us?

As I mentioned before, the prospect of returning to Marlowe House makes me uncomfortable. How to explain the period of experimentation from which this building sprang – the vision of the future we all held back then? And how to square that vision with the conditions in which its residents must live? It won't be easy. I'm not relishing the prospect – I've no idea what sort of reception I'll receive. I only wish I had a fraction of your self-belief when it comes to facing my public. But then again, your folly at Darmstadt was inflicted on us for one evening only. My folly at Marlowe House has been inflicted on its residents for decades.

Yet we both did our best, I think – misguided and foolish though posterity might judge our efforts to have been. And, in our flawed and rather egocentric ways, I also hope that we managed to be courageous. Are we not kindred spirits, then, we two old crazies? Products of the twentieth century's collective nervous breakdown? That century has passed now, and the work we produced (even we, ourselves) are its museum pieces . . . its living exhibits.

We're an endangered species, you and I: the last of the old-fashioned Modernists. We need to stick together while we can. So if it's okay with you, I'd like to continue our correspondence. Then, like living bookends, separated by the quiet and calming distance of the page, we can ruminate on all our glorious failures.

Otto

He didn't bother reading the letter through again. Folding and sealing it into an envelope, he scrawled Laszlo's name across the front and then promptly threw it into the waste bin.

Otto never posted any of his letters, nowadays. They seemed to serve a purely interior purpose.

'Anyway, Laszlo would never forgive me if I sent it,' Otto said to himself. 'He's as touchy about his opera as Pierre is about fucking Foucault.'

The sound of these last two words pleased him, so he repeated them aloud several times to himself as he washed. The acoustics of the bathroom gave the alliteration an extra resonance. Soon the phrase had developed into a little tune. It was only when he heard a faint knocking sound on the other side of the wall, accompanied by a muffled reprimand, that he realised it was probably time to cease his singing. Glancing at the clock, he saw with horror that it was approaching one-thirty. Sheepishly, he turned off the lights and made his way silently to bed.

Ten

Otto stood on the windswept forecourt, looking up at the imposing mass of Marlowe House, and leaned a little more heavily on his cane.

'My goodness,' he said, the words almost carried away by the sharp gust that ruffled his overcoat and hat.

He paused awhile, aware in his peripheral vision of the camera slowly circling him. Yet his focus now was all upon the building. He stepped back a pace, then another, craning his neck in order to scan the upper storeys. It was a grey day, bitter. Chip wrappers and other detritus swirled about the public space. Otto held on to the top of his homburg and squinted upwards.

'My goodness . . . '

The clean lines he had once studied from his seat at the Oval cricket ground remained unmistakable. But the concrete now was streaked and badly weathered. Seen on a summer's afternoon, perhaps, with the sunlight falling at a rakish angle, emphasising the form of the building while darkening out the details, Marlowe House could almost have been the same structure he had known in the mid-1960s. But in the flat and even light of this cold autumn morning, overcast and devoid of all covering shadow, the extent of its decline was clear to see.

Some windows were smashed; others boarded up. A large drainage pipe leaked its contents, the greenish water oozing over the concrete like a slug's trail. Dense graffiti covered its lower reaches, including the giant circular columns that held the structure aloft. One of these, Otto noticed, was singed around its base. Charcoal and other debris, the remains of a small fire, lay close against it.

He saw that scaffolding had been erected across the middle storeys, but he struggled to establish its purpose. Perhaps there was some issue with the lifts on this side of the building.

Chloe stepped forward and spoke off-camera.

'What do you think?'

Otto, who had forgotten momentarily that she was there, glanced at her.

'It doesn't look good,' he said, composed and thoughtful, but with no great wish to expand further. 'Not too good at all.'

He set off on a tour of inspection, carefully studying each side of the building in turn. The picture was uniformly grim. He stopped now and then to disturb with his cane the loose piles of litter that surrounded its walls. Burned pieces of tinfoil, cartons, food wrappers; a crumpled copy of a lifestyle magazine, the smiling face of the celebrity on its cover scratched out by a fingernail or coin. Patches of weed sprouted here and there, in an area that had once been carefully landscaped.

Returning once more to his position before the entrance, Otto turned on his heel to survey the whole scene. The gritty breeze tugged at his coat and trousers. From behind one of the columns, a couple of children peered out, their faces half curious and half hostile.

Otto looked over at the one-time sculpture garden in a corner of the grounds. It was clearly no longer a garden, serving instead as a dumping ground for unwanted mattresses and cardboard boxes. It also lacked sculptures. Just two of the original eight remained. They were balletic, humanoid figures in the style of Henry Moore, and their heads had been sawn or broken off with what must have been considerable effort on the part of those responsible.

Having absorbed the picture as best he could, Otto turned to look at Chloe, who was watching him from out of range of the circling camera. He appeared lost.

'Okay, cut,' she told the film crew. 'I think we have enough for the establishing shots.'

Chloe walked over to Otto, who was staring up once more at the façade.

'That was excellent, thank you,' she said.

'Really?' he asked.

'Yes, really.'

She was already anticipating the final edit, some plaintive classical music, piano or harpsichord, the circling viewpoint, running counter to the swirling of the litter. Otto, shot from below, his noble face pensive, elegant in his overcoat and homburg, his cane pressed into the ground before him, turning now himself, to a different tempo, and surveying the crumbling ruins of his Utopia.

'Would you like to take a break?' she asked. 'There are

some chairs in the van, and there's coffee, too, if you would like some.'

'I would . . . thank you.'

'We're just going to set up elsewhere, and then, if you don't mind, I'd like to ask a few questions about your first impressions.'

'That sounds fine.'

'We'll then take you up to your flat, but please let me know if you feel tired at any point. We want to make this experience as pleasant as possible for you.'

'I feel okay at the moment, but if that changes, I'll let you know.'

They were walking towards the van, Chloe with a woollen hat pulled down over her ears. She disappeared inside while someone brought out a chair and a coffee for Otto.

Lowering himself down and warming his hands around the mug, he noticed that several of the film crew were texting or talking on their mobile phones. As someone whose grip on technology had steadily loosened with the years, Otto felt increasingly bewildered by the gadgets he saw around him. With every new development of the past three decades, he had fought an uphill battle to keep pace with all the changes. From microwave ovens and Betamax videos to compact-disc players and digital televisions, each had proved increasingly difficult to master. Finally, he had given up entirely, to the extent that the current generation of gadgets – the ones named after fruits, and such – were objects both of mystery and fear to him.

Just twenty-five years, he thought, since Cynthia's passing, yet already it feels like a lifetime – such has been the scale and pace of change.

94

Cynthia had never owned a mobile phone or used the internet: she long pre-dated the rise of social media. She barely even understood what a personal computer was. So where were the objects through which she communicated with the world? Where was the typewriter on which her fingers had played, the large red telephone on which she spoke to her friends? Such things were now the preserve of museums, as silent as the grave.

When someone dies, you lose them twice – the first time suddenly and the second more slowly. At first the person goes, then the objects and even the ideas that helped define them in life.

And what would Cynthia make of the world today, he asked himself – how would she have coped with all these advances in technology, with the wider changes in society and politics?

I expect she would feel as disorientated by it all as I do, which, I must admit, would be rather comforting to hear.

Otto's thoughts turned to the interview with Chloe. How should he approach this? What were his initial thoughts on being at Marlowe House once again? He was shocked by the level of deterioration, and concerned at the effect this must have upon the lives of the residents. The atmosphere here reminded him in some respects of the London he had encountered when first arriving in 1951. He still remembered vividly the bomb damage, the poverty, the palpable sense of exhaustion, written onto the faces of the people he passed in the narrow streets near his digs.

But then we seemed to be moving beyond all that.

As he looked once more at the desolate scene before him, a cheery and well-spoken voice from an old newsreel returned momentarily to haunt him. It was accompanied by a piece of generic, Swinging Sixties-style music; all twanging guitars and sunny, optimistic chords.

'The tower block has become a common sight in Britain's cities during recent years. These concrete giants are sprouting up everywhere. But whether you love them or loathe them, you just can't ignore them – not when they come as big as this! Meet Marlowe House, all twenty-seven floors of it, a newly completed tower block in south-east London. One of Europe's largest residential buildings, it is now home to hundreds of local authority tenants.

'And here we see some of them, pictured this week at the official opening. They look delighted, don't they? Take this young family, for instance – they're positively bursting with pride. And as you can see, they're eager to take us inside for a look around their brand-new home. Oops, mind that step there, young 'un. That's right, Dad, you help him up. Here we are, inside, and just look at what we find. State-of-the-art facilities, central heating, a sparkling new bathroom with hot and cold running water. An inside toilet, too, the first this family has ever had. And how about that lovely new kitchen? No wonder Mum and Dad are looking so pleased . . . '

Chloe stepped down from the van and walked over to Otto.
'When you've finished your coffee, would you mind making your way over to that patch of waste ground?'
She pointed to the mattresses and piles of cardboard boxes.
It used to be a sculpture garden, Otto wanted to tell her.
But he couldn't seem to summon up the energy.

*

The interview did not go well. Otto realised, too late, that he had taken it all too personally. The poor condition of the building, of Cynthia's building, had affected him on several different levels. Physical decay was a sensitive subject with Otto. He was surprised at just how irritated he sounded. The clarity of thought shown a few minutes earlier, while sipping his coffee, disappeared in front of the cameras.

Chloe began, 'Now you've had some time to think it over, what are your thoughts on the condition of the exterior?'

'It's a disgrace. An utter disgrace. How on earth was it allowed to deteriorate so badly?'

She seemed to get the wrong end of the stick.

'You blame the residents?'

'Of course I don't blame the residents! Why does everybody *always* blame the residents!'

'The local authorities?'

'It's not that simple. Maintaining a tower block such as this one is no easy task, given the parameters within which they have to operate. There are complex forces at work here. Social. Economic. Political. The problems are systemic. They always have been. I can't just point the finger at some individuals and tell you it's their bloody fault ... much as you would like me to, I'm sure. What I can say is that something has gone badly wrong!'

Chloe looked at him, a little hurt by his brusqueness and patrician tone. He apologised and recovered some of his composure.

'I'm sorry. I'm tired ... I'm not sleeping terribly well. And I'm afraid this whole matter is rather close to the bone for me.'

'The building?'

97

'Yes, but not just the building.'

Chloe said nothing; seeking, through silence, to nudge him towards elaboration. But he wouldn't go any further.

I am not, he thought determinedly, under any circumstances whatsoever, going to mention Cynthia.

'You said there are complex issues involved. Could you explain that statement further?'

'I'm not entirely sure I can. How much time have we got?'

She didn't realise he was asking literally, and so didn't reply to his question.

'Not much time, I imagine,' he continued, thinking aloud. 'You'll need a soundbite, I suppose. Something short, snappy and quotable. Unfortunately I'm not accustomed to that sort of thing.'

Forty years before, when Otto had been a regular in front of the cameras, television had been a very different beast. Invite some thought-provoking guests into a studio, sit them down around a table and give them a couple of hours to engage in an in-depth discussion. Then broadcast the results to the nation. But no one had the patience for that level of engagement any more: there was no time now for complexity or nuance. One must simplify the argument to the point of banality, or else say nothing at all. What is more, one must do it while perched like an idiot on a burned-out bloody mattress.

He tried to explain.

'It's hard to condense the arguments, when it comes to economics and politics. It takes a lifetime of study to begin to grasp the detail. Take *Das Kapital*, for instance. It runs to more than a thousand pages. I got about halfway through, but never finished it.'

He smiled.

'At home, in Hampstead, we used to keep it on a shelf in the downstairs toilet, along with a copy of *Ulysses*. I'm afraid I never finished that, either.'

Otto had lost Chloe completely, not to mention himself. The chance to make an important point was disappearing. Sensing this, he leafed back urgently through the faded pages of his memory. What was it Angelo had said to him a few weeks earlier, when they were speaking on the telephone? Something about used-car lots and a crumbling social fabric. It was pithy and rather good. Just the kind of thing that was needed now, in fact. But he couldn't remember any of it, once the moment of truth had arrived. All thoughts of his own seemed to flee.

They should have asked Angelo to do this, not me.

'I'm sorry ... just a moment ... it's my memory, you see – oh, bugger it!' he said.

Chloe raised her eyebrows in response.

Otto felt tired. His stomach was hurting. Worse still, the building looked so bloody awful, gazing out sadly through eyes of fractured glass.

'I understand you'd like Marlowe House to be given a listing,' Chloe said to him.

He brightened a little and turned once more to face her.

'Yes, that's right, we would.'

'It was an important building in its time, wasn't it?'

Otto had spoken eloquently on this subject on many occasions. Now, unfortunately, wasn't one of them.

'Apparently it *was* important, yes ...'

He lapsed once more into silence.

Chloe was surprised at his failure to take her prompt.

Otto was shocked himself. This was his moment to state the case for saving Marlowe House: the reason he had travelled to London at all. So why didn't he grasp the opportunity? It was something to do with the state of its fabric. The sight of it had totally knocked the stuffing out of him. And then there were the strained faces of the children, peering out from between the columns. That was the kind of detail he hadn't expected. So when his time came, he felt uncomfortable about singing its praises. How could he argue for saving a building that was leaking its lifeblood before him?

Anyway, a small voice inside him seemed to say, it's all right for you, Otto, you don't have to live here. *You* live in a nice big villa in Switzerland.

With the guilt and confusion pressing down, he found that he couldn't say a word. Instead he stared intently at the ground and twisted the handle of his cane.

Chloe gave him a second chance.

'It has some innovative features, I understand . . . architecturally?'

Otto raised his head and looked the façade up and down.

'Yes,' he said, without great enthusiasm, lifting the cane and pointing upwards. 'As you can see, it's rather tall.'

Chloe waited, but nothing more came. The silence burned in both their ears.

With a crushing sense of defeat, Otto lowered the cane and placed it beside him on the mattress. Noticing the other tower blocks in the distance, he added as an afterthought:

'But of course, one must remember, Marlowe House has shrunk a great deal in the years since it was built.'

This was the final straw. It was becoming rather painful. Chloe's professional manner softened back into familiarity.

'I think we've done enough for today. You probably want to unpack. Shall we carry on with this tomorrow when you're feeling more refreshed?'

Eleven

That night, Otto struggled to sleep. It had been a hectic day, filled with unfamiliar people and sensations, and he found it all more overwhelming than anticipated. There was the filming outside Marlowe House and the rather disastrous interview. He had barely been given time to unpack, then it was off to a restaurant for a meal with Chloe and the film crew.

A more pleasant occasion than our dinner the other evening, he thought. No giddiness at all this time. I appear to have conquered the doppelgänger issue.

On his return to Marlowe House, a polite young cameraman showed him to the door of his twelfth-floor apartment, wished him good night and took his leave. Otto, in his tiredness, forgot just where he was, and stood for some minutes staring out into the gloom of the hallway. He couldn't work out how his hotel in Marylebone had fallen into sudden disrepair; or why its porter was now so scruffily dressed. Once the penny had dropped, and the events of the day returned to him, he shut the front door quickly and went inside.

With his head still reeling from the glass or two of wine he had drunk at dinner, he decided he would have a quick shower and retire to bed immediately. But the strangeness of the mattress and the smell of fresh paint that pervaded the apartment meant that sleep, that night, was slow to arrive. When it did it was a sleep of surfaces; insubstantial, devoid of depth. His dreams, too, mirrored waking. They were more like thoughts, near-conscious memories of the day's events and their associations. Cynthia's typewriter, the swirling litter, the howling of the wind between the columns. The smell of paint, in Otto's half-sleep, became a kind of texture on his skin. Then he turned on his side and entered another form of awareness.

He saw Daniel, translucent, on the first day of his life, passed up into his arms by the exhausted Cynthia.

My goodness, Otto thought, looking down at the baby through an unexpected prism of tears. He's so fragile ... a butterfly's wing ... a raindrop.

He saw the same boy at five, his mouth stained with chocolate, grinning and grimacing as the spit-dampened tissue passed across his face. And then the older boy, on his eleventh birthday, sitting at the table in his wicketkeeper's gloves, trying in vain to eat dinner with a knife and fork.

In the holidays, one year, they flew a kite in the fields behind his grandparents' house, Daniel and Cynthia shouting their encouragement while Otto struggled to keep it under control. He could picture Daniel laughing, his head thrown back in pure delight, a gesture he had inherited from his mother.

No sign of that laugh, though, all those years later, as the studious young man boarded the train up to Cambridge. Daniel was shaking Otto's hand, as they stood upon the platform, and thanking him for his support through the years. Cynthia, a little tearful, threw her arms around her son, while Otto hoisted the case up into the carriage.

One year on, he saw the embrace outside the entrance to the hospital; the look of shock in Daniel's eyes, reflecting his own disbelief.

And then, much later, the middle-aged man, a more distant figure, an occasional voice on the telephone.

You should have done more to support him, not run away into the mountains, Otto's conscience whispered deep into his soul.

Eventually he woke, if that was the right word to describe the experience. It was more an acknowledgement that sleep had failed to take him; a shrugging forth into alertness.

He climbed out of bed and walked without hesitation through two rooms and a corridor to the kitchen. It was only once he had got there, removed a glass from the cabinet and filled it with cold water that he realised he had done so without switching on any lights.

How did I do that?

He had barely even noticed the apartment so far. The tour he had taken with the film crew had passed in a blur. Furthermore, the apartment was large (three bedrooms, the biggest available in Marlowe House), with a rather complex configuration of interconnecting rooms for him to negotiate. Yet somehow he had made it to the kitchen, in darkness, without a moment's hesitation. True, the place was sparsely furnished, which meant that there were few obstacles to strike him on the way, but still he was rather taken aback by what he had just achieved.

Even in the villa in Switzerland that would have taken some doing, and we've lived there eighteen years.

It also struck Otto that in total darkness he had known the exact whereabouts of the kitchen cabinets and sink, still in their original positions from the 1960s.

I know it all, he told himself, a little shocked by the discovery. It's still in there.

Turning on the light switch (again he knew its position), it dawned on him that while walking through the apartment he had drawn upon a very precise mental floor plan, seeing each room as though from above. Clearly he must have retained a subliminal mental copy of this plan, unawares, since the early 1960s. There were four types of apartment in Marlowe House, and upon inspection Otto found that each one remained clear in his imagination, together with numerous other details about the layout.

He sipped his glass of water.

It's strange, memory's labyrinth. I can't remember something Anika told me five minutes before, and yet I remember this, all of it, the entire bloody building, as though it were laid out before me in a technical manual.

What a contrast to a few hours earlier, when he had struggled to find a single word to say about Marlowe House. Reinforcements had arrived, but far too late.

Switching on more lights, Otto began to explore the apartment.

We worked damned hard on those plans, though. Cynthia and I . . . the whole team at Unit 5. Months – years – of hard work went into its making. No wonder the details sank in so deeply.

'To me, the key to this whole project is light,' Otto heard a voice say.

How much younger he had sounded in those days.

'The competition brief is to develop residential housing in a densely built-up area. The chief challenge for us, in such a setting, will be to optimise the amount of daylight available to every resident.'

In their office in Fitzrovia, at the less fashionable end of London's West End, the members of Unit 5 sat around the desk on which Otto was perched. In rolled-up shirtsleeves, his tie loosened, he flicked back his fringe from his eyes and handed out some plans.

'We want to lift people upwards, away from the grime,' he continued. 'We want to bring them fresh air and a sense of openness. Give them something they have never had before. Views, space, calm ... '

He remembered, as he spoke, the washed-out faces of the passers-by in the streets of 1950s Lambeth; the cramped and airless terraces many inhabited.

'If we begin our project from a single principle – the principle of light – then I believe that everything else will fall into place. Whatever proposal we submit will be based upon an inherent logic. Form will follow function, if you will.'

The others talked through Otto's preliminary thoughts, making comments and suggestions as they felt the need. Unit 5 was a democratic set-up, based upon socialist ideals. In theory, everyone in the collective had an equal voice in its running. In practice, there was a certain unspoken hierarchy within its ranks. With their burgeoning reputations, and their constant flow of new ideas, Otto and Cynthia found that their suggestions often held sway.

In the weeks that followed, the members of Unit 5 considered several alternative designs. One, suggested by Otto, looked like a series of concrete cubes, placed at angles, one on top of the other; in the manner of a child's toy bricks, imperfectly aligned.

'I'm not sure,' said Cynthia, as Otto showed them all a pencil sketch. 'It looks impressive, technically, but it feels a little cold to me, a little too precise in its execution.'

She passed the drawing round to the others at the table. They gave a low murmur of agreement. Glancing at Otto, she noticed the look of disappointment on his face.

'Sorry, O,' she mouthed to him silently.

'A passing thought, nothing more,' he said. 'What would you suggest instead?'

'Something more fluid,' she replied. 'More organic. Easier on the eye. Rather than a design based on the right angle, on pure geometric forms, why don't we look to the softer lines of nature for inspiration? The tower block as a flower, for example.'

The other members of Unit 5 nodded their approval.

Cynthia began conducting a painstaking programme of research. She borrowed dozens of library books, which formed a small structure in themselves as they stood piled on her desk in the office. She studied photographs of sunflowers – their fat heads turned towards the sun, of seashells, trees and curling leaves, before considering the human form. Ballet dancers, athletes and figures depicted in classical sculptures. Cynthia was trying to capture the grace of natural forms; the fluidity and economy of movement. Finally she turned for inspiration to the fluttering movements of fabrics. One day she arrived at the office with a headscarf she had bought on a trip to Istanbul, pinning it with clothes pegs to a washing line she had strung across the centre of the room. To everyone's amusement, she took the fan from her desk and positioned it before the piece of fabric, studying and sketching it in pencil as it rippled and revolved in the currents.

Otto also took up his sketchbook, visiting the parcel of land that was the location for the development. Like an astronomer from the ancient world, dressed incongruously in morning suit and a large sunhat, he sat each day atop a pile of rubble, studying the movement of the sun across the sky. Hour after hour, he drew the changes of light and shadow on the surrounding buildings, noting carefully the times within the margin.

The final design they submitted for the competition had a classical simplicity. Everyone was happy with the proposed structure, twisting slowly upwards through its levels like a piece of fabric caught in a gentle breeze. The proposal fitted well with Unit 5's aesthetic. All of them disliked unnecessary flourishes, or what Otto once called 'attention seeking'. He, like the others, favoured a certain austerity of form. While the six other designs submitted for the competition tended towards the brazenly futuristic, the team at Unit 5 had opted instead, the judges decided, 'for a technically complex yet outwardly graceful form, allied to a highly sensitive exploitation of light and space'.

It had won them the competition, and cemented their professional reputations.

Drawing back the living-room curtain, Otto noted again the width and height of the window – it was almost like a glass wall – and the depth of the balcony outside. He thought then of the 'principle of light' that had guided so much of their work on this and subsequent inner-city housing projects. He knew the underlying reason for his impulse to maximise light and space. Cynthia understood it, too, although the subject was never spoken about directly. During the two years Otto and his family spent hidden in a cellar in Antwerp's diamond quarter, they were shut away for much of the time in near-total darkness, with only the thin light of candles to see by. For a few short hours each day, however, they were able to go outside into the courtyard to snatch a glimpse of natural light, which the young Otto would absorb with an intense and never-forgotten yearning.

He retreated from the thought. Now really wasn't the time. Tomorrow there would be a full day of filming, and he wanted to face the experience with the clearest possible head. Besides, there was something else he ought to do, before retiring for the night.

Twelve

Dear Anika,

I'm afraid I've been less than honest with you in explaining my reasons for coming here to London. This note is my attempt to set the record straight. Not that it will ever reach you. It will go into the bin, I suppose, like every other letter I write, nowadays.

It is twenty-five years since I last set foot in this city, and almost as long since I reflected on what occurred here. But London has never left me, Anika, in all that time. It has never left me free to dwell in peace. And so I must revisit them, those places and memories – the various events that help explain me.

This compulsion to revisit the past, I now realise, is not the consequence of my journey here, but its cause. It is the reason I am here at all, above and beyond the documentary and our belated attempts to save this broken building. I suspect you already know this, that you grasped the truth of it long before I did. That strange look in your eyes, whenever I mentioned my trip, now makes perfect sense to me. I understand your concern, the cause of your unease, aside from general worries about my health. Yet these other concerns, I want to assure you, are entirely without foundation.

What I'm trying to say, in my convoluted fashion, is that this journey into my past, into the past I shared with Cynthia, is in no way a reflection upon you and me. It worries me that you might see it that way – that you think of me as restless or dissatisfied. My feelings for you today are as strong as when we first knew each other. And goodness, what you meant to me, back then!

Your friendship in those early days was a constant balm to pain. The love that blossomed between us was an unexpected flowering. And what was it that drew me so strongly towards you, beyond your more obvious attractions? It was your voice, I suppose – to me the most beguiling of your qualities. I heard you, in fact, even before I saw you, on that afternoon in Talloires, in the hills above Lake Annecy, when a random series of events caused our paths to cross. I was there on a simple whim, an impulse to see the outside world again. You were there for lunch with the Dutch ambassador, a lunch that was unexpectedly cancelled.

Sitting at a café table and scanning the lake through my binoculars, I caught the sound of your voice behind me, ordering a cup of coffee. I was drawn by your accent, the distinctive burr of the Netherlands, and also by its timbre, deep and assured. When I turned in curiosity to see the owner of this striking voice, the face that turned to meet mine was also striking. Some similar feeling must have sparked inside you, for within minutes you had engaged me in conversation.

111

No, I shall never tire of the sound of your voice; the way it can curl around a phrase. It was there at the start, when you asked if you might share the view – the way you asked to borrow my binoculars! Yet if your voice explains my initial attraction, what deeper forces held us together? We are similar characters, first and foremost, companions cut from the same emotional cloth. Yes, a rather starched one, I have to admit. The same formal manners, the same awkwardness when discussing matters of the heart. Temperamentally, we could almost be twins. And I believe it is that emotional reticence, the one mirrored closely in the other, that drew us together but also now holds us apart.

Our mutual shyness has become a kind of barrier, preventing us from sharing our concerns. Take your pained expression as we stood before the Departures building. I wonder just how deep those feelings run in you. I hate the thought of my baggage weighing you down – and no, I'm not referring now to my suitcase. I hope I still make you happy, Anika. I hope you don't feel trapped by a sense of obligation. I know you take lovers, I don't judge you for doing so, and I realise the needs they satisfy aren't just physical. If I felt it would be of any assistance, I would free you from me completely, but I know that such a suggestion would be misinterpreted.

I wish that I could tell you all this, reach out to you beyond the silent page. But I know from experience it would be hopeless to even attempt it. It is not, to put it simply, how you and I conduct ourselves. It isn't who we are together, nowadays. And so, when we speak, I must express my feelings for you in other ways. In questions about your topspin, or the advice I offer on the azaleas, in the tone with which I describe the autumn forest.

I would like you to know that my passion for you remains, though its expression, these days, is somewhat muted. Beneath the surface frost of age I sense the pulse of former springs, and I hope I have conveyed some sense of that now.

Until next week, my dear . . . Take care of yourself and the chickens.

Otto

Thirteen

'Good morning, Otto,' said Chloe, as he answered the door of his apartment. 'How are you feeling today?'

It was the kind of harmless-sounding question he had come to dread with the passing years. Where on earth did he begin? With the constant pain in his abdomen, eased only by bending forward? Or the constant pain in his spine, eased only by leaning back? Or with the more general pain, the one that ran like a malignant current through his nerves first thing each morning – and seemed beyond all reasonable hope of remedy? Better, perhaps, not to mention any of them. The question, after all, was largely rhetorical.

'I'm fine, thank you, Chloe. How are you?'

'Terrific. Ready for a busy day's filming?'

'I am.'

Stepping back, Otto ushered her inside the apartment, closely followed by the film crew. Chloe had warned him the previous evening that they would call round early to see him. He had readily agreed, forgetting that nowadays he emerged from sleep in stages, rather than all at once. His daily rebooting was not yet quite complete.

'Can I get you some tea?' he asked, as they made their way through to the kitchen.

'Do you mind waiting until we've set everything up? We'd like to film a few shots of you preparing breakfast.'

'Breakfast? Do people really want to see that sort of thing?'

'It won't be anything too complicated. Buttering the toast, putting on the kettle. Do you think you can manage it?'

She flinched at her own words.

'I'm sorry. That sounded patronising, didn't it?'

Otto smiled.

'Life, at my age, is all about diminishing expectations: one's own, and those of others. But fear not. Even if I no longer design large buildings, I'm reasonably confident I can still boil a kettle.'

It was, as Chloe had warned, a busy day. After filming Otto at breakfast – he poured out the tea, twinkle in his eye, with a rather exaggerated flourish – they went on to shoot at a number of locations around the building.

First stop was one of the four main lifts. To his dismay, Otto saw that it was in a shocking state of repair; worse, even, than the others he had used so far. His face looked deathly pale, lit from above, as they descended creakily through many floors, the camera placed just inches from his nose.

'How would you feel about using this lift each day?' Chloe asked him.

Was there an edge to her question, he wondered, beneath the natural warmth of her voice?

'It's an unpleasant experience,' he confirmed. 'I wouldn't

wish it upon anyone. And that strange vibration? The one that's making the camera shake so badly? It definitely wasn't there in the 1960s.'

He would like to have explained things further, but the smell from a mysterious pool of liquid in the corner was making him feel slightly nauseous. He wanted to tell Chloe that it wasn't supposed to be like this; that it hadn't always been so, in fact. Age could play strange tricks on a building, just as it could upon people. In the 1960s, the lifts at Marlowe House had been a source of excitement to many of its residents. People used to ride in them for fun. The lifts were intended to ease life's burdens, yet somehow they only seemed to add to them. Even now, during the daytime, surrounded by the film crew, the atmosphere inside this confined and oppressive space made Otto feel uneasy. Alone, late at night, it must have been most unnerving.

Next they took some film of him wandering alone through the dimly lit corridors. His footsteps echoed in the silence, while the tapping of his cane provided a rhythmical counterpoint. He passed almost no one on his travels, but he sensed, in the graffiti-covered walls, the ghostly presence of several generations of residents. The tangled mass of words and images surrounded him as he walked.

Now and then, he halted to inspect some of the more colourful examples he came across. He squinted up and down the walls, mouthing to himself some of the phrases. There were insults, threats, cries of despair, accusations and boasts. And then, occasionally, something surreal or whimsical, a burst of bleak humour amid the gloom. To Otto, it seemed as though an entire community had been placed on a psychiatrist's couch, their answers then broadcast to the world.

Sigmund Freud would have loved this stuff, he thought. Clearly he was born in the wrong century. If he were alive today he would be analysing walls instead of people.

The graffiti formed a kind of visual hubbub: the messages conveyed were quite confusing.

It's like some dysfunctional dinner party, he continued, where everyone is speaking at once and not listening to each other.

Chloe spoke up.

'I guess the graffiti weren't here, the last time you visited Marlowe House.'

'That's right. The walls of the corridors were painted a rather delicate lemon colour, if my memory serves me correctly. We felt it would give the common areas a bright and friendly feel.'

He looked around.

'We were hoping that these corridors would become attractive places for the residents to wander. We pictured them stopping to chat to friends and neighbours as they passed each other during their evening walk.'

He set off once more along the corridor, as though in demonstration of his words.

'Our aim was to encourage an indoor version of the *passeggiata*, the communal evening stroll seen in the towns and villages of Italy. We saw the corridors as a means of bringing people together.'

He smiled sadly at Chloe, who was walking now alongside him.

'Sounds absurd, doesn't it, all these years later? Pretentious . . . a conceit.'

She shrugged her shoulders, unsure of what to say to him.

'It was a nice idea,' she said, finally.

'Yes,' said Otto, stopping to look at an obscenity daubed upon a wall. 'It *was* a nice idea.'

'Is it a shock for you to see it like this?'

'Not really. Graffiti have become ubiquitous now, on residential estates such as this one. At the time of Marlowe House's construction they were less common, certainly on this kind of scale. It was more a case of the occasional slogan.'

'What's behind it, do you think? Why do people feel the need to do it?'

'Who knows? I find the phenomenon curious, I must admit, but I can't explain its cause.'

Otto could never decide where he stood on the question of graffiti. Was it wanton vandalism or the most democratic of art forms? A cry for attention or simple showing off? He had read all the theories and not been convinced by any of them. To him, graffiti felt more like a glimpse into the city's unconscious – into the fragmentary sensations, perceptions and impulses that were a part of the modern urban condition.

'And are you upset by what you can see here? Disappointed, maybe?'

Otto halted.

'Upset is the wrong word. Disappointed, too. It puzzles me, I suppose, like so much else in life, these days. It puzzles me.'

He turned on his heel again, his eyes scanning the walls with a single sweep.

'I think I preferred the pale lemon.'

Later that afternoon, they did some filming on the roof of Marlowe House. The light and space were a welcome change from the subterranean murk of the lifts and corridors. Chloe wanted to recreate a scene from the original documentary, one in which a confident young Otto had stood near the edge of the parapet – one hand shielding his eyes – and surveyed the wide panorama of London below.

Many years later, the older version shuffled slowly towards the drop, stopping some ten metres short of the edge. It was as far as he dared go this time.

'Just a little further, if you don't mind,' Chloe prompted him. 'It's going to look spectacular.'

It certainly will, if I topple over the edge. I'm an architect, not a bloody stuntman.

Not wanting to disappoint her, however, Otto inched forward with painful slowness. Finally he halted, three metres or so from the drop. His head swam madly: his dry throat burned. He didn't dare look up or down.

'That's perfect, thank you,' he heard her call out to him, from what seemed an unconscionable distance.

'No problem at all,' he managed to call back, in a sing-song sort of voice, as he sought to control the shaking in his knees.

With the cameras rolling behind him, Otto swallowed uncomfortably, shutting his eyes to the giddying immensity of view.

Yet another negative development of recent years – I now appear to suffer from vertigo. And we live in Switzerland, of all places.

His hands began to tremble; he was losing all feeling in his legs.

Much more of this and I won't be able to move at all.

And if this were to happen, he wondered, what exactly would they do? Perhaps they would just leave him there, frozen to the spot, perched on the rooftop like a petrified gargoyle ... right until the moment that the wrecking ball struck.

Otto opened his eyes and saw London swimming below him. The tower blocks contracted and stretched; the rows of streets swayed like corn. He began to sway, too, caught up in the city's strange motion.

Looking down, he saw the sculpture garden directly below. If he fell, he wondered, which of those sculptures might he land upon? Or would it be the burned-out mattress, lying near by? Less messy, perhaps, but surely insufficient to break his fall.

This is becoming rather ghoulish, Otto thought.

To steady himself, he tried to focus on the horizon, which lurched less madly than the rest of his surroundings. He noticed the northern heights of Hampstead, coloured like a bruise against the sky.

I suppose, if I survive this circus, I ought to go back for a look at the old place.

'Okay, we're done,' a voice called from behind him.

With some relief, Otto raised a hand in acknowledgement and edged his way back from the abyss.

Fourteen

Sitting shortly afterwards on a more sheltered part of the roof, Chloe plied Otto with words of gratitude.

'I can't tell you how much we appreciate your cooperation,' she said. 'We have some terrific footage.'

'Don't mention it,' he replied, attempting a nonchalant smile. 'I found the experience most invigorating.'

But as he removed the homburg from his head, running his fingers through the thick white hair, Chloe noticed the trembling of his fragile hands and realised she was responsible for his distress. Her shoulders slumped and the easy chatter that came naturally to her disappeared. Only the sound of the breeze remained, to accompany the thoughts of both.

With the wind tugging his hair into gravity-defying shapes, and his hands playing restlessly with the brim of his hat, Otto gazed out once more at the view. It remained enormous, but was held at a safer distance than before.

'It's still a magnificent city,' he said. 'Even after all these years.'

Chloe looked up, glad to be distracted from the image of his shaking hands.

'Do you have any favourite buildings here in London?' she asked him.

'Of course. I have several. I could talk about the architecture in this city all day long, as poor Anika would no doubt attest.'

He tried pointing out some examples as he spoke, while Chloe sought without success to follow the wavering line of his forefinger.

'Some of them are obvious, the grand set-pieces. St Paul's and Westminster Abbey. Then certain streetscapes, from various periods. Fournier Street in Spitalfields is a particular favourite. A terrific ensemble of eighteenth-century townhouses. So many others: the Nash terraces of Regent's Park; the former warehouses on the Thames; the typical streets of Victorian housing in weathered brick. I also love some of the twentieth-century tower blocks, works by Denys Lasdun and Ernö Goldfinger. That's one of his, by the way, the Trellick Tower, over there.'

He pointed to an elongated smudge on the horizon, far off to the north-west. Chloe had no idea what she was meant to be looking at, but nodded to him politely.

'And yet, oddly enough, my favourite structure here in London is a relatively tiny one. It's not really a "building" at all. It wasn't even designed to be used by people.'

'Whatever is it?' she asked him.

'The penguin pool at London Zoo. Built in the 1930s. Do you know it?'

She thought a second.

'I've seen the new penguin beach – I went there earlier this year. But I don't remember an old pool.'

'It's no longer in use – hasn't been for some years.'

'They haven't knocked it down, surely?'

'They couldn't, even if they wanted to. It's Grade 1 listed, you see. A mere slip of a structure, but important in its way. As far as I'm aware it's now a water feature. It was designed by Berthold Lubetkin's Tecton practice, and is widely regarded as a masterpiece of modern architecture. It has a wonderful pair of concrete ramps, interlocking and spiralling down into the water. A most graceful composition.'

'You've whetted my appetite. I must go back and search it out some day.'

'I don't think you'd regret it; although, as with so many twentieth-century constructions, it did attract its fair share of controversy over the years.'

'Why was that?'

'Some people claimed it didn't work – as a practical structure, I mean. They said it was fine as a work of art, as an eye-catching piece of sculpture, but apparently the penguins didn't much care for it.'

Chloe smiled.

'No wonder it was closed,' she said.

'Yes ... well ... it's quite understandable. I'm sure they'll be much happier with their beach.'

'When did you last go there?'

'Many years ago, now. My first wife and I took our son, Daniel, when he was just a young boy.'

Otto paused a moment in reflection.

'I'm afraid it wasn't a terribly successful outing.'

*

123

On a balmy spring Sunday in 1972, they had taken him to the zoo to see the lions. At five years old, Daniel liked all sorts of animals, but lions were his particular favourite. He had spoken to his parents about little else for weeks.

Within minutes of arriving at the ticket desk, he was running ahead of them on the pathway, eager to reach the scene he could already picture in his head. He anticipated with excitement the deep growling sound in the lions' throats, the way they prowled the perimeter fence of their compound. But as he neared the bend in the pathway that would take him to this magical place, he heard the sound of his mother's voice, calling him back.

'Daniel. Just a moment. Daddy wants to look at the penguins.'

It was some time since Otto had seen the penguin pool, and the sight of the ramps down which they were waddling had stopped him dead in his tracks. He was staring in fascination at the scene, unable to tear himself away.

A reluctant Daniel turned and ran back towards them.

'He won't be long, I promise,' Cynthia whispered with a smile. 'He's having one of his architectural moments.'

Daniel, however, was not amused.

'What about the lions?' he asked.

'In a minute, darling.'

'But we came to see the lions.'

Otto, who was gazing intently at the watery light on the underside of a ramp, failed to notice Daniel or his mounting frustration, even when his son began pulling at his sleeve and pleading with him to move on.

'Daddy, let's go. I want to see the lions. I want to see the lions in their garden.'

At this point, Otto did something he later regretted. He pulled away his sleeve – not angrily, but absently, without even glancing down at Daniel. It was as if he were a thorn on which the sleeve of Otto's shirt had become caught. Straight-away, Daniel's tears began to well.

Cynthia, who had been watching closely, sensed the effect that Otto's unthinking gesture might have. She tried to pre-empt any reaction by distracting Daniel.

'Don't you want to see the penguins, darling? Look, there's a really fat one, coming down the ramp. See him go now into the water. Splosh!'

But it was already too late. Daniel's snivels mounted to a wail. Before Otto had noticed that anything was amiss, Daniel had turned on his heel and was fleeing at speed along the path.

'Daniel, wait . . . ' Cynthia called out, setting off in rapid pursuit.

But she couldn't avert the accident she saw approaching.

Daniel was struck hard on the shoulder by the bicycle that flashed across his path and sent spinning backwards onto the gravel, where he lay on his back, sprawling and stunned.

By the time Cynthia and Otto reached him, he had regained a sitting position and was crying loudly. His elbows were grazed and there was a nasty cut on his knee where it had been hit by a pedal. The young man who had struck him was trying to untangle himself from the aluminium frame. The bicycle lay upended on the grass, its front wheel revolv-ing slowly.

Having established that no one was badly hurt, and with apologies issued all round, Cynthia took Daniel to the first-aid post while Otto went to seek out his son's favourite ice cream at a nearby kiosk. Returning with a giant cone, he apologised and suggested that they go and see the lions. Daniel, a wad of dressing round his knee, looked up at Otto and firmly shook his head. There was nothing they could do to persuade him to change his mind. The eagerly awaited afternoon at the zoo was soon abandoned.

Driving back home to Hampstead, Cynthia cuddled the still-fragile Daniel as he lay on the back seat of the car, his head resting limply on her lap. Otto, silently gripping at the steering wheel, cursed his own stupidity and self-absorption. He had ruined Daniel's day, and there was nothing he could do to remedy the situation. Why was it that he seemed to get these things so wrong so often?

'Daniel's an architect too, isn't he?' asked Chloe.

Otto recovered from his reverie.

'Yes, he is. A talented one. He's won himself a number of awards.'

'You must be very proud of him.'

'I am, of course, although our relationship, these days, is rather broken.'

'Really?'

'There was more or less a complete rupture between us, several years ago. We've not spoken directly since.'

'I'm sorry to hear that,' she said.

He glanced away again at the view.

'It was some silly argument about a railway station he was designing. He was over in Geneva on business and asked me to take a look at the plans over lunch. I made some critical comments that upset him. I should have let it drop, of course, had the wherewithal to sense how annoyed he was becoming.

But I didn't. I kept going, nagging away at him, and finally something seemed to snap.'

He thought again of Daniel, gathering up the plans in his arms, his features contorted with unexpressed hurt. Then the stride to the door; its slamming shut behind him.

Otto looked again at Chloe.

'There was more to it than that, of course. It was a catalyst for the emergence of other, pre-existing tensions. The problems between us lay much further back in time.'

He halted, momentarily, surprised by his own candidness.

'If you'd like to talk about it . . . ' Chloe said to him cautiously.

'It's a complicated matter. I won't bore you with the details. But I must do something about getting back in touch one day. Families are so important, you see.'

Chloe wanted to know more about this troubled relationship with Daniel; about the long and eventful life that Otto had led. Yet the sight of his ancient face, the unfathomable depths of his eyes, brought home to her just how great was the gulf that separated his generation from her own. Dare she tread the eggshell bridge that seemed to divide them? No, it was impossible. The chasm in human experience could not be breached. And so she talked to him about other things instead.

'How are you finding the filming? Is everything okay? I hope you haven't found it a waste of time.'

'No, no . . . not at all,' said Otto, worried about his evident lack of enthusiasm. 'It's been most interesting, seeing the old place again.'

But was the building really worth saving? That was what he wanted to ask her. He no longer knew the answer to this question himself.

Fifteen

Stretched out in near-darkness on his sofa sometime later, Otto felt too tired to get up and switch on any lights.

'Exhausted,' he muttered, in little more than a whisper.

Once more he wished he had given a better account of himself that day. Chloe's questions had been rapid and his answers superficial. He hadn't found the space to gather his thoughts. But then she and her colleagues seemed to operate in a different frame of time to him. *Everybody* did, nowadays. They all moved on fast forward; he in slow motion. No wonder he'd been left a little dazed. It was all so different to his life back home in Switzerland. There he would sit for days on end at the window of his study, watching the colours change in the autumn forest.

He was glad they would soon be meeting some of the residents – apparently it was next on the itinerary. He was feeling a little apprehensive, however. Supposing somebody swore at him?

'How would *you* feel about using this lift each day?' Chloe had asked him earlier.

With an extended yawn, Otto emptied out his mind, allowing his concerns to drift off into the shadows. Tomorrow would no doubt take care of itself.

Little by little, the dark night enclosed him, but he felt no urge to turn on any lights. The distant glow from the city below cast a halo onto the ceiling. He lay staring at it for quite some time, the harsh glare softening to a flickering of candles.

The cellar in which he found himself was long and narrow. It had a red-brick ceiling and walls, which sometimes dripped with damp, and a stone floor that at night seemed half alive with the rumours of mice. He knew this cellar, in intimate detail, and recalled its layout now. There were two exits: a door into the apartment of the elderly couple who sheltered them, and a hatch leading up into the courtyard directly above. Of these two exits, they had been told that they should never use the first. The second, however, they could use as often as was practicable.

The light of the candles offered some respite from the darkness, although the children later had problems with their eyesight, and their mother eventually lost hers altogether. Otto's symptoms were less severe than his sisters', although he always needed glasses for his drawing.

The family moved into the cellar in August 1942, just as the deportations began, having fled to Antwerp from Vienna four years earlier. But it was not far enough to escape the forces of persecution, which seemed, to Otto's father, to be personally pursuing his family across Europe. The previous two years had seen increased levels of violence and intimidation against Antwerp's Jewish community. When word spread that the round-ups were starting, the family had almost no time in which to search out a hiding place. Fortunately, they were offered one by friends.

The cellar was always uncomfortable and its low ceiling claustrophobic. It was high enough to allow the four children and their mother to stand up straight, even to stretch upwards a little to exercise. But Otto's father, who was tall, had to permanently stoop in order to move around. Conditions were at their most bearable during spring and autumn. In summer the cellar could become extremely stuffy, and in winter bitterly cold.

There were mattresses for each of them. Otto, who at nine years old was the youngest of the children, had the smallest space in a corner of the cellar. His three sisters slept in a line running along its narrow length to the wider space at the end where their parents slept. A small table and three chairs also stood in that corner.

Their new living arrangements seemed strange at first, but the children quickly adapted and in time their parents did, too. Their father, in particular, suffered from terrible bouts of claustrophobia during the early weeks, but he hid this from the others fairly well.

Before fleeing Vienna, and for a spell in Antwerp, Otto's father had practised as a civil engineer. He was a stern man, taciturn, but given to moments of great tenderness towards his family. These would break like unexpected shafts of light through his rather oppressive persona. He had greying hair and a substantial moustache in the old-fashioned style. Otto's mother, who was dark and petite, with thick and shining locks, had been a ballet dancer until suffering an injury some years before, after which she had become somewhat melancholy.

During the daytime, the children would be given improvised school lessons by their parents in the larger space with table and chairs that doubled as their sleeping area. They called it, half jokingly, 'the living room'. Classes were held in a variety of subjects, including mathematics, geography, physics, biology and rudimentary English. They used writing materials and books that were left for them, whenever possible, outside the connecting door to the apartment of Mr and Mrs Wouters.

These sessions were conducted as formally as possible, but at a volume that was often little more than a whisper. This generated a strange atmosphere, which left Otto with the feeling that the knowledge he was gaining was somehow forbidden. Perhaps in part for that reason, he developed a great appetite for learning, especially in mathematics and the sciences. He would gladly have spent more time reading than was allowed by his parents, who were concerned about its possible effects upon his eyesight.

Twice a day, buckets containing fresh water for the washing of people and clothing were left outside the door for them to collect, along with modest supplies of food. Normally this consisted of black bread and a hard yellow cheese of indeterminate type. Sometimes they were also left items of clothing.

Otto's sisters, kind-hearted girls with long black hair and large eyes, doted on their younger brother, often giving him their rations of cheese or bread. Their mother and father did the same, meaning there were certain days when Otto ate more than the rest of the family combined. This left him with feelings of intense guilt.

For obvious reasons, the most feared presence in the cellar was the large metal bucket that served as the family latrine. Its normal place of residence was a small recess in a corner. Once a day Otto's father carried it over to the door, from where it was lifted out to be emptied by a benign and unseen hand.

In order for Otto to use the latrine at night, he had to crawl across the mattresses of his sisters, then carefully edge past his sleeping parents. In winter, when temperatures dropped below freezing, using the bucket could be a most uncomfortable experience. In an attempt to avoid this depressing prospect, Otto tried to ignore the aching in his bladder that had woken him each time. Instead, he tried to focus on drifting back to sleep. Normally he failed, and so resigned himself to tackling the human obstacle course that lay between his resting place and his destination. As the disorientated Otto plunged and scrambled across the line of mattresses, his sisters would curse and groan, if they had been asleep, or sometimes giggle, if they were already awake. Yet this drama took place quietly, almost silently, as they all knew that to make any kind of loud noise would be dangerous.

Like the smell from the latrine, fear was a constant presence in the cellar, although the family became highly accomplished at disguising it from Otto, who was not yet of an age to fully comprehend the circumstances in which they found themselves. There were moments when he clearly sensed something. His mother's voice was naturally weak, but at times, when she sat at the table talking to his father, it became even more tremulous than usual. The occasional look that his father gave his mother also told Otto that mysterious issues were moving beneath the surface. His sisters, who were older and knew more than he, remained generally playful in his presence. But even they sometimes appeared a little pensive, as they gathered in a huddle on a mattress to whisper among themselves.

Despite the distraction of the daily lessons, life in the cellar was routine. Often the worst thing for the children was not so much the constant fear of discovery as the boredom of containment. For all of them, therefore, those hours away from studying were spent thinking of the courtyard above; awaiting the hour when they could go outside and stand once again in the fresh air.

Three sides of the courtyard were surrounded by the backs of tenement buildings – blank walls offering protection from prying eyes. The fourth side was overlooked by workshops that had once been used by local diamond-cutters, now replaced by unfamiliar faces. When these strangers had finished work for the day, the family would receive a special 'knock from above', telling them that the coast was now clear.

Each day, as they awaited this signal, Otto would sit on his mattress and watch the blade-thin shafts of light – specks of dust swirling in their midst – penetrate down into the gloom through the hatch that was the portal to those few short hours of bliss. He would feel a surge of nervous excitement whenever the knock on the wooden hatch came: two firm blows from a hobnailed boot, and then three more at a faster rhythm. After waiting a few minutes, his father would go first, pushing up the cover and clambering out, before turning to help up the children in their turn. Their mother, a nervous woman, usually preferred to stay in the relative safety of the cellar rather than join the others outside, fretting until they returned safely to their hiding place.

During those hours outside in what seemed like the harsh light of the courtyard, Otto sometimes played with his sisters, who had developed between them a range of improvised games in which they didn't need to make a single sound.

There were 'clapping' games without any clapping, 'singing' games that were extravagant mimes, and games of 'catch' that involved no ball. At other times, Otto walked silently beside his father, who paced endlessly around the perimeter, his hands behind his back and his long head bowed. At every turn, almost without fail, his father's moustache would twitch; a restless antenna, transmitting to Otto his thoughts.

At other times, when Otto was in a more solitary mood, he would stand or sit in a corner, his back resting against the cool brown wall, and study the sky above him. Sometimes he would sketch the view in a notepad, but more often he would settle on contemplation. Only the narrowest of views was visible, of that famously wide Flemish sky, closed in above them between the encircling walls of the tenements. Yet month after month Otto studied in all weathers that small patch of sky: the soft cloud-brushes against the intense blue; the thick and glowing layers of grey; the flakes of snow that tumbled from on high in swirling, chaotic patterns – seeming to take an eternity to reach his face.

While looking upwards, he thought of the skies he had seen in the great landscape paintings his father had shown to him; at one time, in leather-bound books in their Viennese apartment, nowadays by the light of candles in the cellar, in pages torn from old magazines. Some of those paintings were kept here in Belgium, in the fine-art museum in Brussels. His father had promised that one day, when it was safe to venture outside once again, he would take them all.

During summer, they spent two or three hours each evening in the courtyard, fewer in winter. As the afternoons advanced, Otto would watch the shadows from the surrounding tenements lengthen across the courtyard, submerging the light until only a small patch of it remained in a corner by a wall. His sisters would gather in that corner, where they stood and sunned themselves with arms outstretched, or played within the glowing circle, their movements increasingly curtailed by its gradual closing. Until suddenly, almost unnoticed, the scrap of light would be extinguished altogether, casting the last of the courtyard into dusk. Their father, stepping forward in the blueness, would signal with his hand that it was time for them to go, and they would gather in a silent group around the hatch.

At night, Otto lay staring at the red-brick ceiling. It flickered dimly in the candlelight from the corner, where his mother and father sat talking at the table. Their words were indecipherable from this distance, and so Otto would let the low comforting hum of their voices wash over him, his thoughts meandering far beyond the ceiling at which he gazed. Sometimes he would think back to Vienna, although his memories of the city were already hazy. He retained no specific incidents, only vague and abstract impressions, removed from any context. He remembered the clanging of a tram bell, the smell of horse manure and rooms with tall mirrors reflecting layers of chocolate cake. There was also the leather couch in his old home, mottled and smelling of antique books, with a texture that would sink softly against his face as he lay and listened to his mother read him stories. Otto liked to recreate that texture in his mind as he pressed his face into the rough hessian sack that acted as a pillow and often left chequerboard patterns on his cheek in the morning.

Sometimes he would think of Antwerp, which lay somewhere unseen beyond the roof of the cellar. The wide River Scheldt he could still picture, black and swaying hypnotically against the quays. And he could taste the pickled herrings that his mother bought at market, dropping them laughing into his mouth while he grunted and clapped his hands as if he were a seal pup. He also liked to think about the trip they had taken to see the tulip fields at Lisse in the Netherlands, back before the outbreak of war. He remembered riding between the long strips of flowers on the back of his father's bicycle. The individual heads had blurred into thick streaks of pigment, as pure as any squeezed from a paint tube. A long line of pink, and then a long line of red; yellow, orange, purple – each one in turn becoming Otto's favourite. Later, they climbed up to a platform on the edge of a field, and saw the bright colours run in thick bands toward the steeples on the horizon; a landscape as painted by a child.

If these thoughts failed to return Otto to sleep, he would raise himself slightly, his hands behind his head, and look across the narrow cellar, over the mattresses of his sleeping sisters to the far end of the room. There he could see his parents, hunched in conversation over the table. Many years later, when visiting the Van Gogh Museum in Amsterdam, Otto had seen the painting *The Potato Eaters*, and found himself transported with a terrible immediacy back to that scene of his parents in the cellar. The drawn faces of the protagonists in the shadowy candlelit room made his heart contract in a spasm of recognition, forcing him to sit a moment on one of the benches lining the gallery. Later, in the café, he explained the memory to Anika and felt her fingers brush lightly against his face.

One night, some five months after the family had moved into the cellar, Otto was lying awake on his mattress and staring once more at the red-brick ceiling. He was having trouble getting to sleep. The rain was beating down heavily that night. He could hear it, faintly, on the other side of the ceiling above him, more clearly on the wooden hatch leading up to the courtyard. As he pressed his face into the rough surface of the sacking, and imagined once more the leather couch in their old apartment, he suddenly became aware that the hum of his parents' voices had risen in pitch and intensity. Unusually, too, he could now make out what they were saying, and it was clear that his mother in particular was upset. Her weak and trembling voice almost cracked with anger.

'You can't,' she was saying. 'I won't let you do it. It's dangerous and irresponsible.'

Otto's father sounded less angry, but his deep and authoritative voice carried a barely concealed edge of feeling.

'Irresponsible? What do you mean irresponsible? Europe is at war, Maria.'

Otto heard one of his sisters stirring, before readjusting the sacking on her mattress and settling back down to sleep.

'You have four children – you have a family. Your duty lies with them.'

'But there's nothing useful I can do here, can't you see? *I* can't protect them. *I* can't help them – not if they come for us. There's nothing I can do. And meanwhile all I do here is pace about, taking up what limited space there is in the cellar and using up valuable supplies of food.'

'But what about their education?'

'*You* are more than capable of taking care of that, as you have already shown.'

'But it's a comfort for them to know that you are here. It is for all of us. You're their father.'

'We've been here some months now, and the children are

more than accustomed to this way of life. *They*, at least, appear calm and controlled about the situation.'

'Meaning?'

'Please, let's not argue any more. You know how I feel – we've spoken about this many times. I cannot continue to sit here, in a cellar, doing nothing, while people outside are fighting this evil. We hoped at first it would be for a few months only, but clearly it's going to last for some time yet. I cannot countenance years of sitting here passively, waiting for my wife and children to be plucked like chickens from a coop and slaughtered. *I have to do something.*'

'Not so loud.'

The sound of his father's voice dropped slightly, but Otto could still decipher the sharp whispering from across the room.

'This mission will last no more than a few weeks, as I've explained. My expertise will be invaluable. Indeed, it has been specifically requested by those concerned. Already we owe these people our lives. I cannot ignore such a request for assistance.'

A few days later, after the family had taken their usual turn in the courtyard, and finished their supper of bread and powdered milk, Otto's father asked to speak to the three sisters while Otto read on his mattress. They talked softly around the table, glancing over at him occasionally as they did so. Otto looked up, curiously, when one of his sisters appeared to gasp, but the voices dropped back down immediately and the conversation continued. A few minutes later, Otto was also called to the table and told that his father would be going away for a short while.

'Is this the mission?' Otto asked, surprising everyone with his words.

When they said nothing, he continued, 'I heard you talking last night while I was in bed. You said something about a mission.'

His father had recovered himself.

'That's right,' he said. 'It *is* a mission. And do you know what it is for?'

Otto shook his head.

'I'm going to find us some books.'

Otto said nothing.

'I think we need some more books for this apartment, don't you?'

He always called the cellar 'the apartment' in front of the children.

'Why, you've quite worn out the ones we have here, Otto, with all that reading you do. I'm going to go in search of some more.'

His father had tried to adopt a playful tone, which was among the least familiar in his repertoire. Otto did not really believe him, and realised that something was seriously amiss, but he also sensed that everyone in his family wanted him to believe his father's story. So he convinced himself, for their sakes, that he did.

That evening, Otto's father packed a holdall with some belongings, put on his overcoat and a warm leather cap, and went round to kiss each of the children in turn. Later on, when they were fast asleep, they were woken by the thumping of the hobnailed boot on the hatch above, in the same familiar pattern that always called them out to their early evening exercise. Otto, bleary and confused, looked across and saw the dark shape of his father, threading his way upwards through the hatch.

For many weeks they heard nothing. Otto could sense his mother's anguish, her body language and voice taking on an air of desperation. At night he sometimes heard her whimpering, a sound that would never quite leave him throughout his life. As the only male in the household, he tried his best to assume extra responsibilities. He insisted on climbing up first through the hatch during their daily trips outside. He also started lifting the bucket from its position in the recess to the door to the adjacent apartment, leaving it there for collection every day. Otto sensed that it was his role to be positive; to play the carefree child, in order to lessen his mother's burden. So he took on this happy-go-lucky role, almost convincing himself that it was real; while sensing, deep down, that some calamity was about to befall them.

It came in March 1943, two months after his father's departure. Otto, wrapped in his mother's thick coat, was reading on his mattress one morning while his sisters sat and played with a pack of cards. Suddenly, they heard their mother's voice, talking to someone at the door to the Wouterses' apartment, something that had never happened before. She had gone to collect a bucket of water, having received a signal of three quick knocks, followed by the sound of the key turning in the lock. This was normal procedure, so much so that the children barely even noticed. When they heard a man's voice, however, talking to their mother in the hallway outside, the atmosphere in the cellar quickly changed. Otto's eyes met those of his sisters, and all of them carried the same expression. The fear, so well hidden for much of the time, was instantly there.

Raising himself from the mattress, Otto felt the muscles tighten in his legs. His sisters did the same, all of them braced for flight, remembering the instructions that had been drilled into them by their father. Otto repeated them calmly to himself, just as he had been taught:

'If they come for us through the apartment next door, make quickly for the hatch. Once outside, run to the eastern wall of the courtyard, that's the one where the light falls when we play. There are some loose bricks in the lower right-hand corner. Push them all in and help each other climb through the gap. This corner of the wall gives onto a small road. If Mr and Mrs Wouters are able to help you, they will. One of them will be standing there to show you where to go. They might even be able to come with you part of the way. If no one is there, try to remember the following combination of streets: turn to your right, then run along until you reach the old synagogue, left, then to the plane trees, then right again. This will take you to the big street with the trams. From there you must try to get north to the port, where someone may be able to help you. Be careful who you speak to, however. No one in uniform; no officials. Try to talk to one of the ordinary workers.'

While silently reciting these instructions, Otto and his sisters made their way over to the hatch, waiting for a raised voice or the sound of a struggle that would be their signal to flee. The door creaked on its hinges and closed: footsteps approached down the stairs. When their mother re-entered the room, they saw that she was alone. She looked calm, despite the redness of her eyes, and gently told Otto to go back to his reading while she took his sisters upstairs and into the apartment next door.

The news was broken to Otto in stages, in a bid to lessen its impact. At first, he was told that his father had been taken ill and that he was being looked after in the hospital. Later, he was told that there were complications with his illness, and that Otto must prepare himself for bad news. Later still, he was told that his father was dead.

In the weeks that followed, his mother grieved terribly, but what made it all the more difficult to watch was the effort with which she tried, without success, to hide it. Every night she sat weeping on her mattress, while Otto's sisters gathered sobbing in a desolate group around her. It was like one of the Renaissance paintings he had seen in his father's books. The sadness etched onto their candlelit faces was biblical.

Otto, at first, did not feel such grief, but a slight numbness and a sense that this story wasn't quite to be believed, like his father's tale about the mission to hunt out new books. Each night he lay and stared at the hatch, trying to convince himself that his father would never again come through it. But the idea, when he thought of it, seemed absurd.

Finally, some weeks later, he was sitting on his mattress when he thought once more of their trip to see the tulip fields near Lisse. He wanted to talk again with his father about the long strips of colour they had seen. He also wanted to tell him about a new plant he had discovered, in a book that had been left outside the door for him by Mr Wouters. This plant had a red mouth with fangs, and it liked to eat insects for its supper.

From the mattress, Otto's sobbing brought his mother and sisters running quickly to his side.

'I can never talk to him again,' he said, while they did their best to console him. 'I can never show him the pictures in the book.'

Otto's mother held her son in arms that suddenly grew

stronger. During the eighteen months or so in which the family remained in the cellar, the children never again saw or heard her shed a tear.

Otto did not learn the full truth about his father's death until some time after the war had ended. Once again, he heard the story in stages. Shortly after the end of hostilities, when they were living in the Wouterses' apartment, Otto was told by a boy at school that his father had been involved in a plot to detonate a bridge. His experience as a civil engineer meant that he played a vital role in planning the mission. Unfortunately, in the days before it was scheduled to have taken place, a member of the public, walking his dog, noticed suspicious activity inside a warehouse. Immediately he had alerted the authorities. Within half an hour, the warehouse had been raided, the explosives discovered and the men responsible arrested. Two days later, Otto's father and his three cohorts were hanged in a public square in the city. As it was winter, the authorities left the bodies outside on display for several days – the crimes of which they had been accused written out on notices hung around their necks.

Some years later, Otto learned from a family friend that the plotters had been tortured before their execution. The rumour was that they had not given away a single detail to their captors, who did not even know the names of the men they hanged.

After the war, the family remained living in Antwerp, where a formal education in any traditional sense was difficult to obtain. Both books and teachers were in short supply, and schooldays often curtailed. To add to Otto's problems, he developed a debilitating bronchial condition on his return to the outside world, although it did clear up in time.

Despite these setbacks, Otto's teachers were astonished at his rate of academic progress, outstripping the achievements not only of his classmates, but of children several years older than himself. His gifts in a variety of subjects were exceptional. Otto's teachers were not only dumbstruck by the depth and range of his knowledge, but wondered about the sources from which it had come. The headmaster, calling Otto into his office one day, told him he was a true autodidact. He was even more impressed that the boy appeared to know what this meant.

Six years after the end of the war, Otto left Antwerp to take up his architectural scholarship in London. Two of his sisters remained in Belgium – marrying and living long enough to see their grandchildren do the same. His third sister returned to Vienna, where she died some fifteen years later after a short illness. She had never married. Otto's mother, worn out beyond her years by her wartime experience, lived alone in Antwerp for a while, before moving in with one of her daughters and her family as her health steadily worsened. Blind for the last two years of her life, she suffered a stroke one morning while admiring the scent of the spring blooms in the local park. A few days later, she passed away in hospital. She was fifty-three years old.

Sixteen

'Right,' said Chloe, as they approached the door of an apartment on the fifteenth floor. 'The first people we're meeting are Roz and Joe. Middle-aged – late forties. Been living in Marlowe House for several years.'

'And are they friendly?' Otto asked, with a hint of apprehension that surprised her.

'Yes, very friendly . . . Don't worry yourself about anything. It's all been arranged. They know who you are and what to expect. The cameras are set up in there and we're ready to go.'

She rang the doorbell and lowered her voice.

'Joe has a terrific face – quite old-fashioned, in its way. Tough but full of character; like an extra in an old *film noir*. Roz, too, has such powerful features, though her look is a little more contemporary. I only wish we could film them in black and white.'

Otto said nothing, a little taken aback. Was this how Chloe spoke about all of her subjects?

'I'll lead the questioning, if it's okay with you,' she added.

'Just jump in whenever you feel the need to contribute something.'

'Of course,' said Otto, who preferred to take a back seat for the time being.

Memories of the interview on the burned-out mattress remained fresh in his mind.

The latch was sliding back.

Roz answered the door, and Otto fought hard not to express any shock. She had bright-red dreadlocks, released in long streams; a gym-hardened physique; a taste for body art and piercings. Yet her voice was soft and her manner gentle. Her blue eyes smiled as she greeted them. Joe, beside her, had a wiry physique that seemed to bristle with a nervous energy. The lines of his pale face, beneath the cropped grey hair, were deep. This was a man who had clearly been through a lot in life.

Otto learned, during the introductions, that Roz worked as a nurse at a local hospital. Joe, a former musician and mechanic, was currently unemployed.

They settled down; Joe and Roz on the sofa, the others sitting opposite them on armchairs.

'Let's get down to business,' said Chloe. 'What exactly do you both think of Marlowe House?'

Otto flinched at the abruptness of her question. He had hoped that she would be a little more subtle. Yet neither Roz nor Joe showed any obvious signs of hostility, either towards the building, or the man who had designed it. Roz gazed thoughtfully into the distance, while Joe shrugged his bony shoulders inside his T-shirt.

'I was born and raised in Sheffield,' said Roz, 'in a flat on the Park Hill Estate. So you could say I have concrete in my blood. It's always been there, in one form or another, so the look of Marlowe House doesn't bother me. It's a bit frayed around the edges, these days, but then aren't we all?'

It was hardly a glowing endorsement, but Otto heard her words with some relief.

'How long have you lived here?' Chloe asked her.

'Almost ten years now. I moved down when I got the job at the local hospital.'

'And how have you found it . . . as a place to live, I mean? Would you say that you've been happy here?'

Roz smiled.

'Happy isn't quite the word I'd use. It's a part of me, I suppose. If you were to ask me if I regret having lived here, then the answer is definitely no. It's as good a place as any to experience life. Better, I'd argue, than most. You get life with its gloves off here. I like that – it's to my taste. Although the block does feel a little like it's dying these days.'

Otto felt the need to say something on this last point.

'To some extent I feel responsible for the environment in which you have to live. It was a time of great optimism, you see – the post-war period – for architects and town planners alike. We were trying to build the world anew, to ensure a better life for the generations that followed. For people of all backgrounds and classes. Yet within a few decades everything seemed to evaporate.'

Roz felt sorry for Otto, whose face was pale with concern. He must feel protective towards this place. She felt the same way about her patients.

'You did what you thought was best,' she said, in her finest bedside manner. 'You weren't to know it would turn out like this.'

'And how about you, Joe?' Chloe turned to ask. 'What do you think about Marlowe House?'

Beneath the tough exterior, there was a touch of vulnerability in Joe's grey eyes, making him an oddly ambivalent presence.

'I'm not much good at talking in front of the cameras.'

'Try,' said Chloe, with a smile. 'It would be nice to know your thoughts.'

Joe rubbed his hands together, awkwardly.

'I don't have the same connection to Marlowe House as Roz. Just four years here, for me. I'm originally from Harlow, one of the post-war New Towns. Like Roz, I grew up in a world of concrete. It's hard, to be honest, for me to judge this place as a building, 'cos I connect it with Roz and the good feelings she brings. I wake up, most mornings, after she's left for work ... I look up at the ceiling, and even that, a plain white ceiling, brings me a sense of security.'

Chloe sat forward in her chair. It was an unexpectedly candid response. Joe wasn't so bad in front of the cameras after all.

'It ain't always been that way,' he added. 'I have a bad history with ceilings. They ain't always been that kind to me. Ceilings of bedsits ... ceilings of squats. Some of them hold bad memories.'

The camera zoomed in closer. Joe's head in the viewfinder grew enormous. The creases and folds of his pale and pock-marked face looked like footage from a lunar landing module.

'I had a few problems, you see, in the years before I met up with Roz. She helped straighten me out.'

Chloe nodded, willing him to continue, but Joe suddenly faltered.

148

'I shouldn't really talk about this . . . '

Otto sensed it was time to interject. The intrusion was making him uncomfortable.

'Would you miss anything about Marlowe House?' he asked Roz. 'If it were to be demolished?'

A look of gratitude crossed her face.

'Apart from my friends?'

'Yes.'

'I don't know . . . let me see. Several things, I suppose. The staircase, for a start. I've always liked that staircase. The way it spirals upwards as you stand at the bottom. It needs some renovation work, and it looks a lot less nice from six storeys up, when you still have another nine to climb. But even when the lifts aren't broken, I still make the effort to walk up the first few floors, now and then.'

'Anything else?'

'There's a view of it, sometimes, when I'm walking back across the bridge after my shift. As I look up, I can see Marlowe House, diagonally, in profile, jutting out in the distance on the other side of the river. The sunlight catches the windows near the top and there's a flash, a flare, just briefly. It looks like a great flint being struck. And it feels, to me, almost like a welcome, as though it's sending out something personal to me. And the feeling I get then is about other things. About Joe, who'll be waiting here, and a beer together on the balcony, and the sun slowly setting on our faces. I can feel my footsteps quicken as I walk across the bridge.'

The smile that briefly lit her face was a boon to Otto's heart. It reminded him, faintly, of those scenes with the residents from the newsreel in the mid 1960s. Maybe things weren't so negative here, despite his initial impressions.

It was Chloe who spoke to Roz now.

'And would you like to see Marlowe House saved from demolition and given a listing?'

'I think so, yes . . . certainly if it means carrying out some improvements. Otherwise, I'm not so sure. Personally, I have strong memories of this place, so for sentimental reasons I'd like to see it survive. But life moves on – we may do soon ourselves. A flat's become available nearer work. So I'd only want the building to stay if it meant a better life for the people who remain here.'

'And you, Joe?'

He shrugged again.

'I don't really care much either way, to be honest.'

After a pause, he decided to explain himself further. He might as well finish what he had started.

'I've moved around a lot over the years, lived in dozens of places. I was even on the street for a while, when things got really bad. Sleeping in bus shelters, in supermarket car parks, staring at abandoned factories through sheets of rain. I remember staying in a roofless shed at the site of the old Dagenham car works. The stars that night were shining overhead. The thing is, after something like that, I've moved beyond feeling any connection to places. The only connection that I feel now is to Roz.'

Joe looked questioningly at Otto.

'Does that sound strange to you?' he asked.

'No,' Otto replied. 'I'd say it sounds like wisdom.'

If Joe was largely indifferent to the fate of Marlowe House, then Ravi was a different matter. Born and bred on the eighteenth floor, he was rooted in the soil here as deeply as the concrete columns. They interviewed him that afternoon in the apartment where he lived with his mother and sister. About the same age as Chloe, with lively eyes, tousled hair and a fine-boned face, Ravi sat on the edge of his sofa in a hooded top and jeans. Unlike Joe, he was confident in front of the cameras, wanting to state his point of view while he had the opportunity.

Throughout the interview, he asked as many questions as he answered. He wanted to know about the film they were making; about Otto, and the history of the building. He questioned them about the legal process that would be needed to halt the demolition. Otto's knowledge, on this last point, was rather vague. Nonetheless, Ravi sensed that he had found himself an ally, and his passion for saving Marlowe House soon became clear.

'This place is getting more run-down each year,' he told them. 'Nobody seems interested in its upkeep. Yet at the same time a lot of redevelopment work has taken place near by. Luxury flats, fancy restaurants. It don't take much to see what's going on. I had a feeling, some time ago, that our days here might be numbered.'

'What do you mean?' asked Chloe. 'I don't quite follow.'

'This ain't a well-heeled neighbourhood, but it *is* well placed. Only a short journey from central London. Land in this area has become like gold dust in recent years. You telling me the sharks in suits want thousands of council tenants taking up valuable space? Not when there's money to be made from developing this land as private apartments. They can't wait to see the back of us.'

'Do you have any evidence of this?'

'No, but then how could we? It's just a feeling. Everyone

151

round here knows the score, the way the wind has been blowing these past few years. There's been a lot of social engineering going on in London, clearing inner-city areas of poorer people so that richer ones can move in. And yet it's *not* social engineering – that's what we're told. It's all about regeneration – one of those well-meaning words. Though it's hard to feel regenerated when your home is knocked down and you're sent to live fifty miles away.'

Otto, who had yet to speak, was shifting about in his seat, looking agitated, unhappy. Ravi's words were bringing back some painful memories of past professional battles.

'So what would you say to those people who think that Marlowe House should be demolished?' Chloe asked.

Ravi thought for a while.

'People of many different nationalities live in this building: all the world is here. By and large they get on well with each other, even though life ain't always easy for them. That's an example to everyone, no? People make friends here, they marry each other . . . grow up and grow old together. I work for a local community group so I know the real picture, and it ain't the horror story some people want you to believe. As for the idea that everyone wants it demolished? There are people who like living here and people who don't. But the picture's never been all one way.'

'So what would you like to see done?'

'I'd like them to preserve it – to show that it can work. Spend a little money, maybe, 'cos this place certainly needs it. Don't divide people up and break communities apart; put up a few of the residents in nice new flats, with a photo in the local papers, and then send the majority to go and live elsewhere when nobody is looking any more. I don't really care about the architectural value of this building. No offence, but it ain't my speciality. What I *do* know is that I want this community to stay together, 'cos it's time that people like us made a stand again.'

'Hear, hear,' Otto said quietly, his voice thick with feeling. 'It infuriates me to see this happen. A simple necessity, like a roof over one's head, turned into a bargaining chip for speculators. Communities shoved around, given no say in their future.'

Chloe remembered the rather vague old man who had spoken to her the other day on the burned-out mattress. This was an Otto she hadn't witnessed before: fired up; indignant; re-engaged.

Otto looked at Ravi.

'I'm sorry about this – we should have acted long ago, before the fabric fell into such disrepair. Our chances of success would have been much better then. But we'll do whatever we can to save the building. Rest assured, there are people hard at work on it.'

'Thanks,' said Ravi. 'Appreciate it.'

Once they had finished the interview, and the film crew were moving out their equipment, Ravi accompanied Otto and Chloe to the door.

'It's funny,' he told them. 'When I first heard there were plans to make a film here, I assumed you must be from one of those TV police dramas.'

'Police dramas?' said Otto.

'Yeah, you know the ones. *The Bill*, or whatever. Those people are always shooting scenes round here. Once we had two film crews turn up at once! You should have seen the row that broke out between them. People see this place as a visual shorthand for crime. The concrete, the graffiti, the kids hanging round in hoodies. It's a cliché, simplistic, but it gives you some idea of what we're up against. You get used to it, that's how things are, when you come from a place like Marlowe House. Life is one long battle against the preconceptions and stereotypes. Well, I ain't giving up the fight now.'

Otto looked rather moved as he shook Ravi's hand at the door. His commitment to the building, to what it represented, had been reignited.

Seventeen

Otto rose late, showering and dressing at a more leisurely pace than previously. No filming was planned until later that day, so he had a little time to himself. Furthermore, for the first time since arriving in London, he had enjoyed a decent night's sleep. The reaction of the residents the previous day had come as a relief to him.

He made himself toast and coffee and opened the living-room curtains to be greeted by a fine autumn day. It was crisp and windy, with freewheeling clouds and intermittent sunshine that was all the more appealing for its hesitancy. Time, once again, for Otto to consult the virtual *A to Z* that lay inside his head. Even better, he would consult the three-dimensional map of London laid out beneath the balcony of his apartment.

Settling outside on a plastic chair, he resolutely ignored the fact that the high winds were making it a far less pleasant experience than he had anticipated. Finally, when a slice of buttered toast he was about to bite into was whisked from his hand and flung over the edge of the balcony (no fatalities below – he had checked), he accepted that the sensible thing to do would be to finish his breakfast inside.

Never really thought of that one – not much shelter from the north-easterlies. Funny the things you overlook when designing a place. There's always something – it's never perfect.

Through the closed window, Otto scanned the London skyline. But he knew already where he would spend that morning. The heights of Hampstead, seen from the rooftop recently, were only faintly visible in the distance. Yet they held a prominent place on his mental horizon.

I think it's time to go home, he told himself.

Dressed once more in his overcoat and homburg, and brandishing his cane before him, he left the building some half an hour later and made his way down to the tube station.

Although his face registered no emotion as he sat on the Northern Line train, his heart beat a little faster with each stop. Once he had changed trains at Euston, he began to trace his old evening commute from the West End to Hampstead, his lips moving in time to the announcements on the tannoy. Mornington Crescent – Camden Town – Chalk Farm – Belsize Park: the order and rhythm of these names remained as familiar as those childhood recitals from the Talmud.

Are you really prepared for this? he thought. You could always change your mind.

On a practical level, he had little choice. The schedule for filming was tight, and he must take the opportunity to do some proper exploration. Tomorrow evening, he would fly back home – to his comfortable life with Anika in the hills above Lake Geneva. Chances were that he might never return to London again. Angelo, Otto's last real contact here, was not often around in the city these days. His job made constant demands upon his time, and he was forever travelling overseas. As for Daniel and his family . . . well, who knew what would happen? Otto certainly wasn't making any assumptions there. So this was his last opportunity, then, and he would probably never forgive himself if he failed to take it. The memories, circling incessantly around his head, had been stirred too deeply to settle. He must follow his journey through, relive everything to the full. Maybe it would bring him a sense of peace.

The tube train began to slow for Hampstead. Otto rose from his seat a little early and stood swaying in the centre of the carriage, one hand gripping the overhead pole and the other his cane as a counterbalance. When the doors slid open and he stepped out onto the platform, he stopped momentarily to take out his handkerchief and wipe beads of perspiration from his brow. Then he continued on his way.

As he slowly climbed the stairs from the platform to the lifts, a young man in a suit and tie nudged his shoulder as he hurried past. The young man seemed agitated; perhaps he was late for a meeting. He was clutching a briefcase closely to his chest. Turning as he ran, he sharply muttered something before disappearing from sight. Otto glanced up, irritated. There was nothing new in this rudeness. It was only when returning to London after a period of time away that one even noticed it.

The same thing had happened to Cynthia during her illness. Some smartly dressed young woman, pushing past her in Regent Street. What was it she had said to Cyn, again? 'Out of my way, you stupid cow' – that was it. Quite remarkable. She must have thought that Cynthia was drunk, since her headscarf covered the scars from her surgery. And Otto was looking in a shop window at the time and like an idiot completely missed it. She almost lost her balance, too; had to cling to that lamppost to stay upright. And the anger – the anger Otto felt upon discovering. That young woman would have had no idea what she had just done – no doubt she would have forgotten the incident within a matter of seconds. But it knocked Cyn's confidence, badly. It never quite came back to her. She had been trying not to use her wheelchair, in order to hang on to the last of her independence. After that, she starting using it all the time in public places.

At the exit, Otto fed his day pass into the machine. In a series of rapid movements it sucked in, processed and spat out the pink ticket, which he collected from an orifice as the gate slammed shut behind him.

Even the ticket machines in this city are bloody rude.

Stepping outside the entrance, he blinked at the change of atmosphere. It was thirteen stops here from the Elephant and Castle, where his journey had begun, but a world away in many other respects. Whereas the streets around Marlowe House remained urban in character, Hampstead retained the air of a small country town. Its calm sense of affluence was a little disorientating after Otto's experiences of the past few days. It was a reminder once more, if any were needed, that London remained many cities in one.

Otto followed the high street up the hill, eventually turning off into a network of quieter backstreets. Large houses from the Edwardian period dominated the horizon. He stopped before one of them, the front lawn overgrown in the cottage-garden style, and rested for a moment on his cane.

*

'For a couple of avant-garde lefties, you two have pretty traditional tastes when it comes to choosing your own home.'

These words came from Anton, Cynthia's brother, as he wandered around their newly bought house. It was the spring of 1966, and their professional lives were blooming. The handsome building into which they had just moved offered material confirmation of their new-found status.

Anton was climbing up some steps to poke his nose inside the attic.

'I assumed that you'd be living in some kind of rotating concrete sphere. But this is all rather nice. *Very* nice, indeed!'

It was the kind of backhanded compliment Otto had come to expect from Anton. He was fond of his brother-in-law, but in the ten years they had known each other Otto had never quite established an effective method for engaging in conversation with him. Otto always felt caught off guard by Anton's particular kind of sarcasm, affectionate but slightly barbed, and could never find the right tone with which to respond. He feared either causing offence, by being too blunt in his comeback, or giving the impression that he had himself taken offence, by being too polite. Treading the line between the two was no easy task. In time, after several failed attempts, he discovered that the best solution was to smile politely and leave all the talking to Cynthia, who seemed to know much better than he what she was doing.

'Yes, well, when you've finished your little tour of inspection perhaps you could put all that military training of yours to good use,' Cynthia said to Anton. 'There's a rats' nest in the attic that needs terminating.'

Anton, who had trained at Sandhurst and spent some years in the army before taking up a career in the City of London, was quite different in character to his sister. Their tastes, their interests, their ideas on culture and politics – everything seemed to run in contradistinction. There were times when Otto had the impression that Anton's entire personality was defined on the basis of what his older sister was not; a childhood impulse for contrariness, got completely out of hand. Even their looks differed greatly. She was petite and delicate, with an auburn bob and a taste for flowing garments that grew ever more extravagant as the 1960s progressed. He was thick-set, ruddy and fair-haired, usually wearing a bespoke tailored suit, or – at weekends – a starched white shirt and pressed beige slacks. His style, it seemed, was unvarying. Whatever Anton wore, however, he always looked to Otto like an officer in civvies; someone who would never feel at home unless buttoned up in blazing red and standing to attention.

'Does your brother not agree with you about *anything*?' Otto once asked Cynthia, shortly after meeting Anton for the first time. He had been somewhat shocked by the sharpness of the exchanges between them. 'I thought for a moment I must be in the House of Commons.'

'Don't worry,' she answered with a smile. 'It's a kind of game between the two of us, although at the same time we're perfectly serious in our views. Maybe it's just the way some middle-class siblings in this country express their love for each other. It's all that is left over once our natural affection has been drilled out of us at school.'

Otto knew from previous conversations that Cynthia, like her brother, had undergone a strict education. She sometimes described herself, with a hint of a smile, as a 'victim of the British public-school system'. To Otto, this sounded like an exaggeration. Cynthia's privileged upbringing appeared to him to have been a mixed blessing. On the one hand, it had furnished her with her perfect diction and cut-glass accent, a sound that affected Otto like music. It had also given her impeccable posture and natural grace, self-confidence and knowledge in a wide range of academic subjects. Not to mention a number of practical skills: fixing a carburettor, skinning rabbits without flinching, rolling a cigarette in the fingers of one hand.

On the other hand, Cynthia's background appeared to have left some less positive traits, perhaps going some way towards explaining her somewhat troubled character. Her personality combined warmth and frostiness in equal measure. She was capable of showing great vulnerability; breaking into tears unexpectedly, or hugging and kissing Otto in public with an intense, almost passionate affection. Yet she was also capable of sudden retreats into coldness, of closing off emotionally, quite unexpectedly, and sometimes within moments of these outpourings of warmth. To Otto, Cynthia seemed to be locked in a constant battle with herself – these differing impulses wrestling for ascendancy. Was she essentially a warm and passionate person, whose natural affection had been checked by the coldness and formality of a British public-school education? He sometimes believed this to be the case. At other times, however, it appeared to him that her tendency towards outbursts of emotion had in fact been *exaggerated* by that education; that in attempting to suppress those very qualities, it had somehow made them flower all the more, and to a degree that was not always healthy.

In some respects, the dual nature of Cynthia's personality embodied, for Otto, the dual nature of England itself – a country that combined an innate conservatism with an impulse towards free-spirited anarchy. The two sides of its character (militarism and Kipling on the one hand, the Diggers and the Beatles on the other) seemed caught in permanent creative tension; the latter both fighting against, yet feeding off, the former. That Cynthia generally embraced the anarchic side of the divide appealed greatly to Otto. The unpredictable moments of conservatism he accepted from her without question, because he loved her and they were a part of her originality.

Anton, however, Otto did not love, and at times he found his brother-in-law's tirades against socialism, trade unionism and anti-war protesters, not to mention his sarcastic and somewhat personal asides, a little irksome. All the more so, perhaps, because some of these personal asides – and in particular Anton's unerring knack for pointing out inconsistencies in Cynthia and Otto's own lives; what he once called, with a friendly beam, 'saying one thing and doing another' – carried more than a grain of truth. His remarks about their new home in Hampstead – traditional, expensive, perhaps a shade ostentatious, the kind of house that wouldn't look out of place in Purley, Cheltenham or Tunbridge Wells – again hit the mark.

He felt himself inwardly flinch at Anton's observation.

'We can get to work in the attic later on,' Otto said. 'Let's have a beer in the garden first.'

He and Cynthia worried, sometimes, about their increasingly lavish lifestyle, which did not sit comfortably with their political convictions. During their early years together, they had earned very little, although they did have access to money thanks to a trust fund set up for Cynthia by her businessman father. She always referred to this account, somewhat enigmatically, as 'the source', largely because she was embarrassed by its existence. After gaining recognition with their design for Marlowe House, they expanded Unit 5 to Unit 12, and took on an increased number of projects from around the world. While Unit 12 remained a collective, however, with everyone taking an equal salary just as before, an unforeseen and at first peripheral source of income had made the Lairds, over the past few years, very well-off indeed.

Cynthia, at weekends, had started jotting down in her notebook a few designs for textiles. They were abstract patterns, based largely on studies from nature. It was a hobby, as much as anything, something to distract her while Otto was reading or relaxing to some records. Upon seeing the drawings, a friend in the home furnishings industry suggested launching a limited edition of curtains, using them as a basis. The reception they received was so positive that the production run continued. Soon the line was extended to include wallpaper, tablecloths and bed linen. Demand for the designs grew at such a rapid pace that Cynthia was forced to put her architectural work on hold. Suddenly she found herself, entirely out of the blue, cast in the role of 'Britain's queen of interior design', as one magazine had put it at the time. She hoped one day to return to her first love of architecture, although this now looked increasingly unlikely, as the success of her business spiralled, and with it the new-found wealth that she and Otto enjoyed.

Before the move to Hampstead, they had spent almost ten years in Cynthia's flat on Marchmont Street. Being so close to the West End was a major plus in those earlier days, and it was a relatively short walk from their home to their office in Fitzrovia. But with their growing success and the expansion into new premises on Portland Place, not to mention their plans to start a family, Otto and Cynthia – who by now were well into their thirties – decided it was time to move away from the heart of London into a bigger space further out.

They bought the house in Hampstead on an impulse. As Anton had noted, it was a departure, stylistically, from what might have been expected of them. Nevertheless, Hampstead, like Bloomsbury before it, was an area with a slightly bohemian reputation, even though its particular brand of bohemia carried a more expensive price tag.

They settled down onto the garden chairs with beers and Anton in tow.

'So how long to go now, Cyn?' asked Anton. 'I've lost count.'

'Three months,' she replied.

'July, eh? Well, I'm pleased for you. We both are. Gayle talks about it all the time. We were beginning to wonder if you two would ever get around to having children. I thought that maybe Marx had forbidden it, or something.'

'Would you like some nuts?' Otto interrupted, with a hint of irritation. 'I can get you some from the kitchen.'

'That sounds nice, old chap, thank you.'

When Otto returned to the garden a few minutes later, the sun had broken through the clouds.

'Thanks for coming to help out today,' Otto said, placing the bowl of nuts before Anton. 'We appreciate your coming over . . . *really*.'

'Couldn't leave Cynthia and yourself all alone to sort out the unpacking,' Anton said. 'Not when the bun is browning so nicely in the oven.'

Otto looked confused. After fifteen years in England, he

was still coming across new phrases all the time. He was about to head back to the kitchen when Cynthia rested her hand on his arm.

'Otto's already done most of the unpacking,' she said to her brother. 'But if you can help out with a few bits and pieces we'd be grateful. There are one or two heavy items he could use a hand with, and the lawn could do with a trim . . .'

As he looked again at their old front garden, overflowing now with plants and flowers, Otto tried to remember the tightly mown patch of grass it had been in the 1960s and 1970s. Back then, a few tastefully planted flower beds around its periphery had been the only concession to colour. It was odd, Otto noted, that when he looked back at that period now, he could no longer see it as it had been in reality, but only through the home-made Super 8 cine films he had taken at the time. He didn't see Daniel as the flesh-and-blood child, gap-toothed and blue-eyed with a jet-black bowl fringe, but as a grainy and flickering figure zooming in and out of focus; a flash of white, or of burnished gold, haunting the washed-out frame. Technology seemed to be intruding upon past reality, intervening in Otto's powers of recall. Even his memory was being forced through its prism. The situation was similar regarding his earlier memories, from the 1940s and 1950s – sepia-tinged now, thanks to the surviving film and photo-graphs, and captured again in their immediacy only with considerable imaginative effort.

Otto could see, in his mind's eye, Daniel as he played on the old blue swing, or as he kicked a giant football around the front lawn. But it was the film that Otto now saw – not the memory. The home movie had been taken in order to preserve that memory, yet the memory itself had gone. If anything, the home movie had become a barrier to that memory, not its aid. The odd colours of the footage, by turns saturated or ghostly pale, together with its grainy quality were no longer indicative of a primitive and faulty technology. They had *become* the period in question; they defined it in its essence. Thanks to the development of Super 8 technology, Otto thought, the entire period of the 1960s and 1970s would forever have the texture of deteriorating film stock.

While outwardly, for the Lairds, the early years spent in this house had been among their most fulfilling, there had also been a number of underlying tensions in the marriage; tensions that Otto had perhaps glossed over in the light of subsequent events. They emerged for him now, like small weeds among the abundant flowers of the garden, troubling the domestic idyll he had created in memory. It was painful, but he knew he must face it openly.

No more lies, he thought. Not at this late stage of the game. Know thyself, Otto, if you can bear to . . .

The unexamined life must be placed beneath the microscope; the evidence sifted afresh. It was time for that now. No more romanticising of his own past. If old age brought wisdom, it was because it also brought honesty – the laying aside of the ego, of all mental as well as bodily vanity. It threw its unforgiving light upon the misdemeanours of the past, and demanded a closer inspection.

Cynthia, he accepted, had not been happy then, for a longer period than he had previously allowed himself to admit. He could see that clearly now, once he had penetrated in his imagination beyond the images seen so often in those old home movies: of her pushing Daniel back and forth on

166

the swing at what appeared to be unnaturally high speeds; her smile wide, her auburn hair shining and her pale-blue eyes laughing. When he slowed down the frame to a freeze in his memory, the pain behind her eyes was clear enough. She had suffered from post-natal depression, and the lines on her previously youthful face had deepened during the five years after Daniel was born.

Watching him grow from an infant to a young boy had been a source of joy but also distress for her. The sheer speed of time's passing had brought with it mixed emotions. The loss of one stage of her son's development was compensated by the arrival of the next, but it left in its wake a residual sadness. In no time at all, the new-born infant was gone – replaced at first by a toddler, and later by a child. Cynthia must have felt a strong sense of life passing at this time. Her own mortality must have been thrown into relief by the rapid transformations of her son. And at some point, Otto now realised, that feeling must have panicked her. Unable to express it to him, or perhaps even to herself, she had sought escape in other ways – they both had – and for a while it had jeopardised everything.

Otto never did establish for certain which of them was first to lapse into an affair. But for a number of years these affairs had not only defined their marriage but almost broken it in the process. There was, for example, the liaison between Cynthia and a younger member of the team at Unit 12 (soon to become Unit 11). Otto had never worked out exactly when it started. He suspected later that it might have begun after that party, the one they had thrown at the house one evening to celebrate the contract for the public library building in Helsinki.

He remembered glimpsing Cynthia in conversation with him in the hallway; leaning back against the wall in her burgundy dress, a flash of teeth between the sips of wine, her full lips lingering on the glass. He remembered, too, his own slight pang of jealousy; feeling older, suddenly, than he had before. He felt envious at the intimacy of their expression, the way she drank in the young man's smile, his strong jaw and sinuous frame in an open-necked denim shirt – a hint of chest-hair bleached by salt and sun – resonant of exercise and good health. He recalled Cynthia brushing aside her long fringe, in order to gift him her face. Immediately after then, it must have been. Or maybe it had already started by that time. Otto didn't know. He had avoided the details. Even later on, near the end of Cynthia's life, when she had wanted one afternoon to tell him everything; for him to tell her everything, too.

It doesn't matter, he had said to her. It's just life, passing . . . nothing more. None of it is important any more.

But even at the time he knew that he was sparing himself the additional pain – of his own confessions, as much as hers. And why did those affairs happen? The usual mid-life vanities. Boredom, frustration, a sense of time slipping quickly away. A need for some new-found excitement, started and then gone much too far. And then, in hindsight, there were the mundane pressures of working life. Those, too, had played their corrosive part.

Eighteen

'What do you think of that?' Cynthia asked the seven-year-old Daniel, as he tore the latest gift from its wrapper.

The small wooden boomerang, covered in bright abstract patterns, shone with a coat of glossy varnish, fresh from the workshop. Daniel gazed at it, overawed.

'Thanks, Daddy – it's amazing.'

Otto smiled down at him benignly.

'You're welcome. I've missed you all these days.'

Cynthia smiled at Otto.

'We've both missed you, too. And how is the project progressing?'

'Oh, you know. Slow. Difficult. Still lots of problems to iron out.'

A frown creased Otto's brow as he loosened his tie. He rubbed his eyes.

'Would you rather not talk about it?'

'No, I'm happy to discuss it. Why wouldn't I be? It's my

job. I'm just a little fatigued, that's all. I didn't sleep on the plane.'

'Oh no. That problem again?'

'And we were delayed for an age at Singapore. They might at least have let us off to stretch our legs. How much smaller can they make those bloody seats? My knees were nearly higher than my head.'

Cynthia touched his shoulder with a smile.

'No wonder you're so . . .'

'So what?'

'You know . . .'

'I just need time to rest and get my head back into place. Maybe then I'll feel a little more human.'

'Why don't you take a nap before supper? Or a hot bath, maybe?'

'I'll go and run one.'

'Pour yourself a brandy as well.'

'Good idea. Do you want one?'

'No, I'll be fine.'

Daniel tugged at Cynthia's skirt and held out the boomerang to her.

'What's it do?' he asked.

'Well, when you throw it in the air it turns around in a circle and comes right back to you. Then you can catch it and throw it again.'

'Really? Wow.'

'Shall we go and give it a try? Out in the back garden? Supper won't be ready for at least another hour.'

She took Daniel's hand and they made their way towards the french window. Otto, who was opening the drinks cabinet on the other side of the living room, called across to her.

'Do you think that's a good idea?'

She halted and turned.

'What?'

'Trying it out in the garden. I'm not so sure that you should.'

'Why not?'

Cynthia and Daniel hovered by the window.

'Isn't it obvious?' Otto asked.

The sharpness in his own voice surprised him.

'No, not really,' Cyn replied. 'Perhaps you'd like to tell us.'

An edge had entered her voice in response.

Not again, both Cynthia and Otto thought, simultaneously.

He could have let it go, but he chose to ignore the warning signs. Besides, they had just spent a fortune on some new double glazing.

'There are windows everywhere. The neighbours have just built a conservatory. You can't go recklessly flinging a boomerang around the garden. An accident of some kind is inevitable.'

Daniel was studying the boomerang.

Cynthia's cheeks flushed a little.

'We won't "recklessly fling" anything, Otto. I'm not a hooligan, and neither is our son. We're just going to have a little practice, aren't we, Daniel? See what happens if we give it a little throw. It's only a child's boomerang – which won't go very far – and the garden, as you know, is rather large. Don't worry. We'll be careful.'

She walked away and slid open the window. Otto persevered.

'Nevertheless, I think it's a risk. Even if you don't break any windows, you might damage the boomerang.'

Cynthia, halfway through, laughed.

'It's meant to be thrown.'

'I know. I'm just not sure it's such a good idea. It looks rather fragile to me.'

'Otto, I know what I'm doing. Don't be such a mother hen. And don't buy your son a new toy and then tell him he's not allowed to play with it!'

'It's not a toy, it's a piece of craftsmanship. I bought it mostly for its decoration. I thought that Daniel might enjoy it as an *objet d'art.*'

'What's that?' Daniel asked. 'Does it mean that it can't fly?'

Otto reddened at his own pomposity. Now he felt ridiculous. His embarrassment, however, only strengthened his resolve.

'It's a beautiful object,' Cynthia said. '*Anyone* can appreciate that. We'll be careful not to harm it in any way. But children love to throw things, Otto, and that's what boomerangs are for. What's more, it's a stupid present to buy for a little boy if you're then going to tell him he can't use it.'

'Stupid?'

'No, not stupid . . . '

She searched around for a better word.

'Cruel.'

'But that's an absurd thing to say.'

Their voices had begun to flare. An argument seemed unavoidable. Yet they both became conscious of Daniel in that instant. He was holding the upturned boomerang to his face in the shape of a hopeful smile.

'Let's talk about this later,' Cynthia said, with artificial levity.

'Yes,' Otto replied, in an identical tone. 'I think that's for the best.'

She turned to Daniel.

'I'm sorry, Danny. Your father's rather tired. He's been on a big plane ... all the way from Australia. He seems to be in a bit of a grump.'

Otto bristled, but said nothing.

'We'll play with the boomerang another time,' she continued. 'Why don't we go and look for some of your other toys? The ones that Daddy *doesn't* mind you playing with.'

'Okay,' Daniel said brightly.

He was becoming almost as accomplished at hiding his feelings as his parents.

Daniel ran off up the stairs while Cynthia followed after him. Suddenly, unexpectedly, Otto found himself alone. Removing his tie, he went over to close the french window. Why hadn't he just let it go? Why was he starting to turn his own frustrations outwards? He hated seeing that in other fathers; now he was guilty of it himself.

'Just have your bloody bath,' he muttered to himself.

The silence at dinner that evening was oppressive, broken only by the funereal clicking of cutlery on the plates. Otto wanted to speak, but felt ashamed of himself, doubly so, because of the maturity with which Daniel seemed to handle these domestic rows.

Is he getting used to them? Otto wondered to himself.

That, in itself, was a cause for concern.

After finishing his food, he sat awkwardly at the table for a few more minutes, almost like a child who was waiting to be excused.

'I'll wash up,' he said, at what seemed an opportune moment.

Daniel inspected the boomerang at the table, while Cynthia sat staring out into the garden.

'Why did you say I was cruel?' Otto asked her later in bed.

She had no wish to appease him, but she wanted at least to be fair in her assessment.

'It was the wrong word to use,' she replied. 'You're the least cruel person I know. But I do believe you were being rather selfish.'

'But it was a gift . . . for Daniel.'

'It was a gift for *yourself*, Otto.'

'No, it wasn't. That's a ridiculous thing to say. I wanted to get him something nice. I've hardly seen him lately with all this travelling back and forth.'

'You've noticed, then?'

'Hm?'

'How little time you are spending with your family.'

He leaned back against the headboard and sighed.

'Of course I've noticed. It's a cause of constant worry to me. But I can't just cancel this project at the drop of a hat.'

'Of course you can't cancel it . . . *now*.'

His head lifted up.

'Why say it like that?'

'You know what I think. We've discussed all this before. Priorities, Otto. Life is all about priorities. You had plenty of work on your plate already, without taking on some ambitious new commission in Brisbane. You knew you would have to make several visits onsite.'

'You think I'm neglecting my family. Even as I work myself to the bone for us.'

'*I've* managed to find the right balance.'

'That's because you're fortunate enough to work from home.'

'That's not really fair. I work hard, as you know. As hard, dare I suggest it, as you do. Designing, dealing with business enquiries, raising Daniel.'

'With a fair degree of help from the nanny.'

'You're suggesting I could cope without her?'

'No, but she does make things easier for you.'

'I realise the idea of a nanny makes you uncomfortable, Otto. Me, too . . . we seem to be turning into what we used to despise. But there's not really any choice, not as things stand. We've been drawn into a different way of life.'

They fell silent. Perhaps he should take back everything he had said. Cynthia, however, was wondering whether to take the discussion further.

What the hell, she thought. It's time for a bit more honesty in this marriage.

'I find it all a grind, our life inside this house. It completely stifles me, sometimes. I love my son with all my being, but there are days when I miss the outside world. I rarely get to engage with it any more.'

He said nothing. It was dark: the moon lay hidden. He couldn't see Cynthia's face.

'You disappear overseas on business for days and weeks at a time. When you come back home, you barely say a word to us. You're permanently tired and out of sorts.'

She no longer sounded angry, but resigned, Otto thought. These discussions were nothing new, but the tone of her voice was.

'Anything else?' he asked her, hiding his concern behind sarcasm. The sound of his own voice was irritating to him. He should have gone straight to sleep, not started this conversation.

'Yes. You bought Daniel a present and then stopped him from enjoying it.'

'That again. Why are you so annoyed?'

'Because you stopped us from having *fun*, Otto. We wanted to go outside, into the garden and the evening sunshine. You could have come with us, or at least allowed us to go quietly. But you chose to be a killjoy instead. We wanted to enjoy some laughter together. What was so wrong about that?'

'The double glazing.'

'Oh, sod the double glazing! So what if Daniel had broken a window? Would it really have been such a catastrophe? To tell you the truth, I feel like smashing a few windows myself, sometimes – putting a brick though next door's conservatory. I'm tired of it all, Otto. The snobbery; the pettiness. I don't know how we became like this. I preferred it when we were struggling to get by in Bloomsbury. At least we were still alive back then – not inclined to take ourselves so bloody seriously. At least we knew how to enjoy ourselves.'

Otto was shocked.

'I had no idea you were this unhappy.'

'That's because I've become accomplished at hiding it. I *have* to appear positive. I have no choice. There's a young child involved here, remember?'

'But why didn't you tell me this? Why did you keep it all from me? I'm on your side. I'm here to support you both.'

Cynthia sighed.

'You're hardly here at all, these days. And when you are, the best of you isn't. I feel terrible in saying this to you, maybe it's a mistake, but a part of me wishes you had stayed in bloody Brisbane.'

Otto said nothing. Her words had cut deeply. And she wasn't speaking from anger – that was the worst part. This was how she really felt. The calmness in her voice was troubling to him. He remained silent; wanting to speak, but not knowing what he could say to salvage the situation. When he failed to reply, Cynthia drew breath once more.

'Open your eyes to what's happening between us. Please, Otto . . . open them.'

Neither said anything for quite some time. It was he who finally spoke into the darkness.

'I apologised to Daniel. While reading him his bedtime story. I told him we could take his boomerang to the Heath this weekend.'

'What did he say?'

'He was very pleased. He kissed me on the cheek. He asked me if I would stay in London longer this time.'

A deeper silence.

'I'm not sure you appreciate how difficult this is for me, Cyn. I, too, feel like smashing windows, sometimes. It's impossible. So many commitments. It takes up all the energy I have. I don't know how I became ensnared in this work. But if I pull out of the project now they would probably sue the partnership. I have to see it through. Once it's out of the way, things should be better. I'll be able to see more of the two of you, then.'

Cynthia, who had been lying totally still, stirred.

'You've said that before, but it never seems to happen.'

She gripped a handful of coverlet, pulling it across her as she turned away.

177

Several minutes passed before Otto spoke again.

'So what do we do?'

The clock ticked beside him.

'Cyn? What do we do?'

She didn't answer. The clock was ticking. It appeared she had fallen asleep.

Nineteen

It started some months later, in the spring of 1974, while Otto was in Paris on business. Sandrine, a friend of Pierre's, was a lecturer in history at the Sorbonne. Mercantile capitalism was her speciality; capitalism in all its forms her enemy. Her radical views had hardened since the faltering of the student protests in 1968. She now believed that anarchism was the only way forward. Otto was fascinated, if a little alarmed, by the strength of her anger. She made a striking contrast to the people with whom he usually mixed these days. Sandrine, he suspected, would never want a conservatory.

They met one evening at a café in the Latin Quarter, the day after Otto first arrived in the city. He was staying at a modest apartment in the south-eastern corner of the 18th arrondissement, having turned down the chance of something plusher in the 1st. He wanted to free himself, if only for a few short weeks, from the pampered life to which he had become accustomed.

As he left his apartment on that warm spring evening and

caught the Metro down to Saint-Germain-des-Prés, he felt nervous and strangely excited, craving some kind of rupture from the routine and stress of the past few years. He was to find what he desired in his apartment in the 18th and, more especially, in Sandrine.

He remembered now that the discussion became quite heated, on that first night in the café. They were talking about 1968, and the reasons why the protests had failed to bring about fundamental changes in society.

'What would you know about it?' Sandrine asked Otto, drawing deeply on her cigarette, blowing smoke into his face like an accusation. 'All you have heard has come down to you second hand, through old footage and the words of journalists. What really happened on the streets back then is as distant from your own experience as the English Civil War. I was there – I was a part of it. I saw exactly what happened. Where were you when the revolutionary moment arrived?'

Pushing a pram around Hampstead Heath, Otto thought, but he stopped himself short of a confession. Instead he stuttered into an embarrassed silence. Pierre laughed at his crestfallen expression, at the degree to which the fight appeared to have drained from him.

'Has the world of soft furnishings really softened you, too?' he asked, taking his usual swipe at Cynthia's fast-growing fabrics empire. 'Ten years ago you would have risen to such a question, not blushed and stammered like today. You need to wake yourself up again, Otto; get that political consciousness of yours back into gear. Have you not seen what is happening around you in the world, these days? The Red Brigades – Baader–Meinhof: these are violent and uncompromising times we are living through. The stakes are high – capitalism is on the brink. The imperialists have been kicked out of Africa and Asia in the past few decades. Soon, perhaps, it will be time for them to face the music on their own soil. There simply isn't time, any more, for your polite English manners.'

Otto was annoyed by Pierre's ridiculous tough-guy act, adopted, he suspected, as a means of trying to impress Sandrine. He thought it over later as he stood at the urinals, a couple of drunken professors standing and swaying to either side of him.

Red Brigades – who is he trying to kid? Pierre is even softer than I am. He practically passed out when we struck that squirrel on the road to Orléans – he wanted us to take it to the local hospital. He would no more take a life, or support anyone who did so, than play a round of golf with Richard Nixon.

Sandrine, too, had irritated Otto – with her self-righteous swagger and the facefuls of cigarette smoke. Who were these people to start lecturing anyone? Pampered academics, protected from reality by the very state they claimed to oppose; biting the hand that fed them, but only so much. There they sat, talking revolution over an expensive bottle of Bordeaux.

Otto felt himself provoked in other ways, too. The conversation was stimulating; Sandrine's mind sharp. Somewhere in her early thirties, around ten years younger than Otto, she was teaching on a post-doctoral placement. Her thesis had been vivaed the year before and was already on its way to publication: an analysis of the early trading activities of the East India Company. During the course of the evening, she stared nonchalantly at Otto through heavy-lidded eyes, sizing him up as he spoke. Her tall frame was athletic; her short hair, almost a crop, emphasised the graceful line of her neck.

'You're an interesting man,' she said, as they exchanged

telephone numbers at the end of the evening, 'A little uptight, maybe, but interesting.'

Kissing him on each cheek before parting, she allowed her fingers to brush across his chest.

The next day she called and asked him over to her apartment for dinner. She lived in Montparnasse, she told him – would he rather have meat or fish? Otto surprised himself at the swiftness with which he had accepted; almost pathetically grateful, it seemed to him later, and burying in advance all sense of guilt. As he was preparing for the evening ahead, his hands shook visibly as he ran them through his scalp before the bathroom mirror. The thick hair was greying now, but the body was reasonably well preserved. The silhouette of the younger man was just about recognisable; the profile squintable into flattery, as he checked the stomach and pectorals. Physically, at least, he had not transformed into a sad and bloated parody of himself.

Thinking of Sandrine, he once more felt hopelessly flattered – excited by the predatory nonchalance with which she had looked him over the evening before. She had worn a leather jacket and no make-up, he recalled; a plain white T-shirt with no brassiere. As he lay in the bath of his shabby apartment, soaking his private parts like a prospector panning for gold, Otto remembered the heated exchange that had developed between them, the great care with which he had avoided glancing down at her prominent nipples; sensing that, if he did so, she might just tear off his face.

Something new is happening, he thought, as he climbed from the bath and dressed for dinner.

All those soft lines and soft ideals of the 1960s had disappeared somewhere. A harder new mentality had arisen. Sandrine embodied it. But he hadn't noticed any of this; it caught him unawares. It hadn't yet reached as far as Hampstead.

Otto expected a one-night stand with Sandrine, but the affair lasted nearly two years. Or, to be more accurate, the one-night stand lasted nearly two years. There was no emotional attachment on either side, and therein lay its unexpected longevity. During Otto's stay in Paris, they met three times a week and made love to an abandoned, almost desperate tempo. She was demanding and experimental – everything, in fact, he had hoped for when shaking with anticipation before their first meal together. They were ferocious in their lovemaking, using each other up like a fossil-fuel reserve. Afterwards, they fell back onto the bed, exhausted, and worked their way through a packet of Gitanes. Drawing deep on his cigarette, Otto turned and blew smoke into Sandrine's upturned face. She had succeeded, by this time, in putting to flight all of his adopted English reserve.

Her pillow talk veered between the polemical and the personal, flitting around restlessly from one subject to the next. The OPEC crisis, industrial unrest at Renault, hunting for crabs with her brothers in Finistère. Otto struggled to follow her train of thought as he stubbed out his cigarette and drifted slowly from consciousness, the cool sheet sliding from his buttocks as he turned. But then he would feel her hand upon his stomach, her smoky tongue work inside his mouth, and it would start all over again.

He rarely stayed the night; or only occasionally, if it was too late to think of calling for a cab and easier to await the first Metro of the morning. Generally, Sandrine preferred to sleep alone. Otto did, too, but for different reasons. She never once asked him about his marriage, and he never asked her if there were other men – or women. It was something he had taken as read. Just once, she had discussed marriage with him, in a very general sense. As so often, it was for her a political issue.

'It is the greatest barrier society must overcome,' she told him. 'The notion of two human beings possessing each other – body and soul, in their entirety – has to be the craziest lie of them all.'

Otto understood what she meant – theoretically, at least. He knew the argument: the emergence of the nuclear family as an offshoot of industrial capitalism. The modern family unit, Sandrine explained to him, had developed from an economic imperative, the need to maximise productive efficiency, whatever the woolly-headed romantics of this world might choose to believe. At an abstract level, she might have had a point. But life was never lived out in the abstract. It was filled with all these people, getting in the way and staking their claim. Otto's life was filled with Cynthia, with the many events they had experienced, with and through each other over the course of the past two decades. It was also filled with Daniel, with the several Daniels they had already seen come and go during the first eight years of his life. Otto wanted to explain all this to Sandrine, to wave away the smoke that sometimes clouded her thoughts as well as her handsome face. But he felt too tired, too warm in the sheets that carried her scent; and besides, he didn't want to risk bringing his other life into this one. He didn't want to risk waking up.

Otto returned to the city regularly to see her, using as an excuse his connection with Pierre. He even kept on the rundown apartment in the 18th arrondissement, making it easier for them to meet whenever he was passing through the Gare du Nord on his way to somewhere else. For almost two years, Otto now conceded to himself, the betrayal of his family had been absolute.

No more excuses. You probably lapsed before Cynthia did, so face up to it.

Yet throughout the duration of the affair he had continually played odd games with himself, establishing little rules and regulations that, to him at the time, seemed to make his behaviour more acceptable. He had never once telephoned Cynthia from Sandrine's apartment, for instance – always returning to his own in order to do so. If he knew he would be speaking to Daniel, he wouldn't even phone home from his own apartment, associated as it was with the odd visit from Sandrine. Instead he would call up from a public booth, in the shadow of the Gare du Nord, feeding in the ten-centime coins and asking Daniel in a distracted voice about his day at school.

Strange, the games that conscience plays, he thought. Did it really make you feel any differently?

Evidently it did, because the affair came to an end only once the two worlds of Otto came into inevitable collision, some time in early 1976. Sandrine telephoned him at the house in Hampstead. He had no idea why, she had never done it before, and later he came to suspect it was her way of bringing the whole episode to a close.

If she was bored with me, he later asked himself, sexually or otherwise – then why didn't she tell me to my face?

Perhaps she was more squeamish regarding such matters than she liked to admit.

Otto had answered the telephone that evening, and there followed a minute or two of frantic and inarticulate whispers.

He couldn't remember what was said, exactly, but Cynthia had been listening on the extension in the bedroom. As they passed in the corridor, she told him she would like a word about the conversation she had just overheard. He nodded and retired to the living room to await his sentence.

When putting Daniel to bed that evening, Cynthia was as smiling, attentive and patient with her son as ever. After tucking him in for the night and kissing him lightly on the forehead, she closed his bedroom door and descended the stairs, carefully closing two more intervening doors before passing through her study to the living room. Shutting that door, too, she walked calmly to the centre of the room where Otto sat waiting for her and let the rage explode from within her.

'What the fuck has been going on?' she asked, not giving him the chance to attempt a preliminary apology. 'Who the fuck was that woman? Just how long have you been fucking her? And what the fuck is she doing calling up my husband in our fucking home?'

Her voice cracked on the final three words; the fury spilling over.

Otto was chastened into silence by her wrath. The middle-aged fantasy he had been living out for the past two years came crashing down around his ears. So it was real, there were consequences. And there they were, in front of him. Cynthia was sobbing hard in her anger, but trying all the while to stop herself. She wiped her face in a matter-of-fact way that made it all the more difficult to watch. It was years since Otto had seen her so upset – not since their early days together, when there had been some silly argument and they had separated for a few weeks. But then they had been in their twenties. Cynthia was in her forties now. Seeing her in this distressed and undignified state both shocked and nonplussed Otto.

What have you done?

His voice was quiet as he looked down at the wooden floorboards and told her the entire story, from start to finish. Her face stayed expressionless throughout. He was careful not to stint on any facts; careful, too, not to linger on the details. He wanted to get it over with as quickly and cleanly as possible. When he had finished speaking, Cynthia left the room without a word, closing the door softly behind her. After staring at the floorboards a few minutes longer, Otto slipped off his shoes, lifted his feet from the floor and raised his long body onto the couch. He lay there motionless until the next morning, curled into a foetal position, still wearing the shirt, tie and slacks from his forgotten day at work. He didn't move all night: either to turn off the light, or to clear away from the table the two glasses of wine he had been in the process of pouring when the telephone rang.

He felt no sense of recrimination towards Sandrine; did not even think, at that stage, as to why she might have called him. There was no space for thinking at all now, and this from a man who rarely did anything else. His consciousness overflowed with guilt – with the two years of guilt that had lain buried away. It had tried to burrow its way out sometimes, and manifested itself in bizarre little rituals, such as the phone calls home, made from public booths. Maybe that guilt was evident in the sheer abandonment with which he and Sandrine used to make love. But there was no need, any more, for this guilt to disguise itself as anything else. It was out in the open, freed once more; stretching itself luxuriantly into

187

the furthest corners of his mind, and not allowing space for anything as feeble as thought.

Cynthia's control at breakfast the next morning amazed Otto. She spoke to him normally, joked and chatted to Daniel, and showed almost no sign of the anguish that must have been devouring her. The small, tell-tale signs were all physical: the slight puffiness of her face, a certain redness around the eyes, and the moment when she missed the glass while pouring out Daniel's orange juice, jumping to her feet with a cry of 'Silly me' and sprinting to get a tissue.

Otto hid it much worse than she did. Sitting silent, sleepless and mournful before his cornflakes, he stirred them absently with a spoon, watching with a vague detachment as they spun in slow circles in the bowl. Daniel was distracted that morning by an upcoming school visit to the National Portrait Gallery. He didn't notice anything untoward in the behaviour of his father, who could be pretty taciturn at breakfast, even on the best of days.

That lunchtime Otto left the office in Portland Place and walked to a nearby phone booth. From there he spoke to Sandrine for the final time. Both of them seemed embarrassed. The conversation was civilised and relatively painless. Sandrine apologised. She told him she had telephoned on a whim, after drinking a bottle of wine, and had not really considered the potential consequences. Otto had given her the number some time before, she reminded him, on the understanding that she would never use it.

So why exactly did I do that? he wondered. Some sublimated need to bring about its end?

Sandrine agreed that it was best to end it immediately. She further agreed that after this length of time their affair had run its course. As they prepared to say their goodbyes, Otto suddenly felt oddly sentimental. A ridiculous feeling came over him – the need to say something heartfelt, even profound to her. He ran through some options in his head. Yet everything he thought of sounded idiotic; completely out of keeping both with Sandrine herself, and with the nature of their affair, which had been physically heated, but emotionally stone cold.

What do I say to her? Thank you? That was most enjoyable? I will think of you now and again? I leave with you a small part of my soul? I almost loved you – in a bodily way?

All were absurd, and none quite true – just knee-jerk manifestations of the bourgeois sensibility that characterised Otto, and which Sandrine herself would ruthlessly mock as they lay in the afterglow, smoking their Gitanes.

So he said none of these things, just 'Goodbye'; as did she.

Although this was the last contact Otto ever had with Sandrine, he did hear about her now and again from Pierre. Occasionally he would come across articles she had written in various academic publications. Once he even saw her picture, thirty years on, and still instantly recognisable. The strong face was holding up well, the grey hair cropped tight to the head. Sandrine enjoyed a successful academic career, becoming a highly respected figure within her field. She spent several more years at the Sorbonne, and then a period at Toulouse University, finally gaining her professorship while in her early fifties. Otto noted from the articles he read that her political position had changed over the years, as with so many academic colleagues of her generation. She still considered herself a radical thinker, but her ideas increasingly focused on single issues: the green agenda, gay rights and feminism. She no longer appeared to believe in the political full monty. The revolution she once advocated had been neatly set aside, disappearing beneath the rubble of the Berlin Wall.

So now there's no one left, Otto thought, with a slight hint of sadness, when reading an article by a sixty-something Sandrine about the 'naive student politics' of the 1970s. It's just poor old Pierre, waving his red flag all alone . . .

Cynthia and Otto did not get to speak again until the following evening, when Daniel was safely in bed. Otto dreaded the exchange – he wondered if she might end the marriage altogether, but the direction of the conversation surprised him. It was a taking charge, on Cynthia's part, but not a throwing out. She was still visibly angry, her top lip shaking, exaggerating more than ever its full redness. But this was a resigned anger, perhaps even a cold one, and she kept her message to Otto brief and unambiguous.

'Our marriage is not ideal at the moment, and it hasn't been for some time. You're not the only one who has felt tempted to stray these past few years.'

He looked up at her, surprised. The questions came crowding in. But he could only manage the shortest of responses.

'Right.'

'Clearly we both feel the need to express ourselves elsewhere, but we have a young and beautiful son, and I won't allow anything to jeopardise his happiness or his sense of security. Is that clear?'

Otto nodded, his eyes once more to the floorboards.

'We don't bring it here,' Cynthia continued, her voice now rising a little. 'Not into the house, Otto . . . not either of us, do you understand? *That's* the arrangement.'

And with those words, a tacit kind of agreement was reached, a recognition that there would be others, for both of them, but that whatever else happened, they would be discreet for Daniel's sake. It was an odd proposal, in many respects, but given the circumstances in which they now found themselves, it seemed the only way forward. The damage had been done, they knew; the bonds between them lay broken. But neither of them wished to see the marriage finish completely.

They stuck to the arrangement for the next three years, each more alienating than the last. There was one more affair for Otto, with a fellow architect in her fifties. She was married, with two grown-up children; as guilt-ridden and fractured by life as he was. They had much in common, but little that was positive. All in all it was a furtive and unhappy eighteen months.

They met in hotel rooms, in the middle of the afternoon, one eye on the clock as they fumbled at their clothing. There was little time for conversation, let alone emotional intimacy. Like Otto, she sought an escape from herself; the last thing she wanted was to bring her life into the hotel room for discussion. Especially not with someone even more miserable than she was.

'I must get back,' she always said to him distractedly, as he helped zip her dress, or searched for a sock beneath the bed. 'I have a meeting.'

Or:

'I must do the shopping.'

Or:

'I must collect my husband from the station.'

Cynthia, Otto believed, had three affairs during their

191

period of estrangement. There was the professor she met at a café in Highgate; the colleague with the chest hair at Unit 12; and an artist friend she had known since her days as a student.

The cumulative effect was to push Otto and Cynthia ever further apart from each other. It seemed at times a deliberate distancing: Otto didn't see how the marriage could possibly survive. As those three years unfolded, they spoke less and less; they had separate rooms for sleeping and even reading. They grew apart, quite literally, in that time. They came to occupy different ends of the house.

Otto lifted his cane before him, as though to ward off any more approaching memories. It was enough for today. Before catching the tube back down to the Elephant and Castle, he wandered for a while around central Hampstead. Passing the Everyman cinema on Holly Bush Vale, he halted for a minute or two to look at the upcoming features. This place held memories as vivid, for him, as any of the moving images that had passed across its screens.

We used to come here all the time in happier days, he thought.

And what was it they had seen together? So many things: Satyajit Ray and Kurosawa, Godard and Tarkovsky – all the greats of world cinema. And Cynthia was always inspired by certain images, bubbling with enthusiasm as they debriefed over a pint. Apu and his sister, running through the tall grasses to see the train passing by – that was one of her favourites. Finding the beauty in everyday moments, she said: the commonplace made balletic through the lens's eye. And the name of the film with the grasses and the train? *Pather Panchali,* of course.

Continuing on his way, Otto glanced in one or two shops. He did so in a neutral frame of mind, to keep old memories at bay, rather than invite them in. Yet looking in the window of an interior design store, he noticed, to his surprise, one of Cynthia's old textiles, sitting at the back of a display cabinet. It featured a striking pattern of ochre, green and luminous blue, and was placed in a section marked *Design Classics*.

After the memories of the house, so changed, with its abundant garden masking the close-cropped lawn of old; after his memories of Daniel, partially captured through the lens of an old cine camera, but not rediscovered in their essence; after his memories of their family life here, more troubled and troubling than he had ever allowed himself to admit before, Otto felt oddly reassured to see Cynthia's fabric design in the window. Some familiar part of it remained, then, the twenty years of life they had spent at that house in Hampstead. The traces had not yet been erased completely.

He paused a moment to press his fingers against the glass pane, the pattern of the fabric seeming to pass beneath his palm, before moving on to contemplate the next window in the display.

Twenty

As he was travelling back on the Underground, a fragment of melody came to Otto; inspired, somehow, by the colours of Cynthia's fabric design in the shop window. Words, too, appeared from within the melody.

Ich bin der Welt abhanden gekommen.

(I am lost to the world.)

This sort of thing happened to him, occasionally. It was many years since Otto had used his German on a regular basis, yet it remained, perhaps, the language closest to his soul – the one through which he funnelled and shaped his innermost thoughts and feelings. Even now, many decades since he had lived in the company of German speakers, words and phrases appeared to him suddenly; flotsam from the past, cast ashore unexpectedly as he scanned the near-horizon of his thoughts. The melodious voice of his mother, the deep baritone of his father – both could bring him comfort still in moments of distress. Yet Otto's relationship with his mother tongue would always be problematic. It remained for him a language of poetry, subtlety and precision – the language of Goethe and Schiller, of Hegel and of Kant. But it was also pregnant with other associations: symbol of a history sometimes dark and troubled.

For occasionally, during moments of quiet, Otto heard another voice from his early childhood, floating across the decades from the radio of their Viennese apartment. Astringent and rasping, half choked with fury, this voice stood out amid the lightness of the waltzes that usually poured from the radio. Its harsh tone – the accent of the countryside, not the Viennese to which Otto was accustomed – made it difficult to understand. The loudspeakers through which it was amplified, and the thunderous cheers of the crowd that accompanied every phrase, only added to Otto's bewilderment as he sat on the living-room floor before the radio. Every time Otto heard this voice, inciting the crowd to roars of anger, he thought of the trainers at the circus, baiting the fierce lions in their cages.

'What's the man saying?' he sometimes asked his father, who was leaning forward intently in his chair, the evening paper set aside and his thin lips pale with rage. But Otto never received a reply.

On the tube journey today, however, it was a different voice from childhood that had flooded Otto's consciousness; one evoking a sense of security and peace. He searched his memory for more fragments of the tune, his lips moving minutely as he did so.

Ich bin gestorben dem Weltgetümmel, Und ruh' in einem stillen Gebiet.

(I am dead to the world's turmoil, and I rest in a calm place.)

The source of the lyrics came to him. They were from a *lied* by Gustav Mahler; from his setting of Rückert's poetry. Otto's mother would sing it to him sometimes, whenever he struggled to sleep at night in their Viennese apartment. Or else, on bright spring mornings, she would play a recording of it on the old wooden gramophone, the daylight slanting through the curtains as they listened. Phrases of the song would return to his mother's lips throughout the day – as the two of them played quoits in the Stadtpark, for instance, or as they walked the long road to the shops, Otto clasping the handles of the huge wicker basket and studying the tram wires overhead.

But why had he remembered that song now, at this moment in time? And what was its connection with the piece of fabric he had seen in the Hampstead shop window? He thought it over once more as the tube train rattled through the tunnels.

Cynthia's textile designs were often influenced by places she and Otto had visited, or by specific events in their lives. They were fruits of a journey both geographical and emotional. She had a gift for internalising their outward travels, for distilling them into abstract shapes and colours. During a trip to see the new library in Helsinki, for example, she had been struck by the purity of the northern light, which emphasised with great clarity the building's brickwork, a chocolate brown against the cobalt depths. Inspired by this light and by the landscapes of Finland – its forests, lakes and wide horizons – she produced a series of designs that would prove to be among the most popular of her career. The one in the Hampstead shop window dated from the same period as her Helsinki Series – the late 1970s. But its inspiration seemed to lie much further back in time. The colours were warmer, more optimistic in tone.

The Helsinki Series emerged at a difficult period in their marriage, amid a growing sense of estrangement. No doubt reflecting Cynthia's mental state at that time, the colours of her palette had darkened. The images were more sombre, less joyful than those that had characterised her work in the 1960s. Yet among the chill blues and greens of the Helsinki Series, an anomaly had suddenly appeared: the design that Otto had seen that day in the shop window.

Even at the time of its creation, Otto had noted the unusually warm colours of this pattern. Yet caught up as he was within a self-inflicted melodrama – the affairs, the loneliness, the nagging sense of guilt that accompanied his every waking thought – he had given the matter little serious consideration. Sitting on the train now, however, he wondered whether this particular design had been of greater significance to Cynthia than he had realised. An incident he remembered from that period only seemed to reinforce the idea.

He was walking past Cynthia's study, he recalled: the door was standing open. Glancing in, he saw her in profile, sitting at her desk as usual. But something in her body language caused him to stop. She was not drawing, but staring down intently at the design she had just completed, her shoulders hunched slightly forward and her fingers to her lips. It was not her usual air of concentration, the one she always had in the midst of creating something. Otto knew that look so well. No, this was different; the expression haunted.

Unsettled, he spoke from the threshold of the study.

'Cynthia.'

She looked up, sharply. The eyes that met his were ringed with moisture.

'Otto. You made me jump.'

'I'm sorry.'

He stepped inside, as she turned back to her design, and reached out a hand to touch her shoulder. But he hesitated, just short of contact, gazing down instead at the vibrant image.

'Very nice,' he said. 'I like the bright colours.'

There was an odd formality about their conversation in those days.

'Thank you.'

Her eyes searched his.

'Do you recognise it?'

The tone of her voice, like the expression, was elusive.

Otto studied the picture again, but met her glance of expectancy with a small shake of the head.

'I'm afraid not. What is it?'

She hesitated.

'It doesn't matter. Just the usual jumble of half-formed thoughts.'

She changed the subject, then, before he had a chance to press her further, and the episode had slipped quickly from his mind.

Yet there was something significant about that incident, he now realised, beneath the seeming inanity of the exchange. Her expression had disconcerted him; it still did, today. And why had she asked him that question? Was the design she had created some kind of message to him – a statement of some kind? Had she reached out in her solitude to share a memory, one that he, in his self-absorption, had failed to notice?

Otto considered once more the image he had seen in Cynthia's study that evening; the same he had seen a short time earlier in the window of the shop in Hampstead. Aquamarine. Sun-baked ochre. The silver-green movement of cypresses. The wave-like pattern suggested an afternoon sun, its heat settling on the skin like raked embers. And then, in one corner, what may have been a floating musical clef, stretched out to an abstraction of flying birds.

Ich bin der Welt abhanden gekommen, Otto's subconscious echoed back at him, as he scanned the details of the image with his inner eye.

And then, as he pictured them, the shapes and colours of Cynthia's design seemed to reconfigure before him into a sequence of events. He leaned back abruptly in his seat, a hand to his mouth. The memory had pierced him – the melody, too – entering his heart to draw out the sting that lay hidden there. Their happiest time together? One of them, certainly. A time that, because of its resonance, had lain buried away all the more deeply during the intervening decades.

In September 1956, they were on their honeymoon, travelling across the Peloponnese peninsula in southern Greece. Now in their mid-twenties, they had yet to fully master the skills of the architectural profession, or form – along with their colleagues – Unit 5. Since they could rarely resist the opportunity to search out fresh inspiration for their work, they interspersed the periods of relaxation with visits to a number of ancient monuments, exploring and sketching in forensic fashion.

In the mid-1950s, mass tourism had not yet arrived in Greece, which was still in a state of fragile recovery following its civil war. Travel there was slow and sometimes complicated. As far as possible, they depended on the local bus network to get around, sometimes hitchhiking to reach the more remote destinations. In the course of their journey down from Athens, they visited several sites from the classical period. Yet they also wanted to see ruins from earlier epochs, buildings more in keeping with the raw aesthetic they were beginning to develop in their own work. And so they ended up spending time at the ancient citadel of Mycenae, with its monumental blocks of stone and celebrated Lion Gate.

As they wandered among the sun-baked ruins, spread out over a hill, the tinkling of bells from a herd of goats seemed to follow them on the breeze. So striking was the view of mountains and sea, glimpsed between the heavy blocks of stone, that they found themselves distracted from the architecture.

Afterwards, they travelled to the nearby town of Nafplio, set around the tranquil Gulf of Argolis. There they stayed for several days in a hotel in the Old Town, amid narrow streets of colour-washed houses and wooden balconies dense with flowers. Each evening, Otto and Cynthia would walk through the streets, lost in conversation. Tall and languid, in cream shirt and slacks, he listened closely to her while seeking now and then, with sweeps of his hand, to prevent his black fringe from falling across his eyes. She strolled serenely beside him, her pale skin lightly tempered in the kiln of the late-summer sun. A stylish sunhat shielded her clear blue eyes, and her hourglass figure was enhanced by a pale-blue trouser suit.

The appearance alone of this striking young couple brought them a certain degree of attention. But it was a near-forgotten skill of Cynthia's that made them the talk of the town that week. She could speak some Ancient Greek, having studied it at school, and during their first day in town she slipped unthinkingly into the untried language, in an attempt to converse better with an elderly shopkeeper. Within moments of Cynthia pronouncing the words, the shopkeeper was curled over with laughter, struggling to reply to her through his tears. The routine was repeated every time she made the attempt. The reason soon became clear. For the people of the town, the sound of this modern young woman speaking an arcane version of Greek seemed bizarre beyond all words. Thinking about it later, Cynthia wondered just how she would have reacted had a tourist in London started addressing her in Chaucer's English.

Word quickly spread about her unusual gift. She and Otto were ushered into busy tavernas, the proprietors asking her to say a few words. The hilarity and applause went echoing across town. Cynthia, it was soon established, not only looked a little like a goddess; she spoke just like one, too. People stopped her in the street and asked her to say something, anything at all. Her crisp English accent only added to the strangeness of the sound.

The fishermen they saw each day, setting down their catch on the quayside, were especially enchanted with her mangling of the antique tongue. Without fail, one of them would press a freshly caught squid, or a basket brimming with fish, into the arms of Cynthia and Otto as they passed. During evening strolls, old men stopped to shake Otto's hand. Then they tipped their hats to his remarkable bride, who greeted them in words that had not been heard in everyday conversation for millennia.

'I'm the human ruin,' she said with a smile, whenever people gathered around her to listen.

On their last day in Nafplio, shortly before moving on to explore the mountainous interior, they spent the afternoon relaxing at a nearby beach. When they weren't walking the shoreline or swimming in the depths, the young couple lay on the sand beneath an ineffectual parasol, Otto in his long trunks and Cynthia in a one-piece bathing costume, their fingers entwined or running restlessly along the other's arm or thigh. Everything around them carried an intense erotic charge. Their heads pulsated with longing like the cicadas in the fields.

Otto gazed at Cynthia's reclining form while she lay half dozing. Unknown to him, she mirrored the gesture while he slept. He studied the glowing texture of her skin, the rise and fall of her breasts, the slight S of her spine as she turned to catch the moving sun. The yellow disc that burned above them and the small brown mole at the base of Cynthia's neck seemed to emanate from the same vital source. Otto felt soporific with a sensual pleasure as he basked in their luminous presence, as he moulded the length of his back to the yielding sand.

Later that evening, they sat on the balcony of their hotel, still carrying the warmth of the beach inside them. The air was heavy with the syrup of bougainvillea, with the far-off scent of citrus groves and salt. Voices reached them, occasionally, from beyond the open shutters of the neighbouring houses.

Over a steadily shrinking bottle of ouzo, they made plans for the next stage of their journey.

'Firstly we could catch a bus to Arcadia,' Otto said. 'And then, if we find the time, that is, we could move on to explore ...'

He stopped as he noticed the twinkle in Cynthia's eye. Something seemed to have amused her.

'What is it?' he asked.

'A bus to Arcadia,' she repeated. 'We can catch a *bus to Arcadia*! Otto, this is like being inside a myth.'

Aided by the alcohol, they sank gradually into silence. Their plans could always wait until the following day. With conversation suspended, they savoured the mauve-blue sky, communicating with the occasional look or touch. To every side of them reared the flower-strewn balconies, the tall wooden shutters of houses. And then, into the evening silence, from somewhere in an upper room, a piano offered up a tune that Otto recognised. Soon it was joined by a strong soprano voice; the familiar words drifting down on the perfumed air.

Ich bin der Welt abhanden gekommen ...

The sound of the *lied* surprised Otto. It was a breath of northern breeze, unexpected in the hot stillness of the South. And then a spray of migrating swallows, fanning outward as they rose, swerved and dipped in a fluid motion that seemed to trace the line of melody against the sky.

He listened to the cool phrasing of the German; the language his own, yet his own no longer, opening up a pathway inside him. It was a meeting of his past and present, a reconciliation of sorts. His inner and outer lives had coalesced. A sense of great peace descended on him, passing yet profound.

Cynthia, sensing this, threaded her fingers through his and lightly pressed her palm into his own.

The light-filled colours, the musical clef in the form of flying birds: Otto knew now the meaning of Cynthia's textile design from the late 1970s. She had spoken to him across the decades, through the window of an interior design shop in Hampstead. It was an eerie feeling that left him rather saddened.

If only I could tell her I understand now, he thought. She was trying to reconnect us with something lost.

He failed to notice either the tannoy announcement or the grumbling that followed as the train drew in at the Elephant and Castle, staying frozen in his seat as the carriage emptied around him.

'It doesn't go any further,' one of the passengers came back to tell him, causing him to start up with a jolt.

Twenty-One

'So ... how can I help you? What is it you would like to know?'

The elderly woman sitting opposite Otto and Chloe looked curiously at them as she spoke. She had delicate features and a dignified manner. Her smiling eyes were youthful but her face heavily lined. Before them all stood steaming cups of tea.

'Well,' said Chloe, as the cameras rolled behind her, 'perhaps we could start with you introducing yourself. Tell us some more about your background and when you came to live in Marlowe House.'

'My name is Pham Thi Huong – people here call me Mrs Pham. I am seventy-two years old and I have lived in Marlowe House since 1975, so around half my lifetime.'

There was a hint of disbelief in her soft voice.

'I understand that you are one of the longest-standing residents here.'

'Yes, that is possible. I'm not aware of anyone who has been here longer.'

'Could you tell us, maybe, how you came to live here? My researchers tell me you have an interesting story.'

Mrs Pham smiled politely.

'You could say that. My family were refugees, from the war in Vietnam. We were among the first of those who were known at the time as the Boat People. Perhaps you may have heard of us?'

Otto and Chloe nodded.

Huge numbers of civilians, Otto recalled, had fled the country in desperation in the years after the war, often in boats that were chronically overcrowded. They spent weeks on the ocean at the mercy of hostile forces. Thousands did not survive the experience.

'My family's story is an unusual one, but it isn't so unusual in a place like Marlowe House. Refugees from many countries have found shelter here at different times. I've been friends with quite a few of them.'

'How long were you at sea?' Chloe asked her.

'Four weeks, in total.'

'What was it like?'

Otto winced a little at the directness of Chloe's question. But perhaps he was being overly sensitive. Mrs Pham appeared unfazed. She had clearly been asked that question many times.

'It was bad, although the spirit on board was good. We escaped from Saigon on a wooden fishing boat, soon after the city had fallen. It was built to carry around fifteen or twenty people. There must have been at least fifty of us on board. We knew the dangers, but we felt at the time that we had no choice but to flee. My family was not rich, we had no interest in politics. All we had ever done was run a small restaurant. But during the war, it became popular with the American

206

soldiers. Even one or two colonels used to eat there. Once the Americans had left the city, and it fell to the Communist forces, we feared that we would pay a heavy price for the hospitality we had shown them. So we decided to take our chances at sea with the others. We were hoping to reach land in the Philippines.'

Mrs Pham paused a moment.

'I'm sorry,' she said. 'I almost forgot to ask. Would you like some sugar with your tea?'

Declining politely, they assumed that she wished to change the subject. But after sipping her own tea once more, she set down her cup and returned to her story, describing events with a sense of measured calm.

'We lived below deck,' she told them, 'squeezed in among dozens of others. It was just as packed up on top. Everyone had the same look about them: staring-eyed, frightened, exhausted by years of conflict. The smell, the lurching waves, the heat that made the sweat run down our bodies in little rivers – all of these things made life on board uncomfortable.'

'And you couldn't move around, I suppose?'

It was Chloe, again, who had spoken. Otto was listening intently, his head inclined forward, occasionally raising his eyes to Mrs Pham.

'We couldn't lift a limb without striking other people. Cramp and seasickness were constant companions. In the heat of day, beams of light would come through the cracks in the timbers of the hull. These were hot enough to burn, like a magnifying glass, if any of us got trapped within their range. I don't know if things were worse for us down below, or for those who were staying up on deck. But we told ourselves that at least down there we were protected from the eye of the sun.'

'What about water and food?'

'Fresh water was kept inside leather bottles, but supplies soon ran low. Everyone was praying for the arrival of the monsoon rains. There were biscuits and dried rice, but again not enough to last us long. We had all left Saigon in such a hurry. There wasn't any time for us to prepare.'

'So how did you manage?' Chloe asked.

'With discipline, I suppose. We adults consumed the least that we could, reducing the size of our intake to that of mice. It was difficult to sleep, though, with the heat, thirst and hunger. I'm not sure that my husband slept at all. Whenever I woke at night, the cramp biting into my ankles, I saw him sitting there, alert, cradling our two sons in his arms. The whites of his eyes were shining in the darkness of the hold.'

'And when the food and water ran low? What then?'

Mrs Pham paused for breath.

'The passengers started to die. Two young children, a brother and a sister, were first to go, followed by more in the next few days. The very old and very young. Their bodies were passed up out of the hold and over the heads of those sitting on deck. There they were lowered over the side and into the ocean, a small space having been made for their families to watch.'

Otto's cup vibrated slightly as he raised his tea to his lips.

'By this time I believe that almost everyone on board was resigned to the prospect of death. I think Binh and I would even have welcomed it at that time, if we had been there by ourselves. But we had to keep going for the children.'

She halted a moment, to sip her tea. 'One morning, just after dawn, a great noise began up on deck. There were screams and shouts – the beams of light through the timbers went out. Another boat, we realised, was pulling up alongside us. Binh and I looked at each other as we hugged the boys in our arms. We did not look fearful, either of us. It was a look that said: "It is over now. We may die in a few seconds, with a bullet in our heads, or we may live for fifty more years. But we have reached the moment of truth, and at last our ordeal on this boat is over, along with the uncertainty of how and when it will end for us."'

'And who was on board this other boat?'

'It was a large merchant ship. The crew were helpful, but a little shocked, I think, by what they found. We were given food and basic medical treatment, then transferred to a camp for refugees in Hong Kong. Conditions there were poor, by any normal standards, but after the weeks at sea, and our years in a war-torn country, we felt as though we had somehow landed in paradise. The boys ran up and down the paths between huts, simply because they could, and they laughed and clapped their hands for joy because the earth beneath their feet was solid, and the horizon no longer moved. But our fears soon returned. What would happen to us? Where would we go? The camp became crowded, there were problems. Finally we were told, after months of questioning and waiting, that we had been given the status of refugees by the British government. We would be going to live in London!'

Mrs Pham said this with a certain nostalgic pride, as she reached out to refill their cups from the pot.

'What did you think of it when you first arrived?' Otto asked.

'It was strange but, in its way, wonderful. Marlowe House

209

was huge, the city even more so. But we were alive, the whole family, in a country at peace with itself, so we were happy enough with our fate.'

'And how did you settle? It can't have been easy. As a foreigner in England, I remember it took me some considerable time. I even changed my surname in a bid to be better accepted.'

'It *was* difficult. Binh had great trouble finding work. The language was a problem, especially during the early years, and there were not so many jobs around for anyone at that time.'

'But he found something . . . eventually?'

'Only ever casual work. Nothing well paid, or secure. I know he found this hard, though he rarely spoke about it. He never again found a real footing in life, the way he had done in Vietnam. One time, when he was serving at tables, in a restaurant belonging to an old friend, I took the children over to meet him at work. I became quite angry at the way some customers spoke to him. People in suits, clicking their fingers, ordering him around. I told him it was a disgrace, that he deserved more respect, especially given what he and his family had been through.'

'And what did he say when you told him that?'

'He laughed and said perhaps we should have stayed with the Communists in Saigon, after all! Binh was a good man, with a fine sense of humour; always better able to cope than I with the difficulties that sometimes came our way. Towards the end, with the struggle of work behind him, he was more or less completely at peace. Knowing he was no longer at the command of others left him with a great sense of freedom. He liked to tend the flowers in our window box, and we would go for short walks together by the river. Once, when he was feeling strong enough, we went to see the gardens at Kew.'

Mrs Pham fell silent as she finished her tea.

'What happened to your husband?' Otto asked her.

'He passed away, three years ago, from cancer of the liver.'

'I'm sorry.'

'It was quick, a few months only. He didn't suffer long.'

'And your sons?'

'They are back in Ho Chi Minh City, which is the modern name for Saigon, of course. The name has changed – the city, too. I hear it's a thriving place, these days. I miss my children and my grandchildren, but we talk to each other all the time. They speak to me every other day on Skype.'

Otto sat staring into space. He was lost once more along the tangled paths of memory; Mrs Pham's, now, as well as his own.

He saw for an instant an open-topped van, weighed down with household belongings. Family photographs, rolls of bedding, the horn of an old gramophone sticking out through the clutter. He felt his father's arms beneath his shoulders, lifting him onto a seat beside his sisters. Then he felt again the sense of confusion, the change of atmosphere in the city that had been their home. The familiar sights – the opera house, tram wires and high tiers of chocolate cake – had taken on a new dimension since the *Anschluss*, one that he had struggled as a child to comprehend. Despite the appearance of calm on the streets, following the celebrations of the crowds a few days before, there was a new sense of fear in Vienna, of dangers unidentified. These were reflected back to Otto through the frightened eyes of his mother, as she helped his father up onto the seat beside them.

Chloe looked at Otto, wondering whether he might express whatever it was that appeared to be weighing on his mind. He turned instead to Mrs Pham.

'Would you ever think of returning to Vietnam? Permanently, I mean.'

Mrs Pham thought for a second.

'My children keep asking me that same question, almost every time we speak. They want to know why I stay in this horrible building.'

She paused.

'Oh dear, I'm so sorry. What I mean to say is ...'

'I understand, don't worry.'

Otto had replied with a small and rueful smile.

'My children think I would be happier in Vietnam. But I'm not really so sure. If Marlowe House is pulled to the ground, I *will* return, but it's many years now since I actually lived there. The idea of going back gives me butterflies. There are memories, you see, from the war. Too many of them, perhaps. So for now, at least, I think I will stay where I am. When I get up in the morning, look out and see the sun rise behind the nearby towers, I see it just as Binh and I did, every morning of our lives for thirty-five years. There is nowhere else on earth that can give me that – nowhere, even in the country of my birth, that has that kind of meaning for me.'

Otto looked thoughtful, remembering his own past.

'It *is* difficult,' he said, 'returning to the scene of a traumatic experience. Once it has happened, life is never the same again. The world changes shape, and there's nothing one can do to restore its contours. And then, somehow, without even intending it, a new life has appeared elsewhere. After that, it becomes difficult to ever think of going back.'

212

He looked at Mrs Pham, and continued, 'It's not easy to explain all this, when talking to other people, unless they've been through a similar experience themselves.'

She smiled, with understanding.

'I'm glad you came to visit today – although, I must admit, I was a little nervous about the cameras.'

She asked him, then, if he had children of his own.

'I have a son, called Daniel.'

'That's a beautiful name.'

'It is. His mother chose it, as a matter of fact.'

'And does Daniel have any children?'

'A daughter and a son.'

'Where do they live?'

'Here in London.'

'And you will be visiting them, your family, during your stay?'

Otto reddened and looked at the floor.

Chloe intervened.

'Thank you so much for your time, Mrs Pham. It was kind of you to speak to us. We really shouldn't keep you too much longer.'

Twenty-Two

Sitting alone in his living room late that evening, Otto looked out at the countless pins of light beneath the window. Gathered together, like the dots on a Pointillist painting, they formed a giant image of a city.

In the distance, he heard the sound of sirens. Somewhere, a helicopter hovered. At midnight, the insomniac capital stirred beneath his gaze.

Such a frenetic sort of place, exhausting to me now.

Yet it was all a question of perspective, he realised. To Mrs Pham and her family, on the day of their arrival, London must have seemed an oasis of order and calm.

Lifting his spectacles from his face, he rubbed the pins of light from his eyes. His outer vision blurred, but his inner one intensified. At this late hour, the past flowed in on him unchecked.

'Do you have any children?' Mrs Pham had asked him earlier.

His memory, now, brought forth to him a son.

*

Daniel arrived in the world two weeks prematurely. He was delivered at home and, unusually for that era, Otto was present at the birth. He held Cynthia's hand throughout, but was of less practical help than he had planned. In this sense, it set the tone for the years that were to follow.

The midwife, a fearsome woman in her late fifties, barked instructions at Cynthia as if she were a contestant at Crufts.

'Push!' she ordered. 'Harder, Mrs Laird ... *harder*. We can have this over and done with by teatime!'

When not haranguing Cynthia, the midwife harangued Otto for not joining in with her cries of encouragement. Instead, he held onto Cynthia's hand, repeating time and again in a soft, plaintive mantra: 'My poor Cynthia ... my darling Cynthia ... there, there, my love ... there, there.'

The birth of a child, for many fathers, is an experience bordering on the spiritual. Otto's memory, in later years, was more of a nightmare fairground ride. He recalled only fragments, such as gripping Cynthia's hand more firmly with each renewed scream (his own palm as trembling and sticky as hers), closing his eyes now and then, whenever his head started to spin out of control, and then opening them – to focus, if possible, on the bay window and the swaying oak tree outside. Occasionally, he would glance down for a glimpse of something purplish and messy, before averting his eyes again to the window. His overriding sensations once it had finished were of relief, both baby and mother having emerged bloodied but in good health from their ordeal, and an awestruck admiration for Cynthia's limitless resistance to pain. Upon seeing her, wan and drained, cradling the sleeping baby in the glow of the bedroom lamp, he had undergone his moment of revelation. But that was later, after the clean-up, once the image of the trauma and viscera had faded.

Daniel was not an especially happy baby, as testified by the albums full of photographs showing a furious, red-faced creature either just recovering from one explosion of rage, or about to launch into another. He suffered greatly from colic during the early months of his life, rendering sleep a sweet memory for his bleary-eyed parents, who took it in turns to walk the infant around the bedroom, gently bouncing and rocking him in their arms in a bid to help wind him. There was a particular rhythm that appeared to work each time, though he struggled so much that it sometimes took a while for him to find it. At weekends, the family walked on Hampstead Heath: at first pushing Daniel in his pram, then watching him move on unsteady legs as he chased after pigeons and toppled onto his hands. Sometimes he would be surprised to tears; at others, distracted by his parents' intervention into laughter.

Like his mother and father, Daniel was a sharp-minded child, observing the world around him with a keen and penetrating eye. Sometimes, Cynthia would catch the tube down with Daniel to the office on Portland Place. He would sit at Otto's work desk, flooded by the light from the window, and practise drawing pictures of houses, frowning in concentration and his tongue protruding slightly from the corner of his mouth.

As Daniel grew to school age, Otto felt conscious that he was playing a more peripheral role in his son's life than he would have liked. Whenever Otto returned from one of his frequent trips abroad, the boy always ran to hug him with a naturalness that brought a tightness to Otto's throat. Yet he sensed that an inevitable distance was growing between them. He felt, even when Daniel was seven or eight, a certain formality on both their parts that, as the years passed, would grow ever more entrenched.

I tried to overcome it, but it's so difficult to alter these situations, once the pattern has been set. Could I have done more, to remove the barriers that grew into adulthood?

What Daniel felt and thought, his hopes, dreams and concerns – these were largely the preserve of his mother. Circumstances, somehow, had conspired to shut Otto out. Like many others of his generation, he had played the role of a father without ever quite being the real thing. That he appeared unable to do anything about this had frustrated him immensely at the time. He was glad to see, with later generations, that the situation had begun to change.

Many moments from Daniel's childhood returned to Otto throughout that evening. Yet for some reason it was the kite that wouldn't leave him. If only there had been more memories like that one.

Looking up, he saw Daniel, at the age of five or six, hovering on the threshold of his study in Hampstead. He was waiting, as usual, to be noticed and invited inside.

'Daniel. Hello. How nice it is to see you.'

Otto took off his spectacles and smiled at his son, laying the partially constructed kite to one side.

The little boy ran into the study and hugged him.

'Hi, Daddy.'

'How did you get on with your sums?'

'Okay. Full marks. What are you doing?'

'I'm making a kite.'

'For who?'

'For you.'

'Really?'

The look of delight on Daniel's face prompted Otto to ruffle his hair.

'I thought we might take it to Grandma and Grandpa's house, the next time we visit. We're going there in a few weeks' time. Remember how windy it gets in those hills during the winter?'

Daniel nodded.

'The scarf.'

'That's right. It's where Mummy's headscarf blew away last time. That's what gave me the idea to build you this.'

The kite gradually took shape over the course of the next few days. Daniel popped into the study two or three times an evening to see how it was progressing. Cynthia, too, glanced in periodically.

'It looks lovely,' she said. 'Good enough to hang on a wall.'

'It's been a fascinating challenge. So different, technically, to what I usually do, yet with certain underlying similarities.'

When completed, the kite had a highly elaborate shape. The wire frame and pieces of fabric formed a delicate series of interconnecting folds.

'Like paper screens inside a Japanese house,' Cynthia told him, admiringly.

'Let's hope it's a little more aerodynamic than they are.'

They were to find out, two weeks later, on a raw and blustery afternoon in the Chilterns.

The three of them stood at the top of a hill, overlooking a field of furrowed clay.

'Do you think it will work?' Otto shouted to Daniel and Cynthia.

He had his doubts. The structure was fragile; the wind that day was high, howling in over the fields towards them.

'Let's try, Daddy,' cried Daniel, in his duffel coat and galoshes, the scarf his mother had knitted for him pushed up around his ears.

Otto handed the kite to him and gently explained what to do.

'By the edges ... that's it. Try not to press too hard. Lift it up, right in front of you, and then, when I give the word, you can let it go up into the sky. Okay?'

Daniel nodded and dutifully held out the kite, while Otto took the spool and wound out the string. He continued speaking as he moved backwards.

'Perfectly still. Won't be a minute ... let's see if this contraption can fly.'

Cynthia, moving closer to Daniel, wrapped him in her arms and kissed the top of his head.

'Ready, darling? This is going to be fun.'

In her arms, Daniel trembled in anticipation. The kite in his hands trembled, too. Otto, his tall body visible over the curve of the hill, appeared to be nearly ready.

'Okay? Hold it up now, high as you can,' he called.

Daniel lifted his arms. The kite flapped and struggled as he gripped it between his fingers.

'The wind wants to take it away, Daddy,' he shouted.

'Not just yet, a few more seconds.'

Otto adjusted his glasses.

'Okay, when you're ready,' he called.

'Let's count down together,' Cynthia whispered to Daniel.

'Three . . . two . . . one . . . GO!'

Daniel loosened his grip on the frame, and the kite sprang eagerly from his grasp, twisting and turning in a series of leaps, mounting the sky as if it were a staircase. He and Cynthia cheered as they watched it go, laughing and clapping their hands. Their laughter then redoubled as they looked across at Otto, who fought to keep control as the kite ascended.

'Oh no,' he shouted, raising another wave of laughter, as the spool escaped his grasp and bounced away across the grass.

'Catch it, Daddy!' shouted Daniel.

'Catch it, Otto!' shouted Cynthia.

He tried to chase it down, a grin upon his face, waving his arms and shouting in a way he knew would amuse Daniel. But his smile began to fade as the spool continued to unravel. The kite rose ever higher into the sky. Gaining ground, Otto reached down to grab the elusive spool, but toppled forward onto the grass at the vital moment. Looking on, helpless, he watched it lifting from the earth to follow into the slipstream of the soaring kite. Within a few more seconds, his master-piece was vanishing over the hills and out of sight. It was an entirely new experience and somewhat disconcerting. That sort of thing didn't happen with his buildings.

'Oh damn,' he exclaimed to himself, as the laughter in the background turned to gasps. 'That thing works a lot better than I anticipated.'

Racing back to the car, they set off in pursuit of the kite. Yet scanning the skies through the windscreen, they could see nothing but fast-moving clouds. All afternoon they drove through the narrow lanes, stopping to peer over gates and into hedgerows. But no glimpse of a broken frame, or a twisted piece of fabric, appeared to solve the mystery of its escape.

As the hours passed, Cynthia and Otto became increasingly worried that Daniel might become upset. Yet he remained in good humour and remarkably philosophical, telling them not to worry as darkness fell and they had to abandon the search.

'It was born to be free,' he explained to them over tea that evening, quoting a line from his favourite wildlife film.

Otto built a replacement kite for Daniel the following weekend, its design a good deal less ambitious than the first. But it was a replacement in name only. While it soon lay forgotten, somewhere at the back of a cupboard, its predecessor became a family legend. They never forgot its disappearance. It remained a running joke between them for years.

'Where do you think your kite might be?' Cynthia or Otto would ask Daniel, closing his book of stories and tucking him down for the night.

'Passing Mars or Jupiter,' he would say. 'Maybe it has reached the Milky Way.'

And he would smile his gap-toothed smile at the very thought of it.

Twenty-Three

Dear Daniel,

I have recently become aware — and this is something to do with age, I think — of all the harm I've caused in life to those I love. Not just the major incidents, but the tiny emotional injuries, inflicted unthinkingly, day after day, and accumulating over a lifetime into something more significant.

I realise now that the pain I inadvertently caused you goes back far into your childhood. I realise that my analytical turn of mind, while serving me well in a professional capacity, made me somewhat ill-suited to be a good father. With the occasional exception (remember your kite?) I must have appeared to you as a cold and rather distant figure. Even adults found me intimidating, so heaven knows what it must have been like for a sensitive boy to be faced with such a personality over the breakfast table each morning. In retrospect, I wish that I could change all that, but sadly I cannot. So I am writing in order to acknowledge my mistakes, to apologise for my emotional coolness. I have to repair at least a part of the cumulative damage.

If the roots of our estrangement can be traced back to your childhood, my behaviour during your adult years has only deepened the division. Firstly, my lack of emotional support towards you following the death of your mother: what a friend once correctly described as my 'running away from reality to the mountains'. What I did was unforgivable. You were still a young man at the time – just twenty-one – and I effectively left you to cope with your sense of bereavement alone. It must have been extremely difficult for you. You were in the midst of your studies, you were dealing with the usual emotional pressures of being young and not yet settled in life. And then you had the additional burden of coping with your mother's illness and death, the nature of which was of a singular, quite breathtaking cruelty. And you had to do all this with minimal support from me, other than the occasional letter or phone call to your digs, because I had disappeared into the French Alps to become a recluse. The timing could not have been worse.

In explaining my actions to you now, I'm not seeking to elicit sympathy, merely to establish a degree of understanding. Furthermore, I hope that by revealing to you my feelings at that time, you may at some point feel inclined to reciprocate the gesture. I would welcome that very much.

As you know, within a few months – almost a few weeks – of your mother's death, I had effectively retired from the architectural practice she and I had formed with our colleagues almost thirty years before, sold up our family home in Hampstead and rented a wooden chalet on the slopes of the Chartreuse Mountains. I took my leave from colleagues

223

and friends without passing on address or telephone number.
Looking back, the thing that amazes me most is that I was
able to do all this without appearing to raise a single
suspicion that I had, in fact, completely lost my mind (there
are benefits, I suppose, to having a natural air of authority). I
now believe this is exactly what did happen.

We have never really discussed this before, and I apologise
for probing old psychological wounds, but the last few days of
Cynthia's life – if that is a suitable word to describe her
condition at that time – were not easy ones. All of us hoped
for a good death, a peaceful one, for your mother. It was, at
that time, the only hope we had left. But I'm afraid even
that small mercy was denied her. You had, of course, returned
to Cambridge by this time, having reached the point of
emotional exhaustion after those weeks of waiting in the
hospice.

I'll spare you the details, but her final hours were difficult.
Cynthia struggled, I'm afraid. And, in the months that
followed, well, I suppose I struggled, too. It was the nature of
the ending – the brutality of it. After she had fought the
disease so bravely, for more than two years, to see it take her
in such a pitiless fashion appeared callous beyond belief. It
seemed to me almost like a glimpse of evil; certainly, like the
end of all hope. And then mixed up with it was this terrible
sense of relief – a relief that her great suffering was finally
over, and with it a sense that time hung suspended, in one
endless moment of trauma. It was logical, I suppose, that I
should have felt this way. I imagine that you did, too. But it
left me with a deep sense of shame, nonetheless. I believe,
with hindsight, that these various factors must have tilted me
over the edge.

For almost four years I lived in that chalet. I went for days, sometimes weeks at a time, without taking the trouble to shave. Most days I wore the same tattered sweater, one bought for me by your mother in Italy some years before. The only furniture I had at my disposal was a narrow bed with a mattress, a chair and a small wooden table. There was no radio and no television – I suppose my lifelong taste for minimalism had reached its logical conclusion. To complete this picture of rural solitude, I suppose I should also tell you that I lived on nuts and berries, gathered from the forest; and upon wild game, hunted down by my own hand with weapons I had fashioned from a beech tree. In reality, however, there was a convenient Carrefour in the nearby village, which I visited twice a week for fresh supplies, alarming the poor checkout girls with my bad French and mighty beard.

Throughout the period of my stay there I did little else besides walk in the Alpine landscape. I was trying, I suppose – in a somewhat obscure way – to re-establish some sense of contact with your mother, even though there were no particular memories associated with that place. Cynthia, as you know, had a great affinity with the natural world. Sometimes, when she and I were out walking in the Chilterns, I could almost sense her disappearing into the wind and the birdsong, into the blades of grass themselves. The landscape seemed to consume her. During our walks she often didn't say a word, her silence could be total. Even her footsteps became softer and her breathing quieter; as they do, for instance, upon entering a church. And in a way I think that this is an appropriate metaphor. Woodlands, valleys, rivers and hills were, for your mother, sacred places. It was

like some long-lost impulse, recovered from prehistory, a sense
of the eternal in nature. Since your mother was not a
religious person, the countryside, I think – and especially her
own, southern English countryside – fulfilled that role for
her. It's only in recent months that I have begun to
understand on a personal level the intensity of Cynthia's
relationship with nature; her discarding of the ego and all
sense of self, her becoming the very landscape through which
she walked. There are moments when I've felt something
similar myself, while wandering in the forest near my current
home in the Jura. When I was walking in the Chartreuse
Mountains, however – back in the late 1980s – I had yet to
really understand these things.

It went on for some time, this aimless walking in the
circumference of my small wooden chalet; trying to catch a
glimpse of Cynthia, or at least capture an inkling of how she
might have felt, upon witnessing the play of light across a
stream, or the puffs of mist hanging low in the valleys as the
rising sun drew their moisture. Autumn, I remember, was an
especially poignant time, being the season that most affected
your mother. The winter months were harsh, but there was
consolation to be found in the depth and silence of the
snows.

It was a poetic time, in its way, but also a deeply selfish
one, as I had a young son back at home in England who
needed my support. The guilt was there, on my part; of that
there is no question. Indeed, the sheer ferocity with which I
used to walk, and my recklessness while doing so, were
probably indicators of that guilt. I would sit on high outcrops
in wet and slippery conditions, lean out over precipices to look
at vertiginous drops. Perhaps – who knows? – such actions

226

embodied a death wish of sorts. But life for me was so different up there in the mountains, it had so little connection to my life down below, that I think I somehow managed to shed both the person I had been and the responsibilities that person held towards others. In brief, I tricked myself into thinking I was someone else. I pulled the plug on my former life, and found instead solitude.

I suppose I would have stayed that way for the rest of my life, until tumbling off a precipice somewhere, or going completely barmy with the lack of human contact. Except that, one day, someone else appeared in my life. On a whim, I decided to take a bus trip to the lakeside town of Annecy. I have no idea why. It was the first time I had gone beyond my usual foraging territory for nearly three years. Maybe I craved for once the noise and bustle of people around me, or perhaps I wished to see again some stimulating architecture. Annecy, as you know, has an especially beautiful medieval centre. Whatever the reason, I ventured for a couple of balmy summer days beyond my familiar daily round, and there I encountered Anika.

She approached me as I sat in a café above the village of Talloires. It was a lovely spot on the slopes with a view of the lake. I'm sure I would never have spoken to her otherwise, and this brings me on to the second issue I would like to discuss with you. I realise you have always believed that I married again too soon after your mother's passing. In retrospect, I can understand how you might feel this way. I understand also that you have subsequently cast Anika in a somewhat predatory role; as the woman who swooped down, talons flashing, upon your father when he was not thinking quite as straight as he should have been.

Please don't deny these thoughts, for I must confess I once heard you express them. I was in the downstairs lavatory of your home, and you were talking with Suzie in the hallway. It was one of those difficult situations – wanting to defend someone against words that were not meant for my ears. I let it pass, then, but I would like to address it now. I can say categorically, and with the clearest of heads (the cabin fever of the Alpine years has long since passed, I assure you), that Anika is a kind and beautiful woman who comports herself at all times with the utmost discretion. When she spoke to me, the impulse that drove her was certainly not a predatory one. Please bear in mind that I looked, at the time, like the wild man of the woods! It was simple human compassion. She saw a troubled soul, if you will, and went to its assistance. The feelings that developed between us were slow in their gestation and entirely honourable. It took a long time, in fact, for us to reach a stage that one might define as love. It began as a friendship, pure and simple, and one that took no small degree of patience on her part to sustain, given the extent of my emotional withdrawal from the world at that time. I do not know, of course, what your mother would have made of Anika as a person, but I do know that she approved, as a concept, the idea of my remarrying. It is one of those strange matters that one discusses in the latter stages of an illness such as hers.

I don't wish to turn this portion of the letter into a lengthy homage to Anika, especially as I would like you to continue reading until the end! Suffice to say that she is a sensitive woman, whose spontaneous generosity towards others I witness on a daily basis. She is a very different character to your mother. Anika is not an artist, able to express her emotions with eloquence. She is practical, with an academic background in political science and a professional career spent mostly at the United Nations. Similarly, her kindness towards others takes a pragmatic and undemonstrative form. But it is there, I promise you, and both you and your family would certainly get to experience it, if only we could somehow break down these barriers that have grown up on all sides.

In some respects, I realise, I have continued to run away from reality for the past twenty-five years or so, to the point where an entirely new reality has evolved for me. I imagine, on those occasions when you visited Anika and me in Switzerland, you were surprised at the extent to which I had changed. You must have noticed how out of touch I was with the wider world, my lack of interest in current affairs, or politics. Anika, as you saw, keeps abreast of these things far better than I.

Having avoided the realities for so long, however, in the past few days I've been forced to face up to them. Returning to Marlowe House (we've been making a documentary about its proposed demolition) has not been an easy experience. The building is in a poor state of repair and there's a tangible sense of decay in the air. Inevitably, in such an environment, I've done a lot of soul-searching, questioned where it was that things went wrong.

Also, at a more personal level, it has reminded me of the world from which I came. Not just London, but the world I knew before then . . . before the change of country, and of surname. I raise this last point, as it's something we've not discussed before. Just once, as I remember, was the matter raised by you. How old were you then: sixteen or seventeen, maybe? You asked me one day, out of the blue, just why it was I had changed my name to Laird. And I could sense in your voice, hence my rather dismissive response at the time, the deep disappointment that underlay your question.

I've never forgotten that moment. I understand your feelings. I know how much our heritage means to you. Perhaps it was my duty, in the years after the war, to maintain the family name. Perhaps it was my duty to all the lost. Indeed, for this very reason, the decision I took remains a source of guilt. But it was a decision made, by a young man, remember, for entirely practical reasons. It was driven by a combination of residual fear – unfounded, perhaps, now that the war was over, but real enough for me at the time – and a wish to avoid any further difficulties.

When I arrived in London, I was in a somewhat confused state. I was a guest here, invited on a scholarship, and yet mentally I remained a refugee. There was still some anti-Semitism around, even after what had just occurred, and occasionally I found myself the victim of it. In another sense, and perhaps rather childishly, I simply wanted to feel included somewhere, maybe for the first time in my life. And so I took the name Laird, somewhat randomly, because I was a fan at the time of the works of Sir Walter Scott, and it carried for me rather romantic associations. In a sense, I suppose, I was adopting a new persona; a character, if you like, for the professional life to come. That character, I now realise, is all played out.

I've never been a religious man. It's years since I visited a synagogue. The last time I went on a regular basis was with my father, mother and sisters. Yet even now, as I close my eyes at the writing desk, I can feel them all around me: the candles and solemnity, the incantations of the Rabbi, the words of the Torah and the music of the Hebrew language. Some memories, it seems, are just too powerful to ever leave us.

I hope that you and I can close this emotional distance, Daniel. You have a wonderful family and I would like, if possible, to properly get to know them. It would also be fun to talk with you about architecture again. How I miss those conversations we once had. I have seen your plans for the cricket pavilion in Mumbai – I must admit I was green with envy when I heard you had secured the contract – and they look tremendous. It's good to know those childhood days we frittered away at Lord's and the Oval turned out to be productive after all.

You may feel inclined to take those last comments with a pinch of salt, remembering the insensitive remarks with which I created this rift between us. I apologise. My criticism of your design for the railway station in Coimbra was harsh, ill tempered and wholly unfounded. Ill timed, too, given the professional pressures you were under at that time. I don't know what came over me that day. I suspect, with hindsight, there was more than a hint of jealousy in my remarks. They were the words of an old man, his powers in decline, raging against the dying of his own creative light. I've lost count of the number of times I've replayed that scene differently in my head; ending, each time, with a warm and forgiving embrace.

There were deeper tensions, of course, underpinning that petty row. Anika's name did not arise directly, but I sensed as ever your underlying resentment towards her. If only we could address that issue, of my remarrying not long after Cynthia's death, then perhaps it would pave the way for the airing of other concerns. On the day you returned to Cambridge, for

*instance, in the final days of your mother's life, I felt in some
unspoken way that you were abandoning me. At the surface
level I understood your actions, and goodness knows I didn't
wish to prolong your suffering further. And yet, as you waved
farewell through the window of your cab, I felt a sudden sense
of dislocation. It seemed that you were telling me something,
deliberately putting a distance between us. In reality, I now
realise, such thoughts were largely misguided. But the heart
has a tendency to fear the worst, especially when it is at its
most exposed, and a single misunderstanding – a slight,
falsely perceived – can soon develop into something more
deep-rooted. I believe I speak for both of us when I say this.*

*I suppose this misplaced sense of rejection partly explains
the subsequent coolness between us; the hesitation I
experienced, in that cabin in the mountains, every time I
picked up the telephone to give you a call. 'Does he want to
hear from me?' I would ask myself. 'Or would he prefer it if
I left him alone?' More often than not, I would find myself
replacing the receiver.*

*Those self-same doubts, the sense of hesitation, return as I
write to you now. Twenty-five years on, we still suffer the
consequences of our inability to communicate. You live just a
few miles from where I sit writing this, yet I feel unable to
turn up unannounced at your door. Please let's try to remedy
this situation now.*

With love to Suzie, Michael, Gillian and yourself.
Your father,
Otto Leibowitz

Twenty-Four

Early the next morning, before his final interview with Chloe, Otto left Marlowe House in the brackish dawn to go in search of a pint of milk. Venturing out like this, into the darkness and the cold, was not an agreeable experience, especially since he had forgotten to take his scarf. But there were guests to be welcomed, there was tea to be made, and he didn't want Chloe and her team to think that his standards were slipping. He walked as far as the Old Kent Road before finding a shop that was open.

Back inside the entrance of Marlowe House, Otto noted that a lift was out of order. It was the same one they had filmed inside a few days earlier. A sign saying COUNCIL ALERTED – REPAIR IMMINENT was stuck to its door. As he pressed the button to call one of the others, he became distracted by the building's central staircase, spiralling above him into the murk. Standing on its bottom step, he saw what looked like an endless wheel of spokes, radiating outward into the many different levels. It was the centrepiece of Marlowe

House, the hub from which its mathematical logic unfolded. Otto remained proud of its distinctive design, which was partly inspired by the lines of a seashell, and partly by the structure of DNA.

Inevitably, the staircase was in poor condition. Its yellow paint was chipped and flaking, in places gone completely, revealing a metal frame showing signs of rust. But its twisting form and sense of movement remained undeniably striking, to anyone who might take the trouble to glance upwards. At the time of its completion, it was described by one critic as 'architectonic perfection'. The other members of Unit 5 had beamed with delight upon seeing these words in the paper, and insisted on taking Otto to the pub to celebrate.

It was quite an achievement, Otto thought, even though I do say so myself. The closest I ever got to transcendence in my own work, although Cynthia could achieve such things as a matter of routine. It was certainly the most poetic effect I created.

During filming of the original documentary, the director had utilised its visual potential to the full. Shooting upwards from the hallway, he had captured the rangy and athletic young Otto as he bounded effortlessly up its bottom reaches, his long legs taking two or three steps at a time. Chloe loved that shot and had insisted on recreating it for her own film a couple of days earlier. This time, however, Otto struggled to even make the first few flights. Slowly and methodically he had worked his way to each level, pausing occasionally to catch his breath. Chloe later told him she would use a split-screen technique in order to juxtapose the two shots (one from the mid-1960s, the other the present day) for the opening sequence of her film. But she sensed from the

234

expression that passed across Otto's face, quickly extinguished though it was, that this might not be such a good idea after all.

With head now spinning from his contemplation of the staircase, he reached out to steady himself on the banister. Next he inspected the tile-work of the mural lining the hallway. The original design, the work of a respected artist of the time, had hovered between the figurative and the abstract. The image depicted was intended to be evocative of small boats bobbing on a bay. Fifty years on, however, there was no discernible pattern to be found amid the chaos of individual tiles. Most of the originals had either been broken or worked their way loose, and been replaced with whatever came to hand.

Otto strolled thoughtfully around the hallway, piecing together fragments other than tiles. The artist, rather than his design, was the focus of his attention.

He was the last of Cynthia's lovers. Such a shame to see his work in ruins like this. He was a very talented artist.

Otto leaned forward to study the cracks on one of the original tiles.

I liked him, too, oddly enough, even after learning about the affair. He had a strong face, an honest face, and he meant much more to Cynthia than the others. To her, I think, he must have represented a parallel but unlived life – the husband she might have had if I hadn't appeared on the scene. She knew him before she knew me, after all.

Had there been something between them, he wondered, in those months in London before she and Otto had met? He doubted it, somehow. But there definitely *was* something later on, during those years of near estrangement. They had even discussed him together back then, early in 1979, on those nights when they started to piece their broken marriage back together.

'*What?*' Cynthia asked him, unable to keep the surprise from her voice.

'Do you love him?' Otto repeated.

He was sitting on the edge of her bed, in his dressing gown and slippers. Cynthia, in her nightdress, was moving restlessly around the room, on the pretext of searching for some aspirin. The tone of the conversation was familiarly awkward. Their words, back then, after several years of strain, had become a sequence of chords without resolution; a perpetual circling, without ever coming to rest. Otto's sudden question had transgressed the unspoken rule between them. They never sought to deny the affairs, but neither did they discuss them.

Cynthia chose not to answer him directly.

'And if I *do* love him? Would that make it any worse than the others?'

'Not worse,' said Otto, 'but different. *Better*, I suppose, in some respects.'

'Better?'

'Yes. It would feel less like some bizarre game of brinkmanship between us.'

'And is that how you regard all this . . . a game?'

'No. To be frank with you I regard our situation as rather tragic.'

They were talking about it now, for the first time, perhaps. They were moving onto difficult territory. Anger, long suppressed, was resurfacing.

'So why did you stray?' Cynthia asked him. 'Remind me again. Were you trying to prove your virility in some way? All those high-rise buildings not enough for you?'

There was a wild glint in her eye as she rifled through the drawers of her dresser. Otto, in contrast, appeared tired and listless.

'I really can't remember. I suppose I wanted to feel more alive.'

'And did you?'

'At first, maybe ... but not later on. By then it had become something else. Painful, for a time. Later still it became deadening.'

Cynthia's tone was challenging.

'Painful? But I thought you and I were supposed to be immune to that sort of thing. We've mastered the art of indifference, haven't we, Otto? Isn't that what our "open" marriage is all about?'

Otto looked up at her.

'I've never been indifferent to your affairs, Cyn. I simply became numbed by them.'

She turned from the dresser to face him, sarcasm spilling into her voice.

'Then why didn't you say something, if they *displeased* you in any way?'

'It would have been hypocritical of me to speak out.'

His answer riled her further.

'So you're saying this whole thing has been some sort of misunderstanding between us?'

'Please, don't get angry—'

'We've both been fucking around these past few years by mistake, is that what you're saying? Exactly how many have there been now, between the two of us? I'm afraid I'm losing count.'

'Please, let's try to talk seriously—'

'*Seriously?* If you were halfway serious about saving our fucking marriage you would have tried to stop this "game of brinkmanship" long ago!'

These last words were slung at him like crockery. Otto flinched beneath their weight.

'I *have* stopped,' he said quietly. 'There's no one else, now. There hasn't been for some time. Nor will there be again.'

Cynthia paused a moment, surprised. Then her anger redoubled.

'And you expect me to stop now, too, is that it? *You* started this, Otto, when you slept with that woman in Paris. Now you want it all to finish, because you believe it's getting out of hand. Is that what concerns you – that I'm having more fun these days than you are?'

She looked defiant, but vulnerable. Her upper lip quivered.

She's at the end of her tether, Otto thought. What on earth have I done to her?

'I'm not asking you to stop,' he replied. 'That's why I've raised the subject now. I realise this one is different to the others. I realise you're in love with him.'

Her eyes flashed at him.

'And what makes you say that?'

'Because I sense, with him, that it's no longer anger that is driving you. I sense he has returned you to yourself.'

She halted and stared down at him. The retort that had been swelling on her lips had died.

'And so?' she said, after several moments of silence, her voice now quieter.

Otto looked at her evenly.

'And so you should think about leaving me, moving in with him, making the break completely.'

'Do you want me to do it?'

'No. Goodness knows, no. But you have to make a decision, Cyn.'

'For your sake?'

'Partly, yes, because it's exhausting me. That much, I'm sure, is obvious. But also because it's exhausting *you*. I've seen your nerves worsen in recent months. And I can't stand to see it any more.'

Cynthia paused for a moment, unbalanced by the direction the conversation had taken. Searching again for the aspirin in the dresser, she gestured suddenly towards the door.

'I'm tired . . . I have to get some sleep now, Otto. Let's talk about this another time, shall we?'

For three nights running, Otto barely closed his eyes. In the small spare room where he now slept alone, he lay surrounded by the remnants of family life. A ping-pong table, a bicycle with stabilisers, objects forgotten or outgrown. Through the darkness, as he gazed, he saw before him the trajectory of his life, tailing off like a falling star. If she decided to leave, he must give them his blessing. She had every right: she deserved to find happiness. It would show great courage on her part to put an end to this. Yet despite these finer feelings, Otto's soul shrank painfully within him. He was powerless to do anything but wait.

When the time came to discuss it again, he sat once more on the bed with his head slightly bowed. Cynthia, standing before him, mirrored his stillness as she spoke. The restlessness of a few days before was gone. She had summoned him to her bedroom to talk things over, and he expected the worst.

'You're right,' she said. 'I probably *do* love him ... Certainly I care for him a great deal. And I've thought long and hard about leaving you, Otto, believe me. But you needn't be worried, if indeed you are, because it's too late for me to do anything about it.'

He hesitated.

'I don't understand.'

She took a small step forwards.

'I won't be leaving you. I can't. It's something I've come to realise in recent days. The affairs were an act of self-deception, you see. I thought I was asserting my freedom, proving I could leave you whenever I wished. But that's because I didn't love any of them. I knew I would never have to face that decision. Now that I *do* care for someone, perverse as it sounds, I realise I am unable to walk out on you. Faced with a real alternative, I've found I can't possibly take it.'

The lines on Otto's forehead eased a little, but returned immediately.

'You mustn't stay with me out of a sense of duty,' he told her. 'It would be worse for all of us, worse for Daniel, if you did that.'

'It's not a sense of duty ... it's nothing to do with that. I wouldn't make that kind of decision for the sake of appearances. I really don't care what the neighbours think. No, this is something deeper. We're *conjoined*, psychologically, you and I. It's hopeless to try to pretend otherwise. Why do you think we're still together? How many other marriages do you think could have survived this sort of strain? If we were able to live apart, it would have happened long ago. It would

240

have happened on the evening Sandrine telephoned you here.'

Cynthia took a few steps towards the door, as if seeking one final escape route, before returning to the bed and sitting down beside him. He tentatively took her hand, and she made no attempt to remove it. She spoke calmly now; the tension between them was dissipating.

'I blame all that time,' she continued, 'the years we spent together. I can't just put them to one side and begin again. I *am* exhausted, you're right about that, but it's *your* unhappiness, not mine, that's exhausting me. It's *your* loneliness that haunts me. I can't stand to see you like this, the desolation on your face. I want it all to stop, and then of course there's Daniel ...'

Otto glanced up at her briefly and then downwards again.

'What a ridiculous mess I've caused. Forgive me.'

These last words were barely audible. He was sitting bent forward and holding onto her hand with both of his, looking defeated. She reached up and pushed back the greying hair from his face.

'I've played my part. We both have misdemeanours to forgive. And it was I who suggested that we go our separate ways. It was a mistake. You're a depressive, Otto, both of us are. We have moments when we get very low. And we sought the wrong panacea to try to make ourselves feel better.'

He stared up at her, a little dazed.

'So you're staying?'

She nodded minutely.

'Yes.'

'I had this mental image of you, as I lay in my room ... You were packing your case. I thought perhaps it was over.' He

241

stared blankly into space a moment, before continuing, 'I'm so relieved.'

She gathered him slowly into her arms and they held each other awkwardly, consolingly. A few minutes later, the emotions reappeared, with a strength that effectively sealed their fate together. All other futures closed off to them in that instant. Despite everything that had occurred, they had somehow hit upon a way forward together.

Otto ran a hand over the broken tiles in the hallway.

She cooled things off with him after that – decided that enough was enough. No more affairs, for either of us – just stability and a new openness.

Somehow their marriage had survived. More than survived – it had flourished. As Daniel progressed through his teenage years, then later moved away to university at Cambridge, Cynthia and Otto discovered a new richness in their lives. They were like pearl-fishers, stumbling upon a new and unexpected catch, somewhere out in the depths beyond their previously circumscribed territory. They were almost absurdly happy together as they entered their fifties, the difficult years of their forties now behind them. Otto was grateful, in retrospect, that they had been given those final years of calm and peace, during which they often revisited the past; taking trips to those places where their happiest memories lay: to India, southern Italy, and – much closer to home – to the Chiltern Hills, where Cynthia had been born and raised.

They would travel there regularly at weekends, sometimes staying over with her elderly parents, who remained living in the family home; at other times booking into a pub or B&B.

In thirty years of visiting the area, it was not only Cynthia and Otto whose faces had become lined by experience, creased by the cares of the world. The countryside across which they travelled at weekends now also bore such marks. The M40 motorway cut a swath through Buckinghamshire and beyond. New suburbs ribboned outwards from High Wycombe and Aylesbury. The rural peace Cynthia had known in her childhood was supplanted by the drone of traffic and the sprawl of new housing estates. She felt these changes, Otto sometimes thought, as though the scars on the landscape were her own.

There was still peace to be found, however, among the hills themselves, and it was there that they would escape whenever time allowed.

One afternoon, in the spring of 1985, as they sat side by side on the high hill of Ivinghoe Beacon, Cynthia asked Otto a question.

'How would you feel about selling up in Hampstead? Moving out to the countryside? Somewhere truly rural.'

A model aircraft buzzed overhead.

'It's a nice idea,' said Otto. 'I know how much affinity you feel with this area. I like to come visiting here myself.'

She sensed the slight reticence in his voice and squeezed his hand.

'I realise you're an urban creature, with a fear of open spaces. But you may find those fears are unfounded, once you give it a try.'

Otto smiled.

'It's not that. My concerns are more practical. What about our professional commitments? Could we realistically fulfil them from the middle of nowhere?'

'Not as things stand, no. We would both need to make some changes; hand over control to others. Maybe I could sell up the textiles firm altogether. But I don't see why not. Neither of us exactly enjoys the business side of things. We could focus more on design, like we used to.'

The engine of the model plane cut out suddenly, causing it to plummet to the ground some fifty yards from where they sat.

'And Daniel?' Otto asked. 'What if he wants to return to Hampstead after finishing at university? We really ought to talk it through with him first.'

Cynthia looked away a moment, the breeze catching her hair as she turned.

'I already have,' she said. 'Dan won't be returning to the family home again. He's not that type of person. Too restless, independent, eager to discover life for himself. He's gone now, Otto. It's just the two of us once more.'

Otto watched the model plane – set upright, by its owner – trundle up the incline of the hill.

'Sounds like you've been thinking this through,' he said.

'I have, I must admit.'

She leaned over and brushed her face against his. Her eyes shone with some of the thrilling intensity of old.

'I've a feeling it might be time for us,' she said. 'We're both in our fifties now. It would mean that you and I could be together properly, without all those distractions.'

She reached up and brushed a stray strand of hair from his forehead.

'*This* is life, Otto, not the other stuff.'

The model plane lifted into the air with difficulty, circling above them once again. Otto watched the shadow of a cloud as it drifted over the wheat fields. Absently, he stroked Cynthia's hand.

'What do you think?' she eventually asked him.

A quiet life in the country was something Otto had never considered before. Yet the idea, now that she mentioned it, seemed revelatory. They could live somewhere peaceful, design and draw each day. They would be able to walk, and talk, sit quietly together in the evenings. In terms of the space and creative freedom, it would be like a return to the old days, before their lives became complicated by success.

Cynthia smiled, even before Otto had spoken. She sensed the spark of excitement, kindling in his eyes.

'Why not?' he said. 'Yes, why ever not? I hesitate only because your suggestion is so unexpected. But, thinking on my feet now, I would say that you are right. We don't need to carry on at breakneck speed. Why should we? We've achieved all that we wanted, in a professional sense. And we come to the countryside as often as practicable these days. That alone must tell us something. Besides, I must admit that I do find London tiring lately. Rattling along with thousands of others on the Northern Line each morning.'

'Tired of London, but not of life. Samuel Johnson was talking nonsense. There's inspiration to be found in new beginnings.'

Cynthia's enthusiasm was becoming infectious to Otto, just as it had been throughout their lives.

'It will complete a circle,' Otto said. 'Not just for you, for both of us.'

He was remembering their first trip to the Chilterns together, as students, thirty years before.

Their plans began to solidify in the following weeks and

months: they discussed them together with a mounting sense of anticipation. They even spent a weekend looking at cottages. But the longed-for move to the Chilterns never took place.

Otto stood and waited for the lift to arrive. The dilapidated state of Marlowe House no longer seemed to oppress him. Memories of Cynthia, of the stolen years together that followed their reconciliation, brought with them a new-found sense of peace.

There's always hope, he told himself, as the doors slid open and he stepped over the shards of broken glass littering its floor. Even in the bleakest of surroundings, even when all appears lost.

Twenty-Five

Back in his apartment, Otto discussed with Chloe his final thoughts on revisiting Marlowe House. He was determined to get it right this time. The cameras rolled as they talked.

'Would you do things differently, if you were designing the building again today?'

'Yes, absolutely.'

'What would you change?'

'The apartments themselves seem to have stood the test of time, judging by the one in which I've spent the past few nights. But the public spaces would definitely need to be reconsidered. The lifts, the corridors: their condition is very poor. Personal safety is clearly something of an issue.'

'But you still believe it deserves to be saved? Given a listing, perhaps?'

'I do. I had my doubts initially, I must admit, when I arrived and saw its condition. It needs some investment, some attention and care, there's no question at all about that. But I still think it's worth saving.'

'And your reasoning for that?'

'A simple one, really. The residents want to stay here; some of them, anyway. They want to remain in the building that's their home.'

'You mean Ravi and Mrs Pham?'

'And a few more people, I hope. Our sample was unscientific, I realise, but it's all I have to go on. For them, at least, Marlowe House is clearly important; a repository of memories and associations. Mrs Pham has lived here half her life; Ravi for all of his. If the demolition goes ahead as proposed, they will take away more than a structure.'

'How do you mean?'

'Memory is such a complex matter. It's not just mental, but physical. It's embedded in the landscape itself. Buildings are deeply interwoven with people's experiences – with their sense of identity, if you like. It's something of which I've become acutely aware myself in recent days.'

'But not everyone feels positive about Marlowe House. Joe, for instance, and some of the others we've spoken to.'

'Clearly, its fate is a matter of indifference to some. For others, it no doubt evokes feelings of hostility. You were kind enough not to introduce me to any of them! But on balance, naturally, I support those with an emotional attachment to this place. And that's because, in the end, I share that attachment myself.'

'Will that kind of argument be enough to save the building?'

'No, not a chance. We need hard-headed, pragmatic arguments in order to win this battle. Technical, legal, financial. Property is such a minefield, these days. The developers are circling, there's money to be made. But fortunately, given my fuzzy state of mind, there are other people who can deal with these hard realities much better than I. Hopefully, Angelo and the others will succeed with the campaign.'

'You don't appear to regard yourself as very important in all this. Surely you retain some influence. Don't you think that the people who decide these things will value your opinion?'

'Not really. I'm just here to raise a few questions. But I certainly don't expect my views to be taken seriously. Not at my time of life. Don't worry – you look concerned. I've grown used to it by now. Though it is, perhaps, the hardest part of growing old.'

Otto smiled, a little sadly, and Chloe signalled with her hand for the cameras to stop filming.

'Thanks. That's it. I think we have all the material we need now.'

'It's over?'

'Yes. We're finally done. We'll move on to post-production in the next few weeks. I'll let you know when we've got a date for the broadcast.'

'Do you think we have any chance?'

'Of saving it, you mean?'

'Yes.'

'If you don't know, Otto, then how could I? But I hope you do. It's a remarkable building.'

He looked at her, a little surprised, and wondered if she meant it. This was the first time she had expressed an opinion on the subject.

'It's sad to see it in such a bad way,' she added. 'But I've seen footage of Marlowe House from its heyday, remember? I admire the vision architects showed back then. They were made of different stuff, your generation.'

'Why, thank you,' Otto said.

Chloe, having embarrassed him, decided to change the subject.

'Can we give you a lift somewhere? Arrange a cab to take you to the airport? Sorry to rush you, but we have another appointment at twelve.'

'It's kind of you, but I plan to stick around a little longer. My flight doesn't leave until this evening. There's somewhere I'd like to visit first. So if it's okay with you, could I pop the key back through the letterbox when I leave?'

'Sure. I don't see why not.'

A short while later, Otto stood on the wind-blasted forecourt, lifting his hat to Chloe and the others as their van sped away into the distance. Seconds before, they had shaken his hand and wished him well for the journey home. He wondered, briefly, just who they might be filming that afternoon. Other lives, half captured. Other stories, partially told.

After pressing down his restless homburg, its brim flapping mournfully like a flightless bird, Otto rubbed particles of grit from his eyes. Through the main doors of Marlowe House, the occasional resident came and went. One of them, a tough young man with close-cropped hair, wearing blood-red sports gear, produced a skipping rope and began exercising on the opposite side of the forecourt. On the back of his sweatshirt were the words *Mikey J*, printed in silver lettering. Laying down the rope, the young man shadow-boxed for a minute or two, then embarked on a series of sprints across the forecourt. Passing close by, he nodded absently to Otto, who touched the brim of his homburg in response. Fifty years earlier, in a more neighbourly age, they might well have engaged in some pleasant conversation. But that was not how society operated, nowadays.

Otto looked once more at the forecourt. If the interior of the building was decrepit enough, it took an even greater leap of the imagination to equate the environs of Marlowe House with what had existed back in the 1960s. The sculpture garden was not the only element ravaged by time. With an effort, he tried to reassemble the landscaped grounds, raising them mentally from among the weeds and broken paving. A sculpted concrete arch, he recalled, once framed the approach along the main gravel pathway. But the arch, like the pathway, seemed to have disappeared completely. It would take an archaeologist to find any trace of it now.

Whatever happened to it? Did it fall down of its own accord? Seems unlikely; it was constructed of reinforced concrete. Was it stolen, maybe? Broken apart by vandals? Where on earth could it have gone?

Otto wandered over to a patch of grass in the vicinity of where the arch had once been, and dabbed at it with his cane. Bending down, he scooped out handfuls of earth in order to reveal the solid surface he had detected beneath. His fingers uncovered a low concrete base. Another, he discovered, lay some yards to its east. From the cleanness of the cuts across both surfaces, he assumed that the arch must have been removed in some official capacity. But no other clues to its fate remained.

Can fifty years of wear and tear really bring about this much change? he thought. It feels like the work of centuries.

With a shake of his head, he abandoned the remains of the arch to walk around the columns that supported the main structure. On one of them, a spray-painted image caught his eye. It looked like a cluster of vine leaves, or they could have been the leaves of a cannabis plant, curling upwards from the base to eye level.

It could almost be a classical ruin. But then again, maybe not. Perhaps that is being a shade too optimistic! Who knows, though? Maybe in the fullness of time such parallels will sound less fanciful.

Time and distance always brought a certain romance, even to the least likely of locations. And Otto remembered that Pompeii, too, had its graffiti; some bawdy, some political and some nonsensical. When was it they had visited again? Once, in the mid-1960s, and again in the spring of 1981. Herculaneum, too. Mount Vesuvius. The Archaeological Museum in Naples. Now that was some city, with its high and cooling alleyways, sheltered from the glare of the afternoon sun. The narrow, crumbling tenements, linked by the criss-cross lines of washing, hung out like gossip above their heads by signoras with work-thickened arms.

And where else did they visit in that part of the world? The Amalfi coast – the hillside towns of Positano and Ravello. It was the usual tourist trail, but not so well trodden on the first of their visits. Less packaged up, back then. And every few days they would take the train to visit the ruins of Pompeii. With notebooks in hands, they sketched out the proportions of the buildings, the width and positioning of the windows, the public spaces and street plan. And then, as a break some days, when the midday sun became too much to bear, they sought shade at the House of the Vettii. The fresco near its entrance seemed to fascinate the jostling groups of tourists, who laughed out loud or stared in amazement at the outsized appendage of Priapus.

The carriages of the Circumvesuviana were scrawled with similar images, but no one took much notice of those. Riding the local train back to Sorrento, with the sun touching the sea beyond the mottled windows. Cynthia, back at the hotel, sketching in crayon the deepening blues of bay and sky. Otto, watching her work in the window, his long body stretched out on the bed. And as dusk came on he had studied his upturned toes, encrusted in dust, dissolving . . .

So there were aspects of humanity that remained the same, despite time's constant remaking. Perhaps, in the next millennium, tourists would flock in their thousands to see the ruins of Marlowe House. Maybe they, too, would queue in line to see the random obscenities on its walls. First things first, however. The immediate priority was to stop that demolition.

Pacing around the columns, which glistened in the chill from the overnight rain, Otto studied carefully the spacing between them – measured out with the help of his cane. He saw again the long months they had spent studying the laws of classical proportion, firstly in textbooks and then later, when they had the money, during their travels across southern Italy.

We tried to recapture some of that here, he thought. The play of light and shadow between the columns as one walked through them.

It was a nice idea, but in retrospect a bloody silly one. They didn't really take account of the conditions here in London. All that miserable English weather, reducing everything, buildings and sky, to a muddy and colourless grey. He was sure there must be moments, though, in the heat of a midsummer's day, when their classical shadow–play was occasionally revived.

A momentary trick of the eye for the casual passer-by, transported, almost without noticing, into the shady folds of a Roman forum. It was pleasant to entertain such thoughts, however far removed from reality they might be. It made the decay and desperation of this place a little easier for him to bear.

He wondered, then, just what Anton would have made of Marlowe House in its present condition. Anton always referred to his sister and brother-in-law as the 'patron saints of lost causes'. No doubt he would see its current state as a vindication of his views.

A more personal thought suddenly troubled Otto's conscience.

I should have supported him, too. He was in a bad way.

Once or twice, in the weeks following Cynthia's death, there had been tensions between the two men. Otto became irritated by Anton's sentimentality, by his tendency to deify his late sister, to speak about her in hushed and reverent tones: 'as if she were Joan of Arc', as Otto described it to a friend.

Anton's eulogies were his own way of dealing with the sense of devastation. But in seeking to come to terms with Cynthia's loss, he had rapidly turned his sister into an alabaster idol, removing all nuance and complexity from her personality. In a few short weeks he had transformed her into a character from myth – and so banished her, without meaning to, into the distant past. It was something Cynthia herself would have found ridiculous. At the time Otto found it difficult to keep the impatience from his voice whenever Anton launched into one of his lengthy lamentations, and they had more or less lost contact with each other after that.

I regret that now – my irritation with Anton. It was unfair of me to treat him so. None of us was exactly thinking clearly then.

It must have been ten years now since Anton died. Otto had sent flowers but felt too awkward to attend the funeral. He wished he hadn't lost touch with him after moving away. Maybe they could have been of some help to each other at that time.

Another image sprayed onto a column distracted Otto from these thoughts.

I haven't seen one of those in years.

He stepped forward to take a closer look. It was an inverted Y shape with an extended stem, set within a circle: the symbol of the Campaign for Nuclear Disarmament. Halting before it, he reached out a hand and lightly touched his fingers to the perimeter of the circle. The sight of it alone was enough to evoke the atmosphere of the late 1950s, back in the days before Daniel came along.

Twenty-Six

The threat of the bomb hung over everything at that time. The arms race appeared to be spiralling out of control. At a personal level, as they had married not long before, this was among the happiest periods of Cynthia and Otto's lives. But gradually they felt a shadow creep across their consciousness and conscience. The prospect of a nuclear conflict was becoming ever more real.

One evening at the apartment in Marchmont Street, Cyn was reading John Wyndham's novel *The Chrysalids* when she put it down and joined Otto on the sofa. Shaping herself around him, she pressed her face close to his. Glancing up from his own book, he saw that she looked pale and disturbed.

'What is it?' he asked.

Nuzzling her nose against his cheek, she ran a hand through his thick mop of hair, admiring its pure black colouring in the light from the reading lamp.

'Let's never have children,' she said.

Otto flinched in surprise.

'I'm sorry?'

'Let's never have children.'

He moved his face back fractionally to inspect hers.

'You're serious, aren't you?'

She nodded.

Otto felt caught off guard – embarrassed by the sudden intrusion of this weighty subject into an evening of quiet reading. His mind was still focused on his own book, a rather dense new work by the philosopher Theodor Adorno, and it took him a moment to find his bearings. When he did, his tone was conciliatory.

'Clearly it's not something we've discussed a great deal, and we have plenty of time ahead of us in which to make an informed decision. Nevertheless, I must admit ... I had hoped that, one day, perhaps, you know ... '

Cynthia felt guilty about her unprovoked lunge. She had put poor Otto on the spot. John Wyndham's descriptions of a post-apocalyptic world had wrought a strange effect upon her. She smiled an apology, but could not deflect the sadness from her eyes. Now she kissed Otto on the lips and hugged him to her. This sudden display of ardour shocked him. There was nothing romantic or sensual in the gesture. She seemed close to tears.

'Of course, a part of me hopes to have children,' she said unsteadily, 'but I'm really not sure, any more. Not because of us, but because of the world – the direction everything is heading. I'm not sure it would be fair of us to bring them into this.'

Having recovered himself, Otto recalled the book that Cynthia was reading. Earlier, he had leafed through some of its pages.

'I understand,' he said, slipping an arm around her shoulder. 'But let's not give up just yet. We are young and we have plenty of time to think the situation over. We also have time to make a difference.'

She agreed with him on that last point. They must channel their concerns more positively. In February 1958, at Cynthia's instigation, they attended the inaugural meeting of the Campaign for Nuclear Disarmament, held at Central Hall in Westminster.

The darkest moment of that era came a few years later, in October 1962. Cynthia and Otto were on a camping holiday in the Lake District when news broke of the Cuban Missile Crisis. Over the course of the next two weeks, before the resolution of the dispute, a war between the USA and Soviet Union appeared inevitable. Everyone knew that it would quickly become a global confrontation. They also understood, in disturbing detail, just what the effects of a nuclear strike would mean.

During the daytime, in that difficult fortnight, they took long walks together in the hills. They wanted to take their minds off events elsewhere, to feel themselves fully alive. In the evenings, they sat nervously beside the campfire, wrapped in thick jumpers and waterproofs, listening to the news bulletins on a transistor radio. Their mood became increasingly sombre as the crisis deepened. The USA was demanding that the Soviet Union remove its weapons from Cuban soil. The Soviets showed no signs of acceding. Both sides, it seemed, were becoming more intransigent with every day that passed.

'Surely the instinct for survival will win out,' said Otto, as they listened to the war of words intensify on the radio. 'Sanity, at some point, must prevail. *Somebody* has to back down.'

He sounded, from the tone of his voice, as though he were trying to convince himself as much as Cynthia.

She said nothing for a while. A slight mist wreathed the fields and trees, causing the glow from the campfire to thicken in the twilight. The wet grass breathed its scent into the evening air.

'I'm not so sure,' she said at last. 'Do you really think they'll act sanely in the face of all this? There's so much fear, such paranoia, on both sides.'

Logs cracked and splintered in the fire. They looked out into the murky twilight, at the vast and looming shapes in the distance. Even the mountains themselves seemed suddenly vulnerable.

'You're right,' said Otto. 'Fear makes people do terrible things. All rationality disappears before it. It's there within our recent history.'

He sounded especially thoughtful as he said this.

Cynthia noticed that the reflection from the fire had transformed the lenses of his spectacles into two miniature flames. She slid an arm through his, their waterproofs squeaking noisily.

'It's the scale of it all that's so hard to comprehend,' she said. 'The scale of what will happen if these things are finally used. Not just to our own generation, but to many afterwards. The environmental devastation, radiation poisoning lasting centuries, maybe millennia. It's almost impossible to grasp.'

Otto was staring intently into the fire. All words of solace had deserted him. Cynthia paused before speaking again.

'As a girl I used to try, sometimes, when out walking in the countryside with my family, to peel back the layers of time – to imagine the long-term development of the landscape around me. I did the same thing yesterday, when we went walking up in the hills. Going back one hundred years or so is never a problem. At that stage, I'm only just moving beyond the curve of a human lifespan, so to some extent I feel able to empathise with life as it was lived back then.

'Moving back further in time, it becomes more difficult. Standing stones. Burial cairns. When trying to find my way back into prehistory, all sense of understanding starts to fade. I can't imagine what life was like, what it must have felt like to be a human being. Their worldview would have been completely alien to us.'

A fat log burst in the wind-ruffled flames as Cynthia pursued her train of thought.

'Once I try to go back even further, into deep time, geological time, to the sculpting of the landforms beneath my feet, then my imagination fails me completely. All those thousands, millions of years become meaningless – an abstract number only. I can't connect them to my own tiny existence. It's the same, I suppose, when trying to look any distance into the future. It's hard enough to picture oneself not existing, let alone the planet itself. I can't imagine how bad things would be . . . for whoever, or whatever, followed us. My empathy can't reach that far ahead.'

Otto noticed that she was shivering slightly, and not only from the autumn chill. He drew closer to her in the firelight, trying to better protect her from the stirring easterly wind.

'Maybe tomorrow things will be better,' he said, finding his

260

voice once again. 'Maybe tomorrow they'll finally come to their senses.'

Throughout the 1960s, they participated in a number of anti-nuclear demonstrations. On one occasion, they joined a sit-down protest before the Ministry of Defence building in Whitehall. Otto was concerned about Cynthia taking part, as she was already four months pregnant with Daniel. Fearing a strong response from the authorities to this act of passive resistance, he tried to persuade her not to attend, but she had insisted.

'It's even more important now that we take part, isn't that obvious?' she asked him.

There was a hint of impatience in her voice as her hand rested on her belly.

Otto, however, remained worried. During the protest, he sat shielding her as best he could, while police officers waded into the crowd and dragged protesters away. Cynthia sat firm when two young officers approached them with purpose, but Otto quickly relented. Climbing to his feet and holding out a hand to ward off the policemen, he announced in a firm voice that his wife was pregnant, causing them to hold back self-consciously while he gently helped her up.

'You should act more responsibly, given your condition,' said one of the officers, as he tried to clear a path for Cynthia through the crowd.

'And so should *they*,' she responded angrily, pointing towards the MoD building, before recovering herself and thanking the officer for his help.

Following a thaw in Cold War relations, the profile of the anti-nuclear movement dimmed somewhat during the

1970s. But in the early 1980s, with a renewed heightening of East–West political tensions, fears of a large-scale nuclear conflict revived. Otto and Cynthia listened at the dinner table with a sense of déjà vu, as Daniel voiced his concerns.

'One push of a button by one of these maniacs in power, that's all it will take,' he said. 'And then we'll be gone . . . everyone.'

Glancing at each other, Cyn and Otto wished that they could somehow put their teenage son's mind at rest, but they didn't quite know what to say to him. Otto thought of offering some comforting platitude, about nothing having happened in the three decades since the Cold War began. But the words seemed to stick in his throat.

'I know that look,' Cynthia said to Otto afterwards. 'I felt exactly the same thing, twenty years ago. It's strange to see it in Daniel's eyes, too.'

In October 1983, she marched alongside her son and a group of his friends at a demonstration in central London, attended by an estimated one million people. Later that night, back home in Hampstead, as they lay in bed in the near-moonless dark, Cynthia described the scene to Otto, who had been unable to go due to work commitments. The top of the swaying oak tree was just visible outside, a softly moving shadow against the window.

Expressing surprise at the size of the protest, Cynthia reflected on the cyclical nature of the peace movement. It had now reached, perhaps even surpassed, the scale and intensity of the early 1960s.

'The old campaigns, the old causes, they never disappear completely,' she said. 'They simply wait their moment to return.'

'The old campaigners, too,' replied Otto. 'I haven't seen you this fired up in years.'

'Do you think so?'

'Definitely. I would say that your views now are more radical than when you were in your mid-twenties. It's refreshing to see, as it is precisely the opposite of what is supposed to happen as one grows older. I must admit I can sense my own energy levels decreasing somewhat, now that we're both turning fifty. I don't have quite the same vitality as before. Yet yours just keeps increasing.'

'Growing old gracefully has never much appealed to me,' Cynthia admitted. 'This might be one more mid-life crisis, or it might be the beginning of wisdom, I'm not sure which.'

Her voice in the darkness sounded fainter as they talked on. It was the end of a long day for her, Otto told himself. Yet it was that hour of the evening when Cynthia's thoughts ran deeply, even as she struggled in her fatigue to express them.

'I was thinking a little about it today,' she continued, 'during the middle of the demonstration. I was watching Daniel as he walked ahead with his friends. They were trying to stop their banner from blowing away in the breeze. It was flapping loose from one of its poles and at one point it managed to wrap itself around his head. The others were laughing and trying to rescue him from the folds. He looked clumsy, as he struggled to escape, but also determined, like a young version of you. And I thought while watching him wrestle with that banner that *he's* the reason I'm growing impatient with those in power.

'Do you remember all those years ago, when we sat beside our tent in the middle of the Lake District and waited to hear if the world would end? I said something about lacking the empathy to see far into the future? Well, I was wrong. They were the words of a young woman, a childless woman. Because all that changes once you have children. Your vision grows, somehow. Your empathy extends into the future . . . into *their* future. I can feel that future now, not as dry abstraction, but as physical reality. In my bones. I feel it pass via us through Daniel and his children, on down through the generations, and I feel how precarious it all is.'

Otto touched her shoulder in the darkness and waited for her to continue.

'It sounds vague, I know. Mystical, almost. But I don't know how else to express it. I feel more urgently these days that we must start to put things right. For Daniel's sake, and the others who follow. Because unlike before, I can sense their *potential*. I feel it, pressing down on me like a weight of responsibility. The empathy is difficult to bear, sometimes – it's like a genetic ache. But it's where all this new-found energy of mine has come from.'

These last words widened into a lengthy yawn, prompting Cynthia to break into a smile as she turned on her side towards Otto. He smiled, too, and stroked back the greying hair from her face. As they settled down to sleep, their limbs entwined instinctively in a complex but effortless arrangement; three decades of intimacy, enshrined in a single gesture.

While Cynthia slept, Otto lay awake a little longer, thinking the day over while listening to the rise and fall of his own breathing. Or was it Cynthia's breathing? He had to pause a moment to make the distinction. As with so many other aspects of their life together, the rhythm of the two had become almost inseparable.

Twenty-Seven

Emerging from Russell Square tube station, Otto absorbed the early afternoon scene. It was unambiguously sunny, the streets thick with tourists, making their way to and from the British Museum.

So here he was, then: the spot where it had all begun, and where it had more or less ended. The Alpha and the Omega, the A and the Z, separated by a few squares and streets.

The site of the old café where he had first spoken to Cynthia lay a few hundred yards to the west. But this was not what Otto had come to Bloomsbury to see. Turning south, he walked to the last destination on his inner map of memories: the leafy space of Queen Square. There he settled on a bench, rested his cane beside him and drew a deep breath.

The evening of 22 June 1985 began like any other. A concert was being given in front of Kenwood House, a former stately home on Hampstead Heath. Like hundreds of other people, Cynthia and Otto had taken along a picnic to enjoy the music and the Saturday-evening sunshine, locating themselves on a spare patch of grass on the hill overlooking the stage. Several friends were there with them, plus Anton, his wife Gayle and their youngest daughter Jessica – sitting and chatting around the large chequerboard blanket they had brought with them. Daniel was unable to join them that evening. He was inter-railing in Europe with some friends after completing his first year of study at Cambridge.

Anton was holding forth to Otto. There was nothing malicious in his tone, but he was becoming rather heated all the same; something to do with the Miners' Strike that had ended a few months earlier. It was a thorny subject between them. Gayle looked uncomfortable as she listened, glancing down at the stage below them and willing the orchestra to begin. There was some Mozart on the programme that evening, plus Tchaikovsky and Handel – the light-hearted, crowd-pleasing pieces rather than the great ones.

Their group was animated and lively, the babble of voices and bursts of laughter indicating a frisson of excitement at the thought of the concert to come. Cynthia, however, was quieter than usual, kneeling and pouring the red wine carefully into a row of plastic beakers. Otto had suggested that they cancel that evening, because of her headache, but Anton and his family were coming up especially from Surrey, and so she had taken some aspirin from the bathroom cabinet and told him with a smile that she would be fine. She didn't look fine, though. Very pale, he remembered thinking. The black rings that had recently appeared beneath her eyes were deeper than in previous days. Her lips looked thin and white.

As Anton continued speaking to him, Otto noticed in the

corner of his vision that Cynthia was swaying slightly, as if to an unheard rhythm. And then the long topple forward, almost in slow motion, her face landing heavily among the plastic beakers and the wine spreading over the rug. A sound, too – almost a sigh – as she did so. There was a momentary silence, shock, slight confusion among the frozen group. And then a stirring into life, a low hum of concern, the hands fluttering around Cynthia as Otto and Anton kneeled by her side. Someone reached for a bottle of water. They assumed that she had fainted from the warmth and believed this would be sufficient to revive her. But suddenly she was moving, a kind of convulsion, her body shaking violently as she lay face down on the blanket. And at that moment everything changed. A sense of fear began to take hold, their voices raised now, questioning. What do we do? We need help here – please help us, what do we do? People were looking over from the surrounding groups, some getting to their feet and coming over to see. One, a doctor, middle-aged, took charge. He bent over Cynthia, saw the foam coming from her mouth.

'We need an ambulance,' he said, 'and quickly.'

But they were a long way from an ambulance – there was no ambulance.

'We're in the middle of the fucking Heath,' Anton said.

And then Jessica was sprinting for a phone box, or to get help wherever she could. Others from their party, too – and people they didn't know – running for help because it was all that they could do. And the convulsions were getting worse.

Otto heard his own voice. 'Cyn,' he was saying, 'Cyn.'

But he almost didn't recognise it was his own voice speaking.

The doctor, sounding urgent, said: 'Help me turn her, we have to turn her over.'

Anton then said: 'She's dying ... I think she's dying,' and because he had used that word the clamour around them heightened.

Gayle tried to calm Anton, who was starting now to shout, and the wine from the blanket was running down Cynthia's face as they turned her over and it was the tongue, the doctor explained, he must stop the tongue from sliding back and blocking the windpipe. Otto's eyes were blind with fear and there was a pounding in his ears but he was holding her head still, just as the doctor had told him, and Anton was helping, too, while the doctor worked his fingers inside her mouth. Gayle was sobbing, and everyone around them was looking and yet not looking, and then suddenly people with yellow bibs appeared, running up the hill towards them. There was an ambulance on site, they said, and they lifted her carefully, as instructed by the doctor, and Cynthia appeared to resist and struck one of them in the face with a flailing arm, but it was the convulsions, the doctor said, keep carrying her down there, keep going.

Otto was walking quickly beside her as they carried her down the hill. Anton and Gayle were following and the crowds were parting before them and the music was starting now, the stage looming straight in front of them, and they were playing the introduction to *Eine Kleine Nachtmusik,* which used to be a favourite of Otto's mother, and they were at the ambulance and lifting her inside and the doctor was instructing them and Otto was getting in. Just the husband, someone said, but then Anton climbed in as well and then the doors were shutting behind them and they were driving away very quickly.

They couldn't see Cynthia, because the paramedics were all around her, but they could hear her moaning and Anton's eyes were large and staring, and they could hear the sound of the siren but it was strange and muffled in a way Otto had never heard before, because this time he was on the inside of it.

One of the paramedics spoke to them and his voice was calm but it didn't make Otto feel calm and he was replying to the paramedic but he didn't know what he was saying, and then they were pulling up at the Royal Free Hospital and the doors were opening and they were wheeling her out fast and through the doors of the entrance. Otto and Anton followed but they could only just keep up and then someone came to speak to them and the crowd of medics with Cynthia at their centre disappeared into the distance. The doctor in the white coat with the clipboard was asking them questions with a controlled urgency and they were answering and the doctor went away and they were offered somewhere to sit but they just kept pacing and pacing, neither saying anything for minutes at a time, and this was unusual because Anton was normally such a talkative fellow and besides they were always arguing, and then they looked up and someone else in a white coat was coming down the corridor towards them, a woman, but different to the one before, a different young woman who looked as though she was going to say something to them and stopped before them and opened her mouth to speak.

'It's a tumour,' the doctor told them. 'She has a tumour on her brain. We've sedated her but we don't have the specialist expertise to operate here. We're transferring her immediately to the neurological hospital at Queen Square. An ambulance is standing by. Mr Laird, you can go with her . . .'

*

269

On the bench in Queen Square, Otto paused to catch his breath. It had become noticeably laboured in the minutes before. He tried to return to the scene imprinted on his mind but his thoughts were becoming confused. In a corner of the square he saw his young self standing, dressed in a tweed jacket and flannel trousers, waiting for Cynthia to arrive. They were going that evening to a local jazz club. One of her favourite artists from the States was topping the bill.

As the young Otto glimpsed Cynthia in her beret, her familiar bouncing walk, approaching him from the other side of the square, he stepped eagerly from the pavement to greet her. But as he did so, an ambulance cut across his path, its blue lights flashing, missing him by a matter of inches. The young Otto stared intently after the ambulance, appearing to realise that Cynthia was inside. *He* was inside, too, his hair now grey, his midriff thicker; holding her hand and whispering softly, trying to keep the panic from his voice. Arriving at the hospital on the opposite side of the square, he jumped out after Cynthia, who had an oxygen mask strapped across her face and was being wheeled into the entranceway on a stretcher. The young Cynthia was no longer walking towards the young Otto, but standing still in the middle of the square. Her head in the beret was turned away from him, looking over at the scene taking place at the entrance to the hospital.

Otto shook his head. The memory that was more than a memory dissolved away, suddenly. It was replaced by another, just as vivid.

*

In a pub located on another corner of Queen Square, Otto saw himself sitting at a crowded table, his black fringe falling low across his eyes, beaming as he raised a pint of bitter to his lips. His colleagues were toasting him, Cynthia too, on achieving 'architectonic perfection'. But the broad smile faded as he caught sight of the older man entering the bar – the expression one of ruin, the eyes deep with something unimaginable.

Time, all times, seemed to converge on this place, merging into one. Otto reached for the cane beside him. He wanted to get up from the bench and go – he wanted to leave the square altogether. But he couldn't move, the dizziness was too strong, the circling memories wouldn't allow him to depart. They were fragmentary, but that was inevitable, for life itself had been fragmentary at that time, after Cynthia's collapse on the Heath. A quick series of jolts, one after another, with no time to adjust to one before another followed hard in its slipstream.

They had warned him that she would probably not survive the emergency surgery, but somehow she did. The pressure was released, and they removed the majority of the tumour, but it was already too deeply embedded to extract in its entirety. It would be a week until they received the results of the tests, to discover whether it was malignant or benign.

Cynthia recovered consciousness after a day or so, but was groggy and heavily sedated, only just grasping the information that the surgeons, together with Otto, gently imparted to her. She looked so ill, so pale and fragile as she lay in the bed; and although Otto had been warned to expect it, the huge scar running across her shaven head had caused him, on first seeing it, to stifle a sob.

271

After two days of trying, Otto managed to get news to Daniel, who returned home immediately from his travels. They embraced for a long time at the entrance to the hospital, without any of the usual awkwardness, but their conversation afterwards was subdued. Daniel, like Otto, had been stunned into silence, overwhelmed by the suddenness and severity of events.

In the ward, Otto found it difficult to watch as Cynthia came round and saw her son.

'Don't worry,' she said, as she held him by the hand. 'Don't worry.'

Daniel could barely speak. His words were little more than a whisper. She told him she was sorry to have spoiled his holiday.

For a few hours each day, Otto and Daniel were allowed to sit at her bedside. At night, back at home, they talked a little about Daniel's travels, but all normal communication was an effort. Silence, when it fell, was a relief. One thing alone occupied father and son. They talked about it, but sparingly, in order to spare themselves. The results of the tests would be through in a couple of days. The wait, meanwhile, was excruciating. Time stretched them out upon its rack.

Twenty-Eight

After that endless week came the second terrible jolt. The tumour was malignant, graded at four, the most malignant form of all. Cynthia could undergo chemo and radiotherapy, and perhaps a second operation at some point. But although the specialists could slow the tumour's advance, they were powerless, ultimately, to prevent it. They estimated that she had eighteen months to live.

It was Otto who broke the news to her, late one afternoon, when she had recovered sufficiently from the initial trauma to be informed. Entering the dimly lit ward, he approached her pale form, resting on the bed. Her eyes were closed and her face turned upwards. Her breathing was as shallow as the breeze that stirred the curtains. She appeared transfigured; spectral.

He lowered himself into the chair beside the bed, and after a few seconds her eyes slowly opened. She seemed to have sensed his presence.

'Otto,' she said, with some difficulty.

Her voice was barely audible above the sound of the

afternoon traffic. Life, through the open window, continued as normal.

He reached across and took her hand. It felt weak and emaciated: the pulse was barely there. The smile she offered up to him was a needle through his heart.

'Any news?'

He looked downwards.

'It's not good, Cyn,' he managed to say, before he was unable to continue.

She was very calm and did not seem surprised. It was her own body, after all, which she could no doubt read as well as the experts. He had anticipated comforting her when breaking the news. Instead, the reverse had happened. She stroked his hair like a small child, whispering words of solace as he kneeled weeping with his head lowered to her lap.

'My beautiful Otto ... my beautiful boy,' she said to him over and again.

The curtain billowed inwards in the afternoon air.

It was then that Otto's initial shock transformed into something deeper. He realised that Cynthia was far ahead of him in terms of understanding what was taking place. She had already crossed the threshold – he was just reaching it now. He had been hoping that this was something else – an interlude, of some kind, in their lives. Dreadful – transformative, even – but an interlude, nonetheless. He had convinced himself that the ship would somehow right itself; normality, in some form, return. But he understood now, as he felt her fingers running weakly through his hair, that it was something he had not dared think about until that moment. It was not a one-off incident, a nightmare that would pass. It was the slow and inevitable unfolding of a tragedy; the beginning of the nightmare, not its culmination. She had already grasped this, had already accepted her own body's betrayal. Otto had not known it until now.

There was almost no time to adjust to this new situation before the various forms of treatment began. At first radiotherapy, which could take place only in a single phase, because of the doses of radiation involved. This was followed over time by two courses of chemotherapy. Each treatment brought suffering, both physical and psychological, yet Otto and Daniel were astounded at Cynthia's resilience. There was an eerie serenity about her. She had moved into a different state to the rest of them – a liminal state, perhaps – and exuded an air of quiet calm while emotion raged around her.

There were times when the chemotherapy rendered her unrecognisable, and on several occasions visiting friends broke down in front of her on seeing its effects. And yet she would smile and try to comfort them as best she could. She appeared to feel almost guilty about her condition – guilty of the mental suffering that others were going through on her behalf. As to her own great suffering, physical and mental, she gave little indication of its depth. It was as though she were trying to shield, as best she could, all those around her from the reality. But Otto knew that the headaches from which she suffered were at best intense, and at worst unbearable, if eased somewhat by the large shots of morphine that formed part of her daily quota of drugs, averting the constant danger that she might bite through her tongue with the pain.

And then there was the question of time, the new form of time in which Cynthia and her family now found themselves. In a sense there was no time now, at least not in the way that it is usually measured out. This could make things difficult.

On occasion, friends would say something without thinking – a reference to some event that was taking place in a few months' time. And then they would pull up suddenly, embarrassed, because they realised that she might no longer be around to see the event of which they were speaking. At first the family tried to avoid talking about the future, but this proved impossible. In almost every conversation, it would somehow arise. Otto realised, then, just how much we live in the future – talking about our hopes and plans. To avoid embarrassment for others, and perhaps to maintain the strength to continue, the family began to allow themselves to talk about the future. It was no longer taboo.

'A holiday would be nice,' Cynthia told them, as they sat beside her bed. 'Not now, of course, or any time soon, but maybe once these treatments are out of the way. When Danny gets a break from his studies.'

Otto smiled and nodded. Daniel took up the theme with some enthusiasm.

'I think it's a great idea. It's been a while now since we went away as a family. Where would you like to go, Mum? Anywhere special in mind?'

Cynthia's eyes shone briefly with a memory of bougainvillea.

'Greece would be nice,' she said. 'It's been so many years.'
She looked at Otto.

'Though I'm not sure I'll be up to clambering over any ruins this time.'

'That's okay,' he said. 'There are plenty of other things we can do. Sit on the beach . . . enjoy the views.'

'Exactly,' she replied. 'And it's the light that I most want to experience again.'

She turned to Daniel.

'You would love the clarity of light there, Danny. Don't you think so, Otto?'

Otto nodded, his look distant.

'It's most unusual,' Cynthia continued, 'especially in the early autumn. Intensely bright yet also soft, like a paradox or puzzle.'

They planned and discussed the future like this whenever Daniel was home from Cambridge: holidays and various projects; redecorating the living room, or undertaking some new architectural research together. And in doing so, they would forget, at times, that the future they were planning was imaginary.

'But then most futures are,' Cynthia said to Daniel one day. 'Life rarely works out as we plan it.'

Otto wondered, sometimes, what time must feel like to her now; what she must think about as she lay on the sofa near the living-room window, from where she could watch the swaying oak tree with the birds flitting in and out of its branches. Cynthia must have entered the time spoken about by mystics and philosophers – one eternal now. Everything was present to her. She didn't talk about it a great deal – just once or twice she made the allusion; telling Otto there were many things she had come to understand; and reassuring him that, at a deeper level, beneath the constant pain, she had found a kind of peace.

When her headaches were not too severe, she and Otto liked to listen to music together. At her request, several months into her illness, he climbed up into the loft to retrieve an old box of vinyl records. It had lain there gathering dust for nearly twenty years, ever since the move from Bloomsbury. They worked their way through these records as circumstances allowed.

One evening, they put on an album by the saxophonist Sonny Rollins. Cynthia, who felt well enough to leave her bed that day, was curled beside Otto on the sofa.

'You didn't tread on my toes, not once,' she said to him, drowsily.

'What do you mean?' he asked.

'At the jazz club.'

Otto's eyes opened.

'My goodness. I thought I recognised this tune.'

There was a sadness about the smiles they exchanged.

'That was quite some evening,' he said to her.

'It was,' she said. 'The best of evenings. Strange how suddenly, and how naturally, everything can change.'

The record played on in the background. No more words were spoken or needed. They were back there now, in the heaving maelstrom of the club – she in a polka-dot blouse and puffball skirt; he in his second-hand tweed jacket and flannel trousers. On stage, through a haze of sweet-smelling smoke, they could see the four-piece band: tenor sax, piano, double bass and drums, playing with dazzling dexterity. On the dance floor, young couples, propelled by the music's energy, spun and flew with the fearlessness of trapeze artists.

'Do you like it?' Cynthia had shouted into his ear, her head nodding in time to the music.

'Yes, it's fascinating.'

'Come and dance.'

Before Otto knew what was happening, she had drawn him out onto the dance floor. Abandoning her body to the music, throwing her hair to and fro across her face, she invited him with a smile to follow her lead. At first he was restrained in his movements, unnerved by the bodies whirling around him. He backed into a young woman, turning to apologise only to find that she had disappeared in an explosion of taffeta.

'Don't worry . . . relax,' Cynthia called into his ear. 'Follow me. Feel your way into the music.'

Otto began to align his movements with hers, adjusting his mind and body to the shifting mass of the dance floor. Spatial awareness had never been his strong point, and here it needed to be especially fine-tuned. And yet, so caught up was he with the sight of Cynthia dancing that soon he forgot all those obstacles around him. Cyn, her face aglow and her eyes sparkling, her mouth a beaming smile, twirled around and against him in a way that was quite intoxicating. His limbs started to loosen in an instinctive response. Soon he was moving around the floor with surprising ease.

'Yes,' Cyn called again, in between breathless spins. 'That's good.'

Gaining in confidence now, Otto began to dance more freely. He no longer felt constrained by self-consciousness, or a fear of causing injury to others. His arms swung loose and his hips gyrated with an ease he had not known he possessed. Cynthia beamed her approval, matching his movements turn for turn. Together, they cut quite a figure on the dance floor. Other couples turned to watch them, nodding their heads and shouting their encouragement.

That evening, after walking Cynthia home, Otto did not return to his bedsit in Lambeth. In the half-light of her tiny bedroom, the engines of the passing cars rattling the window in its frame, a night of heady exploration followed. The alien body usually inhabited by Otto seemed to become his own at last. The sound of Cynthia's voice, even the texture of her skin, became charged with a strange electricity, animating and replenishing his own.

As the record came to a halt, the needle catching in the run-out groove, Otto went to take it from the turntable.

'Beautiful,' Cynthia said quietly.

Did she mean the music? Or the memory? Or was such a distinction possible?

Sliding the record into its sleeve, Otto crouched and placed it in the cardboard box. One of the other fading covers caught his eye. It carried a photo of the soprano Renata Tebaldi – a collection of her favourite Italian arias.

Otto lifted the album from the box and scanned through the titles.

'I'd completely forgotten we had this,' he said, holding it up for her to see. 'Who bought it for us?'

Cynthia peered over.

'*You* did, I think.'

He looked at it again.

'Are you sure?'

'Yes. Don't you remember? It was after we saw her at Covent Garden that summer. *Tosca*, wasn't it, with Di Stefano and Tito Gobbi? You bought the record from that store on Shaftesbury Avenue.'

Otto thought a moment.

'Oh yes . . . so I did.'

'And *I'm* the one who's supposed to be losing my mind.'

He watched as she adjusted her headscarf.

'How is it feeling this evening?' he asked.

'Moderately painful, but bearable. I dosed up on morphine, earlier on, so the music is sounding rather wonderful!'

She smiled at him. He smiled, too, but furrows marked his brow.

'Do you want to get some rest now or would you like to hear another?'

'Another, please.'

'Any requests?'

'You choose. Or pick one at random. I really don't mind what we listen to.'

Otto removed the Tebaldi album from its sleeve.

'I'm glad we found these,' Cynthia said, in a sudden outpouring of feeling. 'I want to hear them before they disappear.'

He looked confused.

'The records?'

'No, the memories.'

He paused while lowering the needle onto the vinyl.

'Your memory is in fine condition . . . as you've just proved.'

The needle touched down, a little heavily.

'For the time being, maybe. But for how much longer, realistically? They said the deterioration could come at any time.'

An aria began. '*Vissi d'arte*'.

Otto returned to the sofa and settled down beside Cynthia.

'It's true, of course,' he said, softly. 'I don't wish to deny the reality. I realise you are only stating the facts. And yet, at this moment in time, we've found a place of shelter within the storm. We must try to make the most of it while we can.'

'You're right,' she answered. 'I love these evenings together.

Talking, listening to music. It's such a treat. The hospital feels very distant.'

Otto smoothed down the pillow on which her head was resting.

'Can I get you anything? Something to eat or drink?'

'No. Things are perfect, just as they are. A whisky would be nice, right now, but that sort of thing is out of the question these days. So I'll settle for this glass of water, these pills and a little imagination. What a beautiful tone Tebaldi had, didn't she? I think I may prefer her voice to Callas.'

It took them several weeks to get through every record in the box. There were quite a few of them, and there were evenings when Cynthia's headaches made it impossible to listen. At such times she preferred to lie in silence in the dark. Otto would sit beside her, or (if she asked for solitude) busy himself with some work in the study; listening out in case she happened to call him.

The last record they reached was Glenn Gould's 1955 recording of the *Goldberg Variations*; the first thing they had bought together in Marchmont Street.

Otto inspected the surface of the vinyl.

'It's in excellent condition,' he said.

'That's hardly surprising. We only played it a few times.'

'And then completely forgot about it, once we had finished our studies and moved into the world outside. Odd, the way these things happen.'

Recently, they had bought Gould's second version of the *Variations*, recorded in the early 1980s. Autumnal and reflective, it contrasted to the ebullience of this earlier recording.

'I remember packing those records into the box,' Otto said,

as the album neared its conclusion. 'It was the morning we moved here from Bloomsbury. You must have been about six months pregnant at the time.'

'I can't remember it now. All I do recall is how rotten I felt.'

Otto smiled, almost in apology.

'It wasn't the easiest of pregnancies. I understand your reluctance to have more children later.'

'I've never vomited so much in my life. Not until the last few months, anyway.'

A look clouded Otto's face. He felt the need to raise her.

'You looked terrific, at the drinks party. The one we held the night before leaving Marchmont Street. You stroked your stomach, through your henna-dyed dress, as you chatted to your friends.'

Cynthia looked surprised.

'I didn't do that, did I?'

'You did, in fact. Constantly.'

She smiled.

'How unpleasant for everyone. What an exhibitionist I must have looked!'

'Not at all. You didn't even realise you were doing it. That's what made it such an endearing gesture.'

She lifted her head from the pillow and leaned it cautiously against his shoulder.

'I don't remember a farewell party at all.'

'I expect it's because you were feeling unwell at the time.'

'No. It isn't that. It's a part of this bloody condition. The tumour has claimed that particular memory. I wonder how many others might have gone.'

They were silent for a while, listening to the rise and fall of the piano.

A thought struck Otto.

'We chose Daniel's name at that party.'

'Did we? You'll have to remind me, I'm afraid.'

'You called me across, when your friends were chatting about something else. You whispered it into my ear. "If it's a boy, shall we call him Daniel?" I just smiled at the time, said nothing.'

'You were pleased, though?'

'I was. Surprised, as well. Until then, you'd been reluctant to discuss any names for the baby.'

'I was being superstitious, I suppose, not wanting to tempt fate. There were so many things I was afraid of at that time. The pain of childbirth, the responsibility that would follow, the state of the whole bloody planet, in fact. Yet I came to feel more comfortable with the idea of having a baby. Mentally, at least.'

Otto nodded.

'Something definitely changed in you. I noticed it the night of the party. You were more relaxed than I'd seen you in a long time, despite the discomfort you were feeling.'

A few seconds later, he felt moved to speak again, his voice just about audible above the piano.

'You had a painterly quality that evening. You glowed with a peculiar light. Brimming and overflowing with life: yours, Daniel's ... It's something I'll never forget.'

Neither spoke for a long time after that. Eventually, the record came to a finish.

'That's it,' said Otto, a few minutes later, reluctantly breaking the spell that had descended. 'We've listened to everything now. Would you like to hear anything again?'

Cynthia didn't answer at first. She was gazing into the distance.

'No. I don't think so. It's been a wonderful experience, an important one, for me. But I think it's probably time that I left them behind.'

He nodded, without surprise.

'Shall I put the box away?'

'Yes, please. You can put it back into the loft, if you like. Or maybe give the records to a charity shop.'

'All of them?'

'No, not all. Keep one or two. You know the ones I mean. But we shouldn't fall too far into the past, tempting though that is in this kind of present. Nostalgia can be such a stupefying drug, if one isn't careful. Worse than anything the doctors have prescribed me. I mustn't allow the memories to cloud what time we have.'

Otto crouched down and began to remove her favourites from the box.

'That would be an error,' he agreed.

Twenty-Nine

They tried throughout Cyn's illness to live each moment to the full, discovering a new-found intensity in everyday things. And, despite the seriousness of her condition, and the dreadful sense of reckoning that hung over everything at that time, there were moments of real happiness; more, from Otto's perspective, than he would ever have anticipated.

Whenever she felt able, they took day trips out, mostly to the countryside, to do those simple and life-affirming things that are so easily taken for granted in the normal course of events. They didn't try to do anything particularly special; discovering, to Otto's surprise, that the most essential experiences in life are also the most straightforward, even the most mundane. It was just such moments that Cynthia craved to experience, once she knew that her time was short.

As summer turned to autumn, for instance, she loved to go blackberry picking in the hedges lining the lanes of the Chilterns. The season was short, just a few weeks from mid-September. While in remission, in October 1985, she was able to walk almost unaided alongside her family, plucking out the ripest berries with an expert eye. When undergoing chemotherapy, however, as in the second year of her illness, even this small act proved difficult. Her fingers, badly swollen from the drugs, would catch on the thorns as she tried to work them between the thickets. Some days she felt too unwell even to climb from the wheelchair and make the attempt. And so she would point out to Otto and Daniel where the best berries lay, instructing them from her chair as they moved along the bushes.

Back at the home of Cynthia's parents – who were elderly and frail, but as stoical as their daughter in the face of her illness – they would transform the blackberries into pots of jam, laughing in the kitchen as Otto and Daniel tried to lend Cynthia's mother a hand and usually ended up getting in her way.

The days spent blackberry picking were uncannily peaceful. It was a soothing experience for all of them. Just once, during that time, was there a brief ripple of distress amid the calm of the berry-rich lanes. It came in September 1986, shortly after Cyntha noticed that her eyesight was starting to deteriorate.

She and Otto were browsing alone. The light in the lanes was dense and golden. From her wheelchair, she pointed out a cluster of berries, high up in one of the hedgerows. She could just make out the purple plump smudges in the distance.

'Those look beautiful, don't they?' she said to him.

Otto, desperate to bring her even the smallest of comforts, stretched up an arm to try and reach them. But he couldn't, he couldn't reach the berries in the highest thickets, even with his great height and his ability to balance on the tips of his toes.

'I can't get to them,' he said to her. 'I can't reach the bloody things . . .'

He drew himself up to his full height, but still the precious berries lay beyond his grasp. As he tottered around, his toes started to sag beneath the strain of his weight, and finally he was forced to give up the attempt.

'Dammit,' he exclaimed loudly, landing back onto his heels, his voice suddenly trembling with emotion. 'I'm so sorry.'

And then, before she could tell him not to worry, he had moved away swiftly, somewhere out of sight behind the wheelchair. Cynthia sensed the slight tremor that shook his shoulders. She wanted to turn and hold him, then; to tell him not to be frightened for her; to assure him she was ready for whatever lay ahead. But she lacked the physical strength to rise and respond as her instincts told her. And so she had no choice but to sit and wait quietly, her hands resting on her lap, while Otto silently recomposed himself behind her.

After a minute or so, she felt him take the handles of the wheelchair once again. His voice, when it sounded above her, was strong and reassuring.

'I never thought I'd say this,' he said, 'but I wish I were a few inches taller!'

He kissed the top of her head and smiled down at her brightly, determined that nothing unsettling should intrude upon the quiet peace of the lanes.

'It's okay,' she told him, with a pat of his hand, as they continued on their way. 'We have more than enough of those berries, already.'

*

During the course of her illness, Cynthia managed two seasons of blackberry picking. They had hoped that she might make a third, as there was a further period of remission following a second operation, in November 1986, and more chemotherapy. For a while her memory and eyesight grew no worse. But the tumour began to grow again, in the summer of 1987, and the doctors warned that a third operation would not be as effective as the others. She elected to have it, anyway; there was a chance it might buy her a few more months. The surgery would take place, they told her, in the next few weeks.

At this point, the tone of their conversations changed. Cynthia became matter-of-fact; practical. There were issues that had to be dealt with; difficult subjects addressed.

'You must find someone, after I'm gone,' she told Otto. 'In the fullness of time. When you feel that you are able.'

He looked at her, almost with incomprehension.

'I don't really know what to say,' he said, quietly.

She steeled herself to continue.

'It's difficult. But we should talk about these things. Sensibly. Without sentiment. After all, it's not the first time we've had to do so.'

She smiled as she said this, but her eyes seemed changed. Still beautiful, but tired. The world they looked out upon was different to before.

'You mustn't grieve alone for the rest of your life. I know you, Otto, in a way that no one else does. I know how susceptible you are to melancholy, however well you disguise it from the world. I know how hard you find life sometimes, even when things are going well.'

She paused then, not wanting to become overly serious.

'I've seen what a gloomy old git you can be!'

She smiled again, and he tried his best to return it.

'Keep the darkness at bay,' she told him. 'Try to live happily, and well. Don't let this illness finish you as well as me. That's what I find so gruelling about the cancer. It's not contained to me alone – the ripples spread far outwards. So many others are affected, psychologically. Family, friends, professional acquaintances. And the closer they are to me, the more I make them suffer. That's the cruellest aspect of all. But you have to go on fighting it afterwards, like I'm fighting it now. *I* can't beat it, but you and Danny can.'

Otto nodded. Despite her wish not to alarm him, deeper fears were starting to emerge.

'I'm worried about the future,' she said. 'How you will both get by. Danny's coping well . . . outwardly at least. But then he's always been good at disguising his feelings.'

'He learned from a master.'

Cynthia sought to keep him positive.

'Don't be hard on yourself. You already have more than enough to deal with. Don't take the weight of the universe on your shoulders. You're a good father, Otto. We've raised a wonderful son. No time now for guilt or regrets.'

He squeezed her hand. She paused before speaking again.

'Look out for each other, won't you?'

'We will.'

'I hope so.'

He glanced at her, perturbed.

'It seems to be something that's worrying you. You said exactly the same thing to Daniel and me a few days ago.'

'I understand the two of you so well, you see. I know how hard you find it to share your emotions.'

Another pause ensued. This was proving rather difficult. Cynthia pushed back the sudden wave of emotion to retain her poise.

'There are other things we need to discuss. Financial things. Practical things. I should draw up a will. I've been avoiding it until now. Cowardly of me, really.'

'Now who's being hard on themselves?'

'Perhaps. But let's make the necessary arrangements. Soon – while there's time. I don't want to leave any loose threads for you to manage. Things will be tough enough without those.'

'I'll make some calls.'

'Thank you. I'm grateful. I realise that none of this is easy.'

The will was arranged in the next few weeks, along with the sale of the textiles firm. Such issues should have been deeply painful to address – in retrospect they were – but at the time Cynthia was so phlegmatic in her approach, so determined not to give in to the kind of maudlin sentimentality that might have swamped them completely and left them useless, that all conversations took place in a businesslike fashion, with the minimum of what she called 'unnecessary fuss'.

The third operation took place in late July. As the doctors had warned, Cynthia did not bounce back this time. She regained consciousness, and could still speak with reasonable lucidity for a few weeks, but she was unable to leave her wheelchair, even to walk a few steps. As the days passed, her conversation became increasingly confused and eventually incoherent. Her vision was deserting her. When it became clear that the tumour was advancing rapidly, she was moved into a hospice in central London. Otto and Daniel were constantly at her side.

The room in the hospice was a hushed and twilit place. The nurses, quiet as ghosts, moved discreetly around the bed, administering drugs or changing drips as needed. They always smiled kindly, exchanging a few words with Cynthia, Otto and Daniel before drifting away to tend to patients in other rooms. Cynthia's parents travelled down twice from the Chilterns, but the frail health of her father made this a difficult undertaking. Instead, Otto telephoned them at home last thing each evening, keeping them updated on their daughter's condition. Meanwhile, he and Daniel sought to make her as comfortable as possible.

Each day they brought fresh flowers and placed them on her bedside table. Within two weeks of her arrival at the hospice, however, she could no longer see or acknowledge them. Her hearing outlasted her sight and speech. She remained responsive for a few more days. They played her favourite music on a tape recorder of Daniel's, placing the speaker a few inches from her ear. Even when she was no longer sentient, Otto sometimes thought he saw the trace of a smile; at the sound of a piece by Bach, for instance, or something by Thelonious Monk. Soon, however, even music could not reach her. All of her faculties had gone.

As they waited for the end, the sense of despair threatened to overwhelm them. Death hovered over Cynthia's comatose form like a physical presence.

There was a café, near the hospice, which became a place of respite for them.

'You look terrible,' Daniel told his father, from across one of its tables.

'You do, too,' Otto replied.

The café wasn't busy. It was the lull before the lunchtime surge. Before them, on the table, stood two plates of untouched food. Daniel, unshaven, his hair unwashed and tousled, had a wildness about his eyes those last few days. Otto looked somewhat less dishevelled: the signs of defeat were less obvious in him. He wore a clean white shirt and his hair was only moderately unkempt. Yet, as Daniel noted, there was a small red nick on the curve of his father's chin, where he had cut himself while shaving distractedly that morning.

Neither of them said much in the café, the pop music from the radio providing a welcome cover for their thoughts, but eventually Daniel felt compelled to speak.

'I'm sinking, Dad. Completely. I'm not sure I can take much more of this.'

Otto prodded his food, sensing that Daniel needed him to say something; to release him from this terrible burden.

'Daniel ...' he said, pausing a moment, buying time to properly order his words. 'Whatever it is you decide to do, I fully understand. It's an impossible situation. She no longer knows us. She no longer knows anything. It makes no difference, frankly, who is around her.'

Gratitude and tears filled Daniel's eyes. He held himself together enough to speak.

'I think I'm going back to Cambridge. I'm so tired ... I can't think straight. I don't know what I can do to help her.'

Hurt and compassion intermingled inside Otto as he found the right words to say to his son.

'There's nothing more any of us can do. She's already gone. As Cynthia, I mean.'

Daniel nodded.

'That's what I wanted to say. When her friends phone each

evening at the house, asking me how she is, how I am, how you are, I no longer know what to say to them. It's gone beyond words now. She's wasted away completely. Yet still, somehow, it continues. It's horrendous.'

I must face this alone, Otto thought.

He tried to reassure Daniel.

'I understand. It's better if you go. You can spend the next few days with your friends. They'll look after you, they seem a nice crowd. It isn't fair to expect you to go through any more.'

Daniel's head was bowed.

'I feel terrible,' he said. 'I'm so sorry . . .'

Otto's voice was gentle.

'I'll call you. I'll let you know what's happening. Let you know when . . . you know . . . when it's finished.'

'Thanks, Dad.'

Daniel's head turned away for a second. The music from the radio no longer covered their silence.

'When do you plan to go back?'

'This evening, I think. I'll catch the train at seven.'

'That early? Of course. As you wish.'

Otto looked down at his plate. Daniel watched him, helpless.

'I'll need to go back to the house,' he added, 'to collect my things. I'll catch the tube up in a little while.'

Otto checked his watch.

'Will you come back to the hospice, first? Or would you rather go immediately? I think it's probably time that I headed back there.'

'I'll come. For half an hour or so. I'd like to spend a little time with Mum.'

Otto nodded.

'Of course.'

'I'm sorry, Dad.'

'It's okay ... it's okay. I understand.'

Otto's gaze was far away, his words sounded strained. He reached for his wallet and signalled to the waiter, but his actions seemed strangely mechanical. He no longer appeared to inhabit himself.

'I understand,' he said again. 'It's okay, Daniel. But please don't catch the Underground back and forth. You look tired. The trains will be busy. Let me arrange a taxi for you, at least.'

For the next few days, Otto remained at Cynthia's bedside, occasionally grabbing an hour or two's sleep on a mattress in a corner of the room. He talked to her often, although she couldn't hear him: about the past, about their lives, the experiences they had shared. He hoped, somehow, that it would ease her final hours, like the palliative drugs that flowed through her system. But the memories, as he expressed them, were increasingly confused.

'I didn't tread on your toes,' he said. 'Your puffball skirt was twirling. And then, at the party, all those years later, you wore that henna-dyed dress. You stroked your belly, with Daniel inside, as you chatted away to your friends. You didn't know you were doing it, of course. I'm sorry if I embarrassed you when I mentioned it that time. But it was unconscious, you see, that gesture of yours, and unconscious gestures are the ones that most reveal us ... they're the ones that stay with those we leave behind ... '

The next morning, Otto was woken by an unfamiliar rustling sound. Cynthia was in a state of agitation.

He jumped up from the mattress and called for a nurse.

'What is it?' he asked her.

She went away quickly. When she returned, several colleagues were with her.

Cynthia died later that day, with Otto at her side. The final hours of disintegration were difficult. Her vacant body clung instinctively to life, refusing to release her from its hold. And yet, by the middle of the afternoon, all signs of struggle had ceased in her. She lay peaceful and still, her breathing increasingly shallow.

Otto held her hand through her final moments, his head lowered and his eyes closed. Her passing, when it came, was indistinguishable from what had gone before. One form of absence became another. Then, as he opened his eyes and looked once more into her ashen face, a voice from somewhere in the room told him it was over.

Afterwards, when he had recovered some strength, he telephoned Daniel and then Cynthia's parents. The words they exchanged were kind and gentle: they briefly discussed arrangements for the funeral. Leaving the hospice, he walked the streets aimlessly, finding himself near an entrance to Regent's Park. There, he sat for a while on a bench beside the boating lake. A chill breeze ruffled its surface. The first of the leaves were turning yellow. It was the blackberry-picking season, Otto realised.

Thirty

Signs greeted Otto on the doors of each lift: COUNCIL ALERTED – REPAIR IMMINENT.

'Blast,' he said, looking around and waving his cane at nobody in particular.

Up to this point, he had been fortunate. Only one of the lifts had been out of action at any one time. This afternoon, all four of them had broken at once. Clearly the central pulley system had given up completely.

Just to be certain, he pushed some buttons and held his ear to the doors. No sound of mechanical activity could be heard inside the shaft.

'*Scheiße,*' he added, not especially wishing to begin the journey up the central staircase. He stood around rather pointlessly for a moment, as though hoping for some alternative route to appear. There was not even a sign of any other residents with whom he could at least have shared his displeasure.

'Fucking building,' he concluded, as a final insult to the

empty hallway, before bracing himself and taking his first tentative steps on the stairs.

This was a nuisance. Otto felt tired, even a little disorientated. He was running late and in danger of missing his flight back to Geneva. If that were to happen, the phone call to Anika would not be one he would relish.

He regretted, now, having made the difficult journey to Bloomsbury. He could have chosen to visit any number of destinations that afternoon, perhaps taken a stroll along the Thames. Yet for some reason he had chosen to inflict that upon himself, and he no longer understood why. The trip had achieved nothing, beyond resurrecting some deeply painful memories, and it had left him feeling physically unwell into the bargain. The tube trains back had been packed and stifling. He couldn't get a seat and his spine had developed a painful twinge. During the walk up to Marlowe House from the station, his stomach had started to hurt once more.

Otto was at a loss to explain his behaviour.

It must be that maudlin streak again, the one that Cynthia warned me about. She would not have been happy about my choice of sightseeing today. The neurological hospital – what on earth was I thinking?

Just three flights up, with nine more to go, he was already feeling breathless. Resting his hand on the flaking yellow paint of the banister, he glanced above and saw the radiating spokes of the staircase, circling to the furthest reaches of his vision. High, high above him, they disappeared into the darkness near the top.

The air felt solemn and heavy. His footsteps echoed in the silence. He would like to rest, but was aware of how many things he still had to do. Use the lavatory, collect his case, make sure the gas was off and lock the door as he left. Oh, and he must remember to post the key back through the letterbox of his apartment. It seemed straightforward enough, but Otto was of an age when even the simplest actions could take him an eternity. Some hours, some days, were much slower than others. Clearly he wasn't up to speed today.

Glancing off to the left, he saw a series of narrow windows, running up the walls like arrow slits in a turret. As the sun broke free of a cloud, needle-thin points of light pierced the gloom.

Otto set off again, circling steadily in his ascent – one hand gripping the peeling banister while the other pressed the tip of his cane into the step above. He thought of their walking holiday in the Lake District, all those decades before. Travelling at a steeply sloping angle had seemed straightforward enough back then. Now it felt unnatural, as though he were asking his body to perform some task for which it was simply not designed. With irritation, he pictured himself just a few hours earlier. He remembered gazing up in self-satisfaction at the endless turns of the staircase. Poetic, he had called it then.

'Silly old sod,' he muttered.

It wasn't for him to judge the building's aesthetic value: he really ought to leave all that to others. Anyway, what was more important: a beautifully crafted staircase or an elevator system that worked properly? This question seemed increasingly pertinent, the higher up he climbed.

Otto wished they had spent more time on the lifts, back when Marlowe House was being planned. They should have focused on improving their quality, maybe at the expense of the ill-fated sculpture garden. Eight sculptures seemed extravagant, with the benefit of hindsight, especially since they had all dis-appeared or ended up headless.

If the place is saved and given a listing, maybe we can do something about that.

He paused again to look up to the roof, but the intimidating spiral above his head did not appear to have decreased by much. More beads of sweat had broken out on his brow. He mopped these away impatiently with his handkerchief. The great dizziness he was starting to feel, however, was less easy to brush aside.

Oh, for a moving staircase right now, an escalator to glide on . . .

And then, as if upon command, as if the thought had somehow brought itself into existence, the staircase began to move. Otto felt himself lift slowly forwards, gasping slightly at the unexpected motion. His feet were no longer moving, but somehow he was moving. His body was being propelled by an invisible force. The staircase moved silently, winding steadily upwards, level by level, with no churning of a motor to reveal the hidden source of its magical power.

Once his initial surprise had passed, Otto found himself starting to smile. He even began to giggle in childish delight. The staircase was taking him ever higher: fifth floor, sixth floor, seventh. He had settled down, and was enjoying the ride, when a troubling thought suddenly occurred to him.

What if the escalator didn't stop moving? Not just on his floor; on any floor. What if it kept going – spiralling ever higher, beyond the rooftop he had stood upon recently, through the clouds and out the other side? What if it kept going until the wind was howling, the sky was deepening from blue to black and he could see the curve of the earth's surface appear below him? What if it kept going until the oxygen ran out?

At this point, Otto decided it was time to halt the rising staircase. But how exactly did one achieve such a thing? Looking down at his feet, he pushed the cane hard into the step before him, trying through leverage to halt its movement. When this didn't work, he tried pressing it between a gap in the banisters, leaning on it with all his meagre strength. Some sparks flew up, but it hadn't quite worked.

As the staircase continued moving, he pulled the cane from between the banisters, steadying himself as he prepared for another attempt. In order to gain greater purchase on the cane, he took a firm step backwards. The staircase seemed to crumble away beneath him. Grasping at the air with both his hands, he tumbled into the void, the only sound the clatter of his cane upon the stairs.

Thirty-One

When he opened his eyes, Otto could see the now stationary staircase stretched high above him, the elegant spokes of its various levels radiating outwards like a mandala. All was peaceful here in the stairwell. It had that special quality of silence – the echoing silence of the old synagogue in Vienna. He breathed in the spacious air, and felt his back resting on cool stone. The experience was pleasant, in its way, apart from the slight aching in his neck and a soreness in his head.

Otto saw his cane lying abandoned on a higher step. He reached out both hands and tried to raise himself towards it, but gravity defied his efforts and he was unable to move very far. Eventually, he gave up the attempt.

He touched his bare forehead with his fingertips. It was coated once more in beads of sweat. With an effort, he reached down and removed the white handkerchief from the inside pocket of his unbuttoned overcoat, slowly wiping it across his brow. He lacked the strength to return the handkerchief to its place, however, and lay there with it reposing in his hand like a small flag of surrender.

Where was his homburg? Instinct told him it was rolling around on another step, somewhere out of sight behind his head. But he was unable to turn around and see. A warmth was spreading outwards around the back of his head, and somewhere he could hear an occasional dripping sound. It was loud and intrusive, disturbing the perfect peace of the stairwell.

Otto noticed that his feet were resting on the steps of the flight above him with the tips of his faded leather brogues pointing upwards. He tried moving his toes, and saw the leather wrinkle and pucker as he did so. For some reason, although he was not sure why, this came as a relief to him. He was still unable to move his head – the warmth around it was making him drowsy. But he found that if he diverted his gaze to the left he could see the narrow window-slits, running up the wall. Through one of them he could make out a patch of blue sky with a cloud moving slowly across it.

Otto centred his eyes once more and lay staring at the radiating spokes above him. He was starting to feel a little cold, apart from his head – which seemed, if anything, to be getting warmer. The warmth seemed to be draining from the rest of his body, downwards into his skull. The toes, he noticed, were coldest of all.

'Most peculiar,' he said aloud and was startled to find that he could hardly hear his own voice. It came to him only indistinctly; muffled as though heard from the other side of a door. Yet the dripping sound behind him remained perfectly clear.

He decided that he should try to move his feet. They were starting to feel fuzzy now, as well as cold. The pins and needles were nipping at his toes. But he lacked the strength to lift them properly, or readjust the position of his body. He would have to try something else instead. With his heels, Otto pushed as hard as he could against the step on which they rested. His body started to shift backwards. As it did so, he realised that his head was hanging over the edge of the top step of the flight below. If he pushed any harder, he might propel himself down even further. Better just to lie where he was, then. Perhaps take a little nap while he waited for someone to come and help him move his feet.

Otto drifted in and out of consciousness. Each time he opened his eyes he saw the tall yellow staircase, drawing him upwards through its coils.

'Partly inspired by the lines of a seashell, and partly by the structure of DNA,' he said aloud to himself at one point.

Some time later, in the silence of the stairwell, he felt a rhythmical vibration begin to tickle the back of his head. It was not the dripping sound – that had stopped altogether. This was a steadier rhythm, regular and solid, and the vibrations were getting louder with every beat. He heard a muffled noise, like an exclamation, at which point the vibrations became very fast indeed. The spiral staircase disappeared from view, replaced by a face that Otto recognised. It was the young man he had seen earlier that day, exercising on the forecourt of the building. What was the name on the back of his top again?

The face above him was filled with anxiety. He felt hands cradling his head and heard a voice speaking to him. But he couldn't understand what was being said. The young man gently lowered his head back down, stood and ran swiftly up the stairs. He was wearing a different-coloured top this afternoon: blue this time, not red. No letters on the back like before.

The name, Otto wondered. What is his name?

He watched the head grow smaller as it circled the stairs up to the higher floors. The young man was ascending at a remarkable rate. He must have been taking three or four steps at a time.

Otto shut his eyes. He was starting to feel quite drowsy. Exceptionally drowsy, in fact. And there was a heaviness about it that was unfamiliar. This was no ordinary fatigue. It felt to him like the weight of many ages, pressing gently on his eyelids.

Moments later, a tiny head appeared in the distance – wheeling its way quickly down the stairs. Another followed immediately behind. The second was not moving as fast as the first, but it was travelling at a fair rate, nonetheless. The two heads made an interesting pattern as they wound their way to where he lay.

Geometry in motion, he wanted to say out loud, but the words would not come from his mouth.

The two bobbing heads continued their descent. Otto now could make out the first. It belonged once more to the young man in hooded top and jogging pants.

The name. What is his name?

Otto also recognised the head of the person running behind. The bright-red hair, bouncing loose in plaited streams, was highly distinctive.

Roz, Otto tried and failed to say, as her face appeared suddenly above him.

Roz was saying something to him, as she looked him over with the calm professionalism of the nurse. Her movements were urgent but unhurried. After a brief examination, during which she appeared to be focusing on Otto's neck, her hands gently lifted his head, while the young man (Mikey – that was it!) took his legs.

Once he had been moved around and placed down flat upon his back, Otto felt a little more comfortable. He wanted to thank them both but couldn't, smiling at them weakly instead. They continued talking for a minute or two – beyond his line of vision. Roz reappeared briefly, looking carefully into his face as she spoke on a mobile phone. Then she was gone from sight once more.

Settling as best he could into a more comfortable position, Otto studied again the geometry of the staircase. The peeling metal banisters seemed to wheel away into infinity. And then, high above him, emerging from the darkened heights of the stairwell, he saw something tiny, falling. It was not descending at a steady velocity, but slowly, even cautiously, whirling its way downwards as though in imitation of the banisters' distinctive rhythm. This tiny object, getting closer to Otto now, seemed almost as light as the currents of air in which it spun. There were moments when it blew off course, or lifted slightly upwards, caught within the draughts from the heating system. But sure enough, the downward motion would re-establish itself once more, as this delicate white object defied all attempts to halt its progress.

Dancing and circling, elegant in its descent, the long journey down from the heavens was reaching its end. Then high above it, Otto noticed, many similar objects were falling – hundreds, thousands of them – obscuring the upper reaches of the stairwell as they wheeled and tumbled to earth in silent chaos. The tiredness that had been encroaching on Otto enfolded him completely. Just before losing consciousness, the corners of his mouth twitched slightly and a peaceful smile spread across his upturned face. The snowflake had landed on his cheek.

Thirty-Two

Anika stood as Daniel entered the ward and came across to the bedside, embracing her quickly and without fuss.

'What's the latest?' he asked.

'He seems to be okay. Still not talking, I'm afraid, but he appears peaceful enough.'

They looked down at the bed. Otto lay with his head raised on the pillows. His eyes were shut and his face as pale as the bandages round his head.

'How much damage has been done? Do the doctors know yet?'

Anika shook her head.

'They're not entirely sure. The injury, apparently, was fairly superficial. It was quite a nasty cut, but it looked worse than it actually was. They say there was no serious damage done, either to the skull or . . . to the brain.'

Daniel nodded.

'That's a relief, anyway.'

He bent over to look at his father, while Anika continued,

'Having said that, they are a little concerned about his slow response to treatment. They told me the concussion would normally have worn off by now.'

'I see . . . '

Anika looked down at the resting face, which evoked a complex range of emotions within her. Sadness, of course, even a dash of pity; but also love, compassion and a certain underlying anger that Otto had been so bloody stupid. He had not been well for some time and had partly brought this on himself.

When she had first received the call from Angelo, Anika had exploded with recrimination. She had built up an additional store of anger while reflecting upon events on the plane across from Geneva. As soon as she arrived in London she was prepared to let Angelo, Chloe and anyone else involved in this ridiculous project have it straight between the eyes. Upon walking into the hospital ward, however, and seeing her husband unconscious, she felt her anger dissolve into something less vengeful.

It had briefly re-emerged, once or twice, in the past few hours; but having been given some time to think about the situation, she no longer especially blamed Angelo or the people behind the film. If anything she blamed Otto, but then she couldn't blame Otto, because he had already suffered the consequences of his actions; and because she now grasped that she couldn't have gone on protecting him for ever. Her impulse, to keep him safely out of harm's way in the villa, had been unrealistic. Ageing and illness were unavoidable, and Otto was ultimately too headstrong a character to stay permanently wrapped in cotton wool. The project in London was foolish, Anika still believed. But it was his final attempt to assert his independence, and to answer the siren call of his own abandoned past. It had always been there, she realised, even though he had never once spoken about it with her.

His eyes opened as they sat waiting beside the bed.

Daniel leaned across.

'Hello, Dad.'

A smile crossed Otto's lips. He tried to speak but failed. Anika reached out and brushed her fingers across his cheek.

'You must try to rest now, Otto,' she said, leaning forward to rearrange the pillows. 'You look very tired.'

He did not respond, but lay staring peacefully at the ceiling.

'He does this,' Anika told Daniel. 'There are moments of clarity, when he comes to and recognises people. But then he drifts off again, who knows where? It seems to be a place that makes him happy, though, so maybe it's best to leave him there.'

The following hours were painful, for any number of reasons. Both Anika and Daniel would have preferred to be alone with Otto. Yet they did their mutual best to be civil and in time they began to relax in each other's company.

During a break, over a shared cheese sandwich in the hospital canteen, Anika asked after Daniel's family. He told her about his daughter's recent difficulties at school. She had struggled to assimilate with some of her new classmates and would be moving on to a different school the following term.

'And Gillian is how old now?' Anika asked him. 'Eleven, twelve . . . ? I'm sorry, I should know these things.'

'She's eleven,' he said. 'It's hardly your fault, Anika. We've not exactly bombarded you with invitations to visit.'

Anika thought for a moment.

'I know you've always felt uncomfortable about Otto and me being together.'

Daniel was taken aback by her honesty, but gave a small nod of acquiescence.

'I won't patronise you with some platitude about knowing how you feel,' she continued. 'I cannot possibly know, it's something beyond my personal experience. But I'm aware that it must have been difficult for you.'

Daniel looked her in the eye at last.

'In the early days, yes. But not so much now. I feel rather awkward around you ... still ... but not resentful. Not any more.'

'That's a relief to hear.'

'The point is that Dad and I should have moved on from this silliness years ago. It's not fair on you, that you should see so little of your stepfamily. Our behaviour must have seemed childish to you at times.'

Anika paused before replying. Her professional background in diplomacy could be useful at moments like this.

'I realise that relations haven't always been perfect between yourself and Otto, but I wouldn't want you to think he has ever said anything untoward about you. Your father's an honourable man, very loyal, as I'm sure you know. He keeps all family matters entirely to himself.'

'I guessed as much. That's his way.'

'I have tried, on occasion, to persuade him to rebuild bridges. But always I have to approach it in a way that is ... what is the word now?'

'Indirect?'

'Indeed. It's no good trying to talk to him directly on personal issues. He has a tendency to seize up, emotionally.'

Daniel smiled as he looked at Anika.

'I must admit I didn't often see him any other way.'

'He cares for you, though ... profoundly. I'm certain he would like to heal the rift. But I'm not sure that he knows exactly how.'

'It's okay,' Daniel reassured her. 'I received a letter from him this morning, just before you called. It was written from Marlowe House and explained some things.'

Anika nodded, a little surprised.

'I see.'

She stared out of the window and bit thoughtfully into her sandwich.

'I believe I owe you an apology, Anika.'

She looked at him, startled from her thoughts.

'Owe *me* an apology? Why?'

'Many reasons. I've been unfair to you. Dad told me some things in the letter I hadn't known before.'

'Really?'

There was nothing stand-offish in Anika's tone. She said this with a wide-eyed, almost childlike embarrassment. It roused in Daniel an unexpectedly protective feeling towards her.

'It's fine,' he hastened to add. 'It was nothing particularly personal. Just straightforward information ... how you first met him in Talloires, for instance.'

'That's one of his favourite stories.'

'They were the sort of details I should have known years ago. I *would* have known them, too, if I hadn't been so evasive in my dealings with you.'

'I see. Well, that's *nice*, then. It's good that you should know things a little better.'

'It is.'

Daniel inspected his hands.

'There was one thing in the letter, something I didn't know before . . . Mum telling Dad that he must remarry one day.'

'He never mentioned that to you?'

'No.'

'I suppose it would not have occurred to him.'

There was a look of concern on Anika's face.

'I wonder, sometimes,' she added, 'whether I could have done more to help solve these problems.'

Clearly it was something that had been troubling her.

'Any issues I had were in my head, in the past,' Daniel told her. 'There was nothing you could have done to alter that. Tensions would have arisen between Dad and me, whoever he became involved with . . . whenever it happened. We were both pretty damaged by what took place.'

'Of course.'

Anika took another bite from her sandwich, mentally adjusting to this sudden shift in mood between them.

Daniel pressed on further.

'You did a good thing, with Dad. It wouldn't be an exaggeration to say that you saved his life. Or at least gave it back to him.'

'I don't know whether I would go *that* far.'

'He was in a bad way, when he met you. It's safe to say you restored him. I honestly don't know whether anyone else could have done that.'

Anika smiled, despite herself.

'Your words are very generous, but it was not an act of charity on my part. I am no saint, I promise you. I loved your father very much, and I still do. There was no hardship involved, as far as I was concerned.'

She measured out her words, before continuing, 'As we both know, Otto is complicated. He is difficult to get to know, and difficult to live with at times. But he's also a special, interesting man – a beautiful man, in my eyes. If I restored Otto, then you might say that in some respects he helped to *build* me.'

Anika smiled as she remembered.

'I was in my late thirties when I first met him. I was divorced, there had been several others. I was very much a woman of the world. Yet I feel now that I knew so little – almost nothing, in fact – before I met Otto. I suppose that's the kind of person he is.'

'It must have been hard for you. The early days, I mean. Given the state that Dad was in at that time.'

'It *was* hard. Painful, at times. Things moved more slowly than I thought I could stand. I was quite swept off my feet, you see. I had never really met someone like your father before. All my life I had mixed with a very different type of person. Ambassadors, diplomats – *buttoned-up people*, as Otto calls them. Otto was buttoned-up too, in his way, but there was also something original about him. He had the brain of an artist, a scientist, a mathematician, all of them rolled into one. He was the Renaissance Man I had read about as a young woman studying in Utrecht. But this wasn't sixteenth-century Florence, I had to remind myself. What was such a person doing sitting in this café in the middle of the Alps?'

'So how much did he tell you, then, about Mum?'

'I sensed straightaway that bad things had happened in Otto's life. At first he gave no indication of what they might be. He was very much cut off from the world at that time. And so I

314

was careful, patient, maybe even a little calculating, if that's not too strong a word to use about someone in love. I was head over heels but I didn't want to drive him away. And so I waited. We would arrange to meet up, now and then, for days out in Geneva. I would sit with a coffee in a bar near the station and wait for his bus to arrive from the mountains. We went to museums, to galleries, the opera and theatre. *The mating rituals of the bourgeoisie* – that is another phrase of Otto's!

'About five months after our first meeting, he asked if I would like to spend the weekend at his chalet in the Chartreuse. It was winter, the snow was falling, but we walked a little in the hills around and I tried to teach him some of the basics of cross-country skiing. He wasn't terribly good at it. In the evening we sat huddled by the paraffin heater, drinking brandy and listening to the compact-disc player I had bought for him. Otto allowed himself no luxuries at first, but I was beginning to wear him down by this time. We only had one disc to play, though – Michelangeli's recording of Debussy's *Préludes*. We must have listened to it ten times that weekend. It was during the first evening that he told me the story of Cynthia. Later, we lay together in his bed. Yet throughout that night, and for some time afterwards, we were as pure as the falling snow outside.'

As she spoke, Anika glanced continually at Daniel, assessing his reaction. He looked down but gave no indication that he wanted her to stop.

'The snow that weekend wasn't just *outside* the chalet. The finer stuff blew inwards through the gaps between the rafters. When we woke the next morning, our blanket was covered with a powdery film of snow. Otto got a stepladder and fixed the problem in the roof, while I shivered beneath the covers

315

and watched him work. The two of us could barely move beneath the many sweaters we wore that weekend. We must have had six layers each.'

'And when did you start living together? I've never known that. I got word while at Cambridge that Dad was seeing someone else. After that I disconnected for a while.'

'He moved in with me about six months later. I remember it was midsummer when we moved his belongings to my apartment. I was living in the Eaux Vives district at the time, in an apartment just south of the lake. It's not the most swish part of Geneva, but it was centrally placed, I was in between jobs and the rent there was pretty reasonable. We stayed there three years before building the villa.

'At weekends, when we lived in Eaux Vives, Otto liked to sit outside on the balcony with a coffee and a cigarette. He would sketch the view of the Jet d'Eau fountain, located near us at the lake's edge. It was especially striking when seen from our balcony. The fountain was perfectly framed, you see, between the rows of the tenement buildings. It seemed to be standing at the end of our street. There was a certain time of day that Otto loved. Late afternoon, on those pulsating summer days that ignite the lake. By that time of day, the shadows from the tenements were lengthening, and the spray from the fountain looked like a vast silver flame between the rooftops. One day, when Otto was sketching that view in charcoal, I sat down beside him and asked if he thought he might like to become an architect again.

'It was quite a big moment, although I tried to play it cool. I had been preparing myself to ask that question for weeks. By this time, Otto was putting his life back together; on a practical level, at least. I felt that this would be one of the final pieces in the jigsaw. I had a friend who worked for the council in Geneva. She mentioned to me a plan to commission a new urban garden, at a 1960s housing estate in Onex. An ornamental fountain would form part of the architectural brief. I knew that Otto had a fondness for fountains at that time.'

'I see. So *that's* why he came back with that particular project. I never really understood that before. You persuaded him.'

'It was not so much persuasion. Otto was ready for it by that time, I think. Maybe he just needed someone to say those words to him.'

The following day, as they sat once more beside Otto's bed, the doors of the ward opened and Angelo peered inside. Daniel shook his hand and Anika embraced him, with no sign of any reluctance or tension. It was Angelo's lunch hour, he couldn't stay too long. He was carrying some chocolates and a book on Frank Lloyd Wright.

'Just been published – very good, apparently,' he told them.

Angelo placed the gifts on the bedside table, where they stood alongside a bouquet from Chloe and the film crew.

Having checked on Otto, who appeared to be dozing, Angelo turned to speak to Daniel.

'I realise this is hardly the time to talk shop, but thanks once again for all your help with the campaign to save the building.'

The look of surprise on Anika's face caused immediate embarrassment all round.

'Daniel didn't tell you and Otto that he was involved?' asked Angelo.

'No,' said Anika.

'Oh, dear. Have I spoken out of turn?'

Daniel jumped in.

'I thought it best to keep it quiet. I wasn't sure how Dad would react, you see. I was planning to tell him later on.'

Anika looked at him.

'Now it is *I* who should apologise. The day before Otto flew to London, I finally plucked up the courage to ask him why you weren't helping out with the campaign. I must admit my words weren't complimentary.'

She looked down at her sleeping husband and continued, 'He brushed the matter to one side at the time. But I know how pleased he will be to hear it.'

'It's the least I can do – he's my father. But it's not just a family matter. Dad's a great architect. Marlowe House is an important building. Work of that quality deserves to be recognised and protected.'

Anika began to readjust the flowers in the vase.

'Otto would like to hear you say that. Architecture was ... is ... his life. For the past ten years he has described himself as retired, but look at what he achieved in that time. Designing constantly – an eco-house, a ski-station, a project to convert an old *fruitière* into a social housing scheme. He was writing endlessly, too. Letters, academic papers. And yet he seemed to feel he was inactive all those years. He was always telling me how lazy he had become. Otto had the mental energy of ten people, even then, even after his various operations. It made me wonder just what he must have been like at the peak of his powers. Back in the day, he and Cynthia together must have been something to behold.'

Once Angelo had gone, and they were sipping cups of

coffee in the hospital canteen, Anika asked Daniel about his own career as an architect.

'Why did you decide to follow in your parents' footsteps? Did they encourage it?'

'You would imagine that to be the case, but in fact, no. They were keen that I should make my own decision.'

'That's the right approach to take.'

'Dad may be a strong-willed character, but he was careful not to influence me on issues such as that. Not *consciously*, at least; although I suspect with hindsight that he did influence my decision in other ways.'

'How do you mean?'

'There was one particular incident I remember as a child. The fact I remember it at all must be significant. We were visiting London Zoo, I must have been five or six at the time, and I remember I was keen to see the lions ... '

He described to her in detail the story about running off and colliding with the bicycle.

'Looking back, I now realise that Dad must have hit upon some idea for his work. Inspiration sometimes struck him like that. He would become completely immersed in something apparently trivial and lose all interest in everything around him.'

'Yes, I know that expression.'

'He meant nothing by it. Dad doesn't have a cruel bone in his body, as you know. It's just his way. But at the time, when I was a young child, it would upset me. On that occasion, it was particularly bad. I suppose, in retrospect, it made me realise just how much architecture meant to him. It also made me understand it was the only means of getting his attention.'

'So, when you became an architect, you were looking to win his approval?'

'To some extent. Life is never that simple, of course, and I'm sure there must have been a wide range of factors. But the incident at the penguin pool, and a few others like it, must have played their part.'

Late that afternoon, Otto woke once more. The first face he saw was his son's.

'Daniel,' he managed to say.

'How are you feeling, Dad?'

'Not bad. A little tired, perhaps. And my head is rather sore. I think I may have done something foolish.'

'Not at all.'

Daniel was looking down at him with filial concern. Otto thought for a moment.

'It's good of you to come.'

'It's good to see you again. I received your letter.'

Otto smiled, weakly.

'I'm glad that you did. I almost didn't post it. Did it make any sense at all? I'm afraid I'm a little confused these days.'

Daniel reached down and took Otto's hand, for the first time since the days of the kite and the penguin pool.

'We'll talk things over when you're feeling better. You need to build up your strength.'

With Otto sleeping once more, Anika and Daniel prepared to leave for the evening. Pulling on his overcoat, he turned towards her.

'Would you like to come back to the house for dinner this evening?'

'Dinner? Really?'

'It must be lonely for you, stuck in that hotel. Suzie and the kids would love to see you.'

Anika looked touched, suddenly, beneath the usual reserve.

'That would be very nice, Daniel. Thank you.'

Thirty-Three

The blackberries were fattening once more in the hedgerows, but Otto waited his moment to begin their gathering. He circled them at distance for a day or two, choosing instead to focus on the flower beds. Once these were done, he raked and replenished the compost heap in a corner of the garden, barely glancing over at the ripening harvest in the hedgerows. From the top of the heap of sweet-smelling compost, he stood and gazed at the milky haze over the lake. Splinters of light illuminated the distant vineyards. He seemed to forget for an instant where he was. Such moments aside, however, his mental faculties had grown no worse in the year or so since leaving hospital in London. If anything, they seemed to have slightly improved.

One day, while Anika was out shopping in town, he decided that the blackberries could wait no longer. They might rot or burst if left ungathered. Anika always encouraged him to wear gloves when working in the garden, but the battered old pair he usually wore lay discarded down by the rose bushes. This happened when she was not around to keep an eye on him. Otto didn't mind the thorns and brambles pricking his fingertips. They made him feel strangely alive.

Having reached a decision, he made his way to the bottom of the garden with the help of his wooden cane. He had regained some strength in the fifteen months since his last episode of surgery, and carried the walking stick as a precaution, these days, rather than from necessity. Once he was close enough to properly view the hedgerows, he noted how abundant the blackberries were this year. Setting aside the cane and reaching upwards, he plucked one of them and tasted it cautiously, wondering if the memories would assail him. But nothing came. Instead he found himself savouring an intense sweetness.

'They're just blackberries,' he said, with a lick of his fingers, settling down on his haunches to begin work.

He had filled two plastic bags when he heard the distant trilling of the telephone from the villa. Anika had turned up the volume on the handset before heading into town, one of countless small acts of thoughtfulness she performed on any given day. By the time Otto had raised himself to his feet and made his way up to the villa, the ringing had stopped. He pressed the playback button on the answering machine, which was also turned up to maximum volume, and listened to the message as he went through to the kitchen. There he washed the juice from his fingers and dried his hands on his old corduroy trousers. He kept forgetting, these days, that there were things called towels.

Returning to the living room, he picked up the receiver and dialled 'return'.

'Daniel? It's your father.'

'Hello, Dad. I thought you'd be out with Anika at your Pilates class.'

'No, that's on Wednesday . . . every *other* Wednesday, to be precise. This new health regime she has devised for me is more merciful than I had feared.'

'I'm glad I caught you at home, anyway. I thought I should let you know the sad news. The demolition of Marlowe House began as planned this morning. We did all that we could . . . I'm sorry.'

Otto paused a second before replying with a note of resignation.

'It's a great shame, but the news isn't exactly unexpected.'

'There are some disappointed people in the profession today. I heard Jorge on the radio just now and he was railing against the decision. Wanted to know why one of our finest living architects wasn't receiving the respect he deserved.'

'Jorge said that? Clearly he's mellowed with age. The last time I saw him – must be ten years ago now – he called me a prick to my face.'

Daniel smiled, despite himself.

'He's by no means the only one who feels that way. Many others are echoing his sentiments. An important building is an important building, whatever the prevailing *Zeitgeist*. It's frustrating that we couldn't get the authorities to see this.'

'You're kind, but I suspect the disappointment is far from universal. Plenty of people will welcome the decision, I'm sure. The real shame is that some of the residents wanted to stay in their homes. I wish we could have done something more, for their sakes.'

Otto was keen to know what had happened to the tenants

he met during his stay there. Mrs Pham, he had heard from; they wrote to each other, occasionally. A few months earlier, she had returned to Ho Chi Minh City, to live with the eldest of her sons. She was readjusting well to life in Vietnam, she had told him.

But what about the others, he wondered – Joe and Roz, Ravi and the young lad Mikey?

'Did you manage to make any of those enquiries I mentioned?' he asked.

'I did, but I'm afraid I drew a blank.'

'Blast. I should have asked you to look into it much earlier. Everything I do is behind the pace, nowadays.'

'I spoke to someone from the local authority, who confirmed they had all moved on some time ago. But nobody was able to give any indication where.'

'Thanks for trying. I imagine they will be okay. It would have been nice to know for certain, that's all.'

Otto reflected for a moment.

'And they never even broadcast the documentary.'

'I know. I'm sorry, Dad. I spoke to Chloe about it a short while back.'

'What did she say?'

'She was embarrassed, naturally, and very apologetic. She tried to persuade her producers to treat it more kindly, but they said the footage was less exciting than they had hoped. "Nothing much happened on camera," they told her. "The old boy didn't give much away." And so they decided to shelve the film altogether. Ran something on a new comedy festival instead.'

'Oh well,' said Otto. 'I never was a great fan of television . . . although Anika, as you can guess, was none too happy about their decision. Nevertheless, all things considered, it was a more productive experience than I'd anticipated.'

Daniel, at this point, seemed to read his father's thoughts.

'That reminds me. Suzie asked me to confirm it with you. We're still planning to make it over with the children for half-term, if that's okay?'

'Absolutely. Wouldn't miss it for the world. We're both looking forward to it greatly.'

Once the call had finished, Otto returned to the kitchen and emptied the blackberries into several airtight containers, colour-coded according to their degree of ripeness. He was following Anika's instructions to the letter.

'I think I'll make us a nice pie this weekend,' he said aloud.

Walking slowly down the corridor to his study, and leaning on his cane a little more lightly than was once the case, he pushed open the door and took his seat at the desk beside the window to study the trees. The soft morning light gave them an autumnal sheen. The forest had shaken off summer's uniformity and wore its multicoloured garb with some style.

Otto paused to observe the orange-yellow patterning of the leaves.

She used to wear bright dresses dyed with henna.

Balancing his spectacles on the tip of his nose, he searched out some notepaper in the drawer, unscrewed the cap of his fountain pen and settled down to begin writing. One elbow rested on the surface of the desk, his fingers touching gently to his temple. His other hand moved across the page in long and sweeping strokes, sketching out the music of his thoughts.

Thirty-Four

Dear Cynthia,

This is the first time I have written to you since your death.
Clearly it is an unusual thing to do, but unusual letters seem
to be my speciality. I hope it doesn't trouble you that I trouble
you again.

Would it upset you, perhaps, to know that I write such a
letter – destined for no eyes but my own? You might think
of it as evidence of a deteriorating mind, but this is not the
only possibility. For if that were the case, then how does one
explain those other, earlier letters – written to you in life but
not passed on? This character trait, you see, is not a new
one.

I wrote a few of them, as far as I recall, completed and
then crumpled them into oblivion. Clarifications, confessions,
attempts to explain or justify my behaviour. If retrieved and
flattened out by a curious hand, they would doubtless make
for rather awkward reading. Other letters, too, less specific in
purpose, offered you expressions of my love. One of these I

composed during the early years of our marriage, in the first flush of discovery and wonder. Another was written in those blissful years before your illness; a third, in the days immediately after.

As they were written when I was at liberty to express my views in person, what did the creation of these letters signify? Emotional repression, I suspect, dating back to childhood. A wish not to make too much noise. Those conversations in the cellar, now I think of it, were always conducted at a whisper.

The truth is I was never too good at expressing my emotions. There were things I should have said to you more often. Haunting the space between heart and tongue are the ghosts of many delicate feelings; experienced, sometimes intensely, but never uttered. The temptation in writing to you now is to pour out those feelings with abandon, to record each moment you made my spirit soar. Your gestures, looks, words, caresses: all had the potential to transport me. Even outwardly trivial events could spark this inner alchemy. Listening together to Beethoven's Sixth, or pruning the flowers in the garden; watching the rise and fall of your breathing as you dozed with your back to the warm sand.

Attempting to list each meaningful moment would border on the absurd, like seeking to isolate drops within an ocean. I could fill a thousand pages without pause. But time is short and I must move on to other, more pressing matters. One thing in particular I have to discuss with you.

Back in 1987, in the weeks before losing your ability to reason, you mentioned something that Daniel and I should do once you were gone. Several times you repeated yourself; at the time I put it down to your deteriorating condition, but

328

in fact you knew exactly what you were doing. You spoke to us calmly, but with an underlying urgency, aware of the dangers that your advice might go unheeded.

'Take care of each other,' you told us.

Twenty-five years later, we are finally doing what you asked. Ridiculous, isn't it, that it's taken us so long? Yet during that time I somehow convinced myself that I was taking care of Daniel. In a sense, I suppose, one could argue that I was. Economically, professionally – I was a model father in all things practical. Yet my responsibilities towards him were also emotional. And that is the one thing I failed to comprehend. I should have reached out to him, in the period after your passing. My mad retreat to the mountains opened a breach that was hard to close. Daniel played his part in what followed, as the years went by and he became older himself. But I should have taken the initiative in clearing the air much sooner. And so a tale of slow estrangement that began in early childhood, with lions unseen and boomerangs unthrown, came to a head some forty years later with my offer to 'correct' a design on which he was working. Could a worse word have been chosen – the mood been more poorly judged? After the years of coolness, the constant miscommunication, my comment finally pushed poor Daniel over the edge.

There was a falling-out, and for almost three years we didn't speak a word. But recently, things have greatly improved between us. Thanks to a letter (posted), a mishap and an unplanned reunion, he and I have become rather good friends. Furthermore, I've learned a great deal about the changing nature of parenthood. With the passing of time, there's a levelling-out in father–son relations. Not a reversal

329

of roles, exactly, but a gaining of equilibrium – a balance between one's waxing and the other's waning. Strange as it sounds, I have only just grasped this, only just begun to treat my son as an equal. I am thankful for his patience in this matter. He is certainly a better parent than me, and probably a better architect, so it is time for me to abandon my sorry attempts to play the patriarch.

Daniel and the family visit us regularly now in Switzerland. The grandchildren love the views of the lake and the flowers in the garden. I wish you could have known Gillian and Michael. You would all have had such fun together. They have the same boundless curiosity and love of life as their Grandma. Michael's a very practical boy, a dab hand at Meccano and always making something new. He's quite a sportsman, too, something clearly not inherited from our side of the family. He tells me he wants to open the batting for England, or maybe become a famous architect. He hasn't yet decided between the two. Daniel, I am sure, will not discourage him in either ambition.

Gillian is more studious – top of the class at just about everything and with a boundless sense of fun. She started at her new school a short while ago, and already she has made lots of friends. She has a particular flair for languages, her command of German is exceptional, and she plans one day to teach herself Ancient Greek. When she told me this, I immediately thought of someone who might have helped her.

Both Gillian and Michael are always asking questions about you. Daniel recently made them an album of old photographs. They brought it over to show me, the last time they visited, and we spent a couple of pleasant hours leafing through it. *A most affecting experience, as you can imagine. Some of those pictures I hadn't seen in years. There was one in particular, taken on our honeymoon, which seemed to be a favourite of Gillian's. I wonder if you remember it. You are wearing a pale-blue trouser suit, perched on the edge of a broken stump of column. You've just removed your sunglasses and your eyes are filled with laughter. Gillian thinks you look like Audrey Hepburn!*

You left another message, as you lay upon your sickbed, and this is something else we should discuss.

'Find someone,' you told me. 'Don't waste what time you have. Try, if you can, to live happily and well.'

In this regard I've been very fortunate, in the decades since you left us. Anika, my wife, is a wonderful woman. I'll forever be grateful that she coveted my binoculars. She gets on well with the grandchildren, and she and Daniel are perfectly friendly, these days. That's something I never thought I'd be able to say. What is more, Anika has struck up a bond with Suzie, Daniel's wife. The two of them are always talking on the phone. You would like Suzie, a serene sort of presence, a perfect foil for Daniel's nervous energy. They have, it is clear, such a stable, loving marriage. I wish you could have lived to see him settled.

By the way, while I remember, there's another piece of news I should tell you. A building we once designed together has been condemned to the wrecking ball. Marlowe House, our one-time 'home of the future', is at this very moment being demolished. We did our best to save it, but our efforts proved to be in vain. Time, I'm afraid, has been unkind to so much that you and I held dear.

How strange it was to wander the empty corridors, to

inhabit those spaces we created together. Rediscovering the spatial logic of the structure was like unearthing the thought patterns of our younger selves. I was constantly reminded of those discussions we all had, round a table in our office in Fitzrovia.

At a personal level, it has all been rather painful, seeing the demise and destruction of something we cared for. But the experience has also restored my sense of resolve. They can knock down people's homes, you see, but they cannot so easily break their spirit. The residents I met were proof of that. These days, as a consequence, I try to write more useful letters: to politicians, newspapers and the like. Who knows if anyone has the patience to read them? I'm not very good at sticking to the point. But it's important, I think, even when one's mental powers are in decline, to try to stay engaged with the outside world.

Well, Cyn, it looks as though our time together is drawing to a close. I must leave you now, for Anika is coming. I see her ride her bicycle past my study window. Soon I will hear the creak of the back door and the sound of her tyres upon the flagstones. She will be weary, after her journey to town, and I must restore her with a lunch of scrambled eggs. Cooking a meal for Anika has become my greatest joy.

We will meet again soon, no doubt, in the memories I hold of you, though I'm glad to say these no longer overwhelm me. They emerge, rather, only when summoned, or when I'm of a mind to set them free. When I'm walking alone in the forest, and the feeling comes upon me, I release those memories like birds into the air. They nestle in the treetops, they sing to me their song, but it's a song of celebration, not a lament. Your memory, these days, inspires and uplifts me – inviting life, where once it seemed to obscure it.

I'm at peace now, Cynthia. I am reconciled with our son. Knowing this, I sense that you, too, are finally at rest.

Sleep well, dear Cynthia. Sleep well, dear Cyn.

Otto

Thirty-Five

She was waiting for him outside the apartment that day. No beret, the auburn hair shining, the lips full and smiling – her dress a simple print of pale orange. As Otto pulled up alongside her, the sunlight glinted on the rich cream paintwork of the open-topped car he had hired for the trip. Cynthia laughed and made fun a little. She didn't even know that he could drive.

'Where did you find this? It must have cost you a fortune!'

He could tell that she was delighted.

'It's just for the weekend. I couldn't resist. And since we're going somewhere that is special to you, I thought we needed a special form of transport to get us there.'

'It's beautiful . . . thank you. It's beautiful.'

She kissed him on the mouth. Her smile was radiant as she turned towards him.

'If it rains we can always put the roof up, of course, but I thought it might be nicer to drive with it down, if you don't mind the breeze.'

'The breeze is perfect,' she said, fastening her seatbelt.

'And there's a hamper in the back, for when we get hungry.'

She kissed him again with vigour.

'You look nice,' he told her.

'So do you. I love the jacket – very elegant indeed.'

'And you've brought the camera?'

'I've brought two, just in case. The light is fantastic so I hope we can find lots to photograph.'

In the mid-1950s, the drive out through north-west London became pleasant more quickly. The ribbon development encircling the city was less pronounced; the countryside, or something approximating to it, arrived earlier. By the time they reached rural Buckinghamshire, it had become a day bathed in near-perfect sunlight: soft and diffuse, without sacrificing any clarity of line or colour.

The car dipped and rose through the softly rounded landscape, hugging its contours as naturally as the hedgerows. Cynthia reclined in the passenger seat, her eyes closed, her arms stretched out and her face upturned to the warmth, as though absorbing secret messages from the sun. Otto and she were talking and laughing; basking in each other's presence. Their relationship, still in its early stages, was deepening in a way that seemed almost miraculous.

'Very green,' he shouted.

'Mm?'

Cynthia opened her eyes.

'The countryside ... here in England. Everyone told me that it would be. *Very* green.'

'You like it?'

'Yes, the tones are exceptionally rich. And the grass seems

335

to glisten, even though the weather is dry today. It's as if the memory of the rain lives on inside it.'

She smiled.

'How poetic. But then I suppose that's England for you. Rather on the damp side, I'm afraid.'

Otto nodded.

'I only wish I had visited the countryside earlier.'

'I can't believe this is your first trip outside London. You've been here several years.'

'I was busy with all those books. The crazy man in the attic, remember?'

She leaned across to kiss him and then pointed off suddenly to the side of the car.

'Look. A Cabbage White. The first I've seen this year.'

Otto was trying to keep his eye on the road.

'Where?'

'There. A few of them, in fact. Flying alongside us. Can't you see?'

'Flying cabbages, you say?'

Cynthia laughed.

'Cabbage White. It's a type of butterfly. Over there ... look, in the hedgerow.'

At a quiet spot on a hill, with a view in the distance of Henley-on-Thames, its outline accommodating the silver flow of the river, they parked the car and removed the picnic hamper from the boot. They had lunch – ham and cheese sandwiches, apples and a flask of tea – on a blanket at the summit. The breeze flapped at Otto's fringe and the orange folds of Cynthia's dress. Afterwards, in a hidden crease of the hill, with no one else around that day, they made love slowly to the rhythms of the breeze and the birdsong, as soporific and timeless as the sunshine on their skin. Back in the car, they glanced over the map and decided to head further into the Oxfordshire Chilterns. The lanes were close and narrow here, the hedgerows thick with white spring flowers, which Cynthia could almost touch as she trailed her hand out over the side of the car.

'There's one. Let's pull over and take a look.'

Otto drew up the car before a ruined cottage, which he estimated must date back to the early nineteenth century. It was steadily being reclaimed by the foliage coiling up its walls. The roof sagged badly in the middle, but just about held aloft. There was a sense of melancholy about the building, picturesque though it was. And then, higher up, a few hundred yards beyond it, lay the remains of an old outhouse, totally collapsed. Once a barn for keeping cows, it was now a pile of rubble on the crest of a slope.

Cynthia made her way up the hill, camera in hand, while Otto peered inside the broken windows of the cottage. No furniture was visible in the gloom, just bare walls and a few loose beams. Some broken glass was strewn across the floor. Wading through the tall grass at the side of the house, he gave a little wave to Cynthia, who was nearing the top of the hill. The retaining wall on this side had fallen down entirely. The empty rooms gave no clues about the lives of their former occupants. Otto snapped some pictures of the crumbling wall and exposed interior, kneeling down to get a satisfactory frame. Dusting the thick spores from the knees of his corduroy trousers, he rose to his feet and followed Cynthia up the hill.

'The view is magnificent, come and see.'

She was standing at the top of the pile of rubble, reaching behind her to Otto with an outstretched hand. She smiled as he stumbled upwards to join her, losing his footing on the loose stones, but never halting. Sensing her broadening smile, he exaggerated his movements to please her; arms out sideways, swaying from side to side with each new step. Unable to control herself, Cynthia laughed, her head thrown back, delighting in the moment. A halo of sunlight burst between the trees.

Ever since his childhood, people had laughed at Otto: at his great height, his clumsiness, his eccentric demeanour and the impenetrable flow of his ideas. But this laugh was different. It told him it was all okay. No, more than that: that he was loved. Otto was laughing too, now, as his hand reached out towards hers.

'Shall we get married?' he asked her late that afternoon, as they sat in the car and watched the shadows lengthen on the hills. The question seemed to come naturally from him, without awkwardness or nerves. Otto himself could hardly believe how relaxed he sounded. To the casual observer, he might easily have been commenting on the view. Cynthia's reply sounded equally unruffled. She was unhurried and at ease, allowing his words to play across her like the sunlight.

'Yes,' she said, matter-of-factly, leaning across to kiss him on the cheek. 'Of course.'